Inside the Grey House

Also by Cat Stark

Novels
The Elven Prince
The Grey House

Collections
Enter the Maze

Inside the Grey House
A World of Contagion Trilogy Book Two

Cat Stark

www.catstark.com

ISBN: 978-1-7333985-1-0

DEDICATION

This trilogy is dedicated to Travis Legge for allowing me to use his world as a setting for this trilogy.

This book is dedicated to Maman, who doesn't like fantasy but loves that I write.

ACKNOWLEDGMENTS

I want to thank my readers for picking this book up after waiting so long for the second one to come out.

As with the first book, I had a large amount of people who helped me edit this book. A short list includes: Richard Pulfer, Caitlin Campbell, Michele Perry, Kelly Fields, Paul Stanek. Thank you to all who helped.

Cast of Characters

These are the characters that appeared in book one and are in book two, in case a refresher is needed. They are in alphabetical order not in order of appearance.

Anthony: Vincent's trusted friend, who does not trust Natalia

Ben: Vampire medic who works for Vincent

Bethany: Natalia's human best friend

Charlie: Werewolf who works for Vincent, and Rebecca's husband

Christopher: Edwin's sire and Captain of San Francisco (missing)

Dean: Human who helps Slayers

Donald: Vampire who killed Natalia's mother

Doug: Werewolf who works for Vincent.

Dr Elving: Doctor/vampire who works for Vincent

Edwin: Acting Captain of San Francisco

Joseph: Vincent's trusted friend, and Mierka's lover

Judith: Slayer who works for Zechariah

Justin: Vampire who works for Vincent/Anthony

Kari: Edwin's lackey

Kimberly (Kim): Vampire who works for Vincent

Lorraine: Vincent's Sire

Markus: Human who works for Vincent

Mierka: Vincent's trusted friend, and Joseph's lover

Miguel: Slayer who works for Zechariah

Morgan: Edwin's lackey

Natalia: The female lead

Orlando: Werewolf who works for Vincent

Rebecca: Vincent's Alpha werewolf and Charlie's wife

Richard: Maître d' of Ocean's Edge, Vincent's restaurant

Vincent: The male lead

Zechariah: Slayer who kidnapped Natalia

1

The jet landed on the private runway, barely causing a bump. Vincent and Mierka were off the plane within five minutes of landing and were being greeted by Lorraine's valet within seven. It was very close to sunrise, making the vampires grateful for Lorraine's private runway. She owned an incredible property in upstate New York. She had a private runway and hangar, which was large enough for Vincent's 16-seater jet. Human servants led Vincent and Mierka to separate bedrooms, gave them blood, and told them Lorraine would meet them in the evening.

The next evening Vincent woke up craving blood, his head still swimming in his dream. He narrowed his eyes and snarled. Lorraine had a habit of drinking his blood while he slept. She had apparently crept in sometime during the day and taken her fill. She told him once she did it because she was his sire and could do as she pleased with his body. Grumbling to himself about his beloved sire, Vincent threw back the bedcovers and got out of bed, the dream cobwebs making his vision a little fuzzy.

He groaned a bit as the image of Natalia floated before him then ran away into the darkness. The dream, like all his dreams of the human, was simple. It started with the fight at the cabin: she was surrounded by the Slayers but was able to incapacitate all of them with her staff before anyone else could move. She and Mierka, with the help of the werewolves, killed all the Slayers in seconds. When she was done proving herself as a fighter, she came to him, wrapped her arms around him and kissed him deeply. The dream dissolved into the night, and left Vincent with the image of himself taking advantage of all of Natalia's many abilities.

As he stood and looked toward the closets for clothing, he wished briefly that he had not ordered his people to destroy the cabin. It would be lovely to take Natalia back there and give her memories she would cherish instead of loathe. Vincent shook his head trying to clear it, but as he was learning, it was difficult to remove her from his mind. As he walked slowly to the clothing hanging on the closest door, he wondered if he should have brought Natalia with him instead of ordering Charlie to take her home. If she were here, she would be healed in less than a day. As it was, it would be longer than he wanted to wait until he could see her again.

Vincent's jaw twitched as he forced himself to stop thinking of Natalia. He would see her soon enough. He did not need her here as a distraction and Lorraine was expecting him. Vincent closed his eyes and took a very deep breath, letting it out slowly. Once his mind was clear, he turned his attention to the set of clothing hanging on the closet door. He examined the jeans and button up shirt, smiling. They were his forgotten clothing from his last trip.

Not wanting to waste any time with cleaning up, he slipped on the clothing and hurried out of the room. If Lorraine were anywhere, she would be in her study. She always began the night by looking over complaints and potential problems. There was generally a group of people waiting to talk to her each night. As Vincent descended the stairs, he noticed three people sitting on the couch outside Lorraine's study. Not bothering to acknowledge their presence, he strode past them, barging into his sire's study. One started to protest but was stopped by the slamming of the study door.

Lorraine was on the phone, pacing back and forth, speaking rapidly to the person on the other end. She was dressed in a blue silk robe and nothing else. She was a shapely woman and stood five foot four. She had been turned at twenty-five, but looked to be about twenty because of her small stature. "Is there any way you can get her here sooner...? Is there someone who can come sooner...? How experienced is she...? And you don't need her...? When can she be here...?" She looked toward Vincent. "But no one today...? That'll have to do. Just get her here as soon as you can. Thank you. You will be well compensated."

Lorraine hung up the phone, sat in her chair and looked toward Vincent, who was leaning against the door. "All of my healers went down to North Carolina for a ritual. They can't spare anyone until this afternoon. Lilly will be here at sunrise. It's the best I can do."

Vincent stared at her, fuming. "You said you had someone here."

Lorraine leaned back in her chair, placed her feet on the desk and her hands behind her head. The robe slid open revealing every inch of her pale petite body. Vincent felt himself reacting, knowing what she was capable of. "I told you I <u>thought</u> I could have someone here. And I really thought I could Vincent, love. I've been trying since you called."

Vincent's eyes slowly traced the line of her body from the crook of her elbow down her torso to her tight thighs. She had shaved recently. Catching the ogle, Lorraine slowly drew her hand down her body to her thigh, showing off her manicured nails. The blood red polish was a sharp contrast to her ghostly white skin. Transfixed, Vincent's eyes stayed on her hand as it traveled back up her thigh. He shook his head to clear it then realized the trail of red he hallucinated was actually her blood. Her fingers were digging hard enough into her skin to pierce the flesh and draw blood. He was by her side in an instant, kneeling by her thigh, waiting for permission. He was highly agitated, and very hungry. He wanted, no, needed blood.

Lorraine caressed his head, then wrapped her fingers in his soft, blond hair and pulled his head back. The other hand went to her thigh. She dipped her middle finger into her blood then touched her finger to his lips, tracing his flesh with her finger. She healed herself and stopped the blood flow. Her thigh was still streaked with blood. She lowered her feet to the floor, and turned to the side as she did so. She placed her feet to each side of him, and scooted forward to trap him between her legs. Even though on his knees, as tall as he was, his head reached her breasts.

Vincent allowed her actions, as his nostrils filled with the smell of her blood. He enjoyed playing the submissive with her. It had always been the same between them. He could overpower her, take what he wanted and leave her whimpering for more, but had no desire to do so. Since their first encounter, she held the dominant position. After nearly three hundred years, neither felt the need to change roles. The massive vampire allowed the diminutive woman to do as she pleased, as his wants and desires grew.

Lorraine leaned forward and brought his head toward her lips. She licked his lips clean, then dipped her tongue into his mouth, and ran her tongue against his. He took in a shaky breath and let it out in a growl. She heard his craving in the rumble and threw her head back to laugh. It had been a long time since she brought him to this level. She had to drain a good deal of his blood in order to get him to this point, but it was well worth it. And she wasn't even trying. She smiled as she bent forward to kiss him.

Vincent placed his hands on her thighs, feeling the tackiness of the blood on his left hand. The kiss grew more intense as she bared her teeth and bit his tongue. As the blood flowed into their mouths, his hands moved to her back to pull her out of the chair. He stood and set her on the desk. Her arms went around his neck to tighten the gap between them. She continued to suck on his bleeding tongue. He plunged one hand into her red tresses and pulled her head away from his. He healed the wound and glowered at her.

"Haven't you taken enough?" He could feel his control slipping. If she didn't satisfy at least one desire soon, he could become ornery.

"Vincent, love… you forget your place." There was a hard edge to her teasing tone.

"And you, lady sire, forget my nature." He caressed her breast and though he loved the feel of her soft skin, he wished she were warm. He closed his eyes, tried to pull away, then realized she wasn't letting him.

She caught the look in his eye, not really surprised. They had been in this situation before. He always tried to run; she never let him. "Vincent? Why pull away? Let your desires loose upon me. At least I can take it."

"You're not whom I wish to be with." He reached around to pry her hands loose.

"She's quite the human, to keep my favorite from my bed." She moved her hands from his head to the waistline of his pants.

He ground his teeth, and tried to control himself. He covered her hands with his to stop her questing fingers. "Sire, release me."

"No." Her tone was once again hard.

"Lorraine…" He tried to pull her hands free. She wouldn't allow it.

She pulled him forward, and snaked one hand up his chest to his head. Tangling her hand in his hair, she pulled his ear to her mouth. "You have a whole night here before you can leave, Vincent. I have a present for you—something we haven't done in a long, long time. Do you wish to see it, or do you wish to spend the rest of the night hiding in your room, sulking because you can't have your human?"

Vincent pulled back a little, not wanting to give her a chance to bite his neck. His mind thoughts spun. There were many things they hadn't done in a long time. Ravenous and now rather curious, he picked Lorraine off the desk and set her on her feet. Reaching around her he set her robe to rights and tied it closed.

"All right, love. Show me what you have, but make it quick. I'm hungry and you haven't offered me dinner yet."

"I will." Her voice was slightly melodious. She turned, headed for the door, and left him to stare at her back. He was right behind her as she opened the door. She was accosted as soon as she set foot in the hall.

"Lorraine. You were supposed to speak with me next. This," the smaller man paused and gave Vincent a sideways glare, "whelp had the audacity to step in front of me and take my place."

"Vincent is my child and is older than you by decades, Morton. Take your complaints to Max. He'll listen to your prattling; I'm bored with it. The rest of you, please return tomorrow. I have other things to take care of tonight."

"Lorraine. There are things we must discuss." This came from an older vampire, one Vincent recognized.

Her voice was kinder when she spoke to this one. "Rowland, please, I know your grievances. I can address them tomorrow. Vincent is here for one night, and as I told you when he called, I will have my fun with him.

It's been a long time since I've seen him, and I don't want to argue about it. Go about your duties and I'll see you again tomorrow night after he leaves."

Rowland seemed to shrink back into himself, unhappy with the situation. All Lorraine's children were aware Vincent was her favorite. All who lived near her were happier when he wasn't around. Rowland gave Vincent a nasty look but bowed to his sire and left. Morton continued to glare, and the third vampire left without a word. Lorraine gave Morton a smug look as she took Vincent's hand and led him away to her dungeon. Morton glared after them until he was led to the door by two of Lorraine's humans.

2

Lorraine's dungeon was not as expansive as Vincent's. His sire didn't like keeping her enemies around. She generally killed them quickly rather than storing them for future enjoyment, as Vincent was notorious for. Lorraine's dungeon consisted of one twenty by twenty-foot room with five sets of shackles. In the past, Vincent tried to convince her to create an oubliette, but she refused.

When Vincent found out that one of his people planned to betray him, he allowed the deceit to continue to its fruition. He had the betrayer watched until the full extent of their treachery was revealed. Then, when he was sure the betrayer was at his or her peak, Vincent snared the person and exacted revenge befitting the depth of the treachery. Lorraine believed in stopping the deceiver as quickly as possible and found that killing a betrayer swiftly was just as meaningful a deterrent. Consequently, Lorraine hardly ever used her dungeon.

Tonight though, two people were shackled to the wall. A naked man hung on the chains, seemingly dead. The woman, also naked, was wide-eyed and alert, with a ball gag in her mouth. Dried blood streaked their arms from the shackles. The chamber had five rows of small ceiling lights, each illuminating a different part of the room. Depending on necessity, all could be turned on, or just enough to see by. The only row on tonight was the one pointed toward the wall with the shackled humans.

"What did they do?" Vincent chose to study them from the far wall. The smell of blood aggravated his hunger.

"They're squatters. They were found in my woods, wandering around lost. The farmer who found them took them in and tried to help them. He put them to work, and for a while they seemed interested in helping. Then they started using drugs. My farmer wasn't sure where they were getting them until they foolishly tried to sell them to my humans. They had the audacity to grow them in my woods."

Her voice grew harsh. "As none of my people were interested in being killed, they refused. These two decided to try and sell the drugs to dealers in my city. It took one day for the farmer to find out what was going on. After he told me, I decided to play along and allow them to think that I was interested in a cut of the profits. When they arrived, it took me three seconds to convince them they made a big mistake. I've been researching their lives for the past month. As no one is looking for them, we can punish them as we see fit."

Vincent regarded the two humans before him. Something didn't feel right about his sire's story. Something didn't fit. He caught the female's eye, staring her down. There was true terror in her eyes, but something else as well. It was that unidentifiable something that made it impossible to take Lorraine at her word. Vincent pushed away from the wall and walked slowly toward the humans. He stopped at arm's reach from the woman and placed his cool hand on her beating heart. He closed his eyes as the beats grew more frantic. Natalia's face swam into his head, and he imagined he had her chained to the wall. His eyes opened again, and he failed to suppress a growl.

The woman before him had brown eyes and dyed black hair. Her lighter roots were showing. She was shorter than Natalia, but she was roughly the same shape. It was easy to pretend it was Natalia shackled before him.

"How long have they been here?" His hunger was so acute he could almost hear the blood flowing through her veins.

"One month."

Vincent opened his eyes. "If your story were true, they would be suffering from withdrawal. They look too healthy to have been users." He turned to Lorraine, who now stood beside him. "What are you doing, Lorraine?"

She leaned sideways against the wall with her arms crossed. She was between the two humans and could feel their warmth. "Wouldn't you love to tear her throat out, Vincent? To feel the blood stream down her neck as you lap it up like the dog you are? To use her in every way you can, just to hear her beg for more?"

The growl came from deep inside his throat. He turned to snarl at his sire, but his hand stayed on the human's chest. "That was a long time ago, Lorraine, and I'm a different man. Why do you insist on testing me in this manner?"

Her eyes grew hard as she regarded her favorite. His hand was under the human's breast; his thumb caressed the skin over her heart. "How long has it been since you've had a human lover, Vincent?"

"All save you, started out human." He turned back to the woman

7

chained to the wall. Fear shone brightly in her eyes. It grew as he leaned in to place his lips on her jugular. She started to struggle but stopped when his hand pressed her into the wall. The woman felt his strength and shuddered.

Lorraine saw the tension in his actions; the barely controlled aggression that threatened to burst through his calm exterior. He was close to the edge, but she wanted him over it. Lorraine moved to stand behind him. She reached her hands around him and gathered his shirt in her fists. She pulled hard and smiled when the buttons popped. He allowed her to pull the shirt off, then slipped his bare arms around the human's torso. Her warmth made him shudder. She tried to scream and couldn't. Vincent laughed softly, intoxicated by the terror seeping through her pores.

"What's the longest you've had to wait until you changed one of your human lovers, Vincent?" Lorraine's voice penetrated his clouded thoughts.

"Six months. What are you getting at, sire?" He looked at her with clouded eyes as she came around to stand against the wall once more.

"I spoke with Mierka. She told me about Natalia. Why does she want to be with you, Vincent? What are her intentions?"

Vincent leaned into the human's neck again, and breathed her scent into his lungs. His answer was a whisper against the woman's neck. "Pleasure."

"Are you sure?" Lorraine ran her hand up and down his side, tickling him slightly.

"No." He answered through clenched teeth and Lorraine saw his fangs.

"What do you want with her?"

Vincent's hands moved to the wall, to either side of the human, as Lorraine's hand moved to the front of his jeans. She rubbed his already obvious erection. "To use her in every way she allows."

Lorraine leaned in to whisper towards his ear. She could feel him quivering as her hand snaked inside his jeans. "Long run, Vincent. What do you want from her in the long run?"

His vision cleared as he turned his head to stare hard at his sire. "I want to change her, make her mine for as long as she'll stay."

"Have you considered she might not want to be changed?" Her hand came out of his jeans to undo his button and zipper.

"I'll keep her human until I convince her." He shut his eyes tight as Lorraine slid his jeans down and pushed him against the woman. He growled as the fire of her skin seared his chest and erection.

Lorraine whispered as her hands roamed his back. "And if she doesn't want to be convinced?"

His hands dug into the wall. The limestone crumbled as his fingers caught in minute crevices. "I'll keep her as she is."

"Look at the woman in front of you Vincent." She whispered but her voice grew severe when he didn't obey her. "Look at her, Vincent."

Not wanting to, he pulled back anyway, and regarded the frightened human in front of him. Tears streamed down the human's face; her eyes wide as saucers.

"What would you do to this human, if I let you?"

His answer was to growl as the girl whimpered.

"And what will you do to Natalia the day you confront her with the same amount of hunger?" Her voice was rather mild.

Vincent reeled back; surprised his sire had voiced his thoughts. He took a good look at the terrified human chained to the wall. She slumped against the wall and whimpered in relief. Vincent pulled his jeans up, buttoned them, and gave Lorraine a nasty look. "This is why you brought me down here? To teach me a lesson?"

Lorraine leaned against the wall, once again between her two captives. She started to caress the male, to get a reaction out of him. He moaned as she ran her hand along the inside of his thighs. Vincent was taken aback. He had assumed the male to be dead. Lorraine smiled at their reactions.

"Reminding you of the danger was one of my reasons, yes." She stopped touching the human and he went limp.

Vincent took a deep breath, and let it out slowly. "I wouldn't do this to her."

"Mierka told me Joseph had to pull you away from her the night you freed her. It's dangerous to be with a human for any length of time. Especially one with as dubious a background as hers."

He slammed his fist into the wall, and grew hungrier as he healed his bloody knuckles. "I'm not letting her go."

Lorraine smiled at his reaction. She sounded amused. "She's gotten into your blood. How interesting, and only after what, three meetings? I'm impressed."

"Four."

"What?"

"Four meetings. I've met her four times." Vincent smirked. He would bet that Joseph had not told Mierka of Vincent's encounter with Natalia at the restaurant. Vincent would have the pleasure of telling Lorraine every lustful detail. He would have the upper hand tonight.

"Vincent, listen to yourself. You've lost control. You care about how many times you've seen her, and not what you will one day do to her. What will you do when you accidentally kill her?"

Vincent was starting to get bored with the conversation. His hunger was returning and there were two humans chained to the wall. He was still quite turned on and Lorraine wore only a robe. Except he couldn't do anything until she told him he could. He sighed heavily. "This is all irrelevant until I know if she's willing to be changed or not, Lorraine. We both know that." He took some steps toward the door, stopped then turned back to the humans. "Why are they really here?"

"Both were born here, on my farms. They decided they didn't want to be here anymore, but they didn't ask my permission to leave. They had it in their heads I would never allow anyone to leave, because no one has wanted to in a long time. They knew what I was, of course, and somehow contacted a Slayer. Hired one to kill me. They confessed to wanting my riches as well. I killed the Slayer in front of them and their parents."

"What did their families think?" Vincent came close to the female again to caress her naked body. He was starting to understand Lorraine's intentions.

"Their parents were also born here. They live by my rules and believe their children are foolish. They can't understand why they would want to leave when I provide everything they want. All the money they could need, all the food, everything. They have the freedom to come and go as they please, as long as they give me what I need and keep quiet. Their parents understand that. They are among my most loyal."

"And what did they say when you caught their children?" Vincent had one hand around the female's throat, and squeezed her breast with the other, as he pressed her into the wall. She whimpered again.

"These two are old enough to take care of themselves. They took my oath with their parents many times." She shrugged. "Their parents think they're already dead."

"And what will you do to them?" He kissed the spot just behind the girl's ear, and nibbled on her earlobe. She sobbed through the gag in her mouth.

Lorraine pulled him away roughly, and turned him toward her to slap him. "They receive no pleasure." She slapped him again, mostly for the fun of it. She enjoyed controlling a man so much larger than herself he could snap her in two. "How hungry are you, Vincent?"

He pulled his sire into his arms, and held her tight against him. "I could drain her in seconds."

"Then do it, my love." She held onto him, not letting him move. "But imagine that it's Natalia chained to the wall. Take all the aggression Mierka couldn't assuage, all the hunger for your human you can't yet release. Take it all and channel it into her." She inclined her head to the woman now struggling with futility against the chains. "Take her blood only. I want to reap the benefits of the aphrodisiac."

"You're a very strange woman, Lorraine." His hand plunged into her rich red hair; his lips crushed against hers. There was no passion in the kiss, only hunger. She had given him permission to take what he needed. He allowed his craving to blossom fully as he let his sire go and turned to the human, who shook her head violently.

Vincent closed the distance between them and reached out to encircle the human's neck with his hand. The crazed look in his eye stilled her movements. He reached out with his other hand and ripped the leather ball gag off. She started pleading then, some inane babble that had no meaning. He showed her his teeth, elongated his fangs as she watched, and drooled as she started to scream. The sound was bliss. To live as a civilized man, he had donors to feed from. It confined the predator in him. It was a delight when the prey fought back. He reached up, pulled the chains out of the wall, and smiled as faint hope glimmered in the girl's eyes.

She immediately started to fight and tried to hit him with her heavily shackled hands. He let the chain hit his chest. It stung. He had clearly lost more blood than he realized. If he let the fight drag out, he might get hurt. His smile grew wider as a growl passed his lips. His hunger took over and he backed up to give her room to move. Lips quivering in a slight snarl, he let her pass. She swung the chain, as if to gain her freedom by fighting, most probably. Although the girl had lived with the knowledge of vampires all her life, she evidently knew nothing about fighting them.

The girl started swinging in tighter arcs, hoping to get him with one good hit. She did look like Natalia but had none of her grace or talents. He could take this one down with one punch. He waited though, allowing her to land one hard slap with the chain. He felt and heard the crack on his shoulder bone. Vincent healed quickly, felt his hunger grow, and then it was too much. He had used and lost too much blood to continue as a thinking creature.

With an animal howl, he launched himself at the being in front of him and slammed it against the wall. He sank his fangs deep into its neck, and pulled back to rip the skin apart. He heard the feminine scream, and rejoiced in the sound. He plunged his teeth into the being's neck again, felt his fingers as they sank into flesh and ripped through to the bone. Even as blood flowed freely down the human's neck, the creature that could barely be called Vincent bit through skin and muscle. Crimson liquid stained the girl's paling skin as it poured down her body.

Vincent drank her down, and lapped up all he could. Fingers clawed into her skin as his need grew and changed. In less than a minute, her blood was gone and his need for blood had abated. He pulled away from the girl, only to find himself on his knees. His chest, fingers, hands and arms were streaked with arrant blood and bits of flesh. He turned when he heard his name being called softly. Lorraine stood to his left, untying the belt on her robe. As he watched, the robe slid off her shoulders, then off her arms to pool at her feet. She took a step forward into the light. It illuminated her pale body, and made it glow.

A dark red line slowly traced its way down her neck, between her breasts. As Vincent watched, it pooled in her belly button. He growled at her, pulled himself completely away from the carcass and crawled to her on his hands and knees. He locked eyes with her as he moved, and held her steady with his gaze. He rose to his knees a foot away from her, and bowed his head as he spoke.

"Give me leave sire, to do with you as I please." His voice trembled with restrained, controlled passion.

She reached out a hand to raise his head and looked down into his eyes. Her gums and lips were stained scarlet. Blood dried on her chin in two streams. "I don't like it when you control yourself around me, child. Show me what you're holding back, and you can do as you please."

His eyes flashed as he was granted permission. Now it was his turn to control her. He reached out slowly and placed his hands on the side of her thighs. He bent his head a bit to lick the blood from her navel. Carefully, slowly, he licked his way up the stream of blood. When he reached her neck, he bit carefully into her jugular and took a few swallows. His hands traveled up and down her torso, squeezing, pinching, caressing, as was his mood. Her hands were in his hair, down his back and up his chest. Drunk, the taste of her blood swam in his mouth, and he pulled gently out of her neck. She healed the bite, pulled her head up and locked eyes with him. His frustration boiled his blood. She had been teasing him the whole night; it was his turn now. She didn't agree.

"Let yourself loose on me, Vincent. Give me what I desire. Now." It was an order.

His laughter bubbled up from deep within his chest. It was not a mirthful laugh, but an evil, gleeful laugh of one in absolute control. "You will have what you wish, lady, when I feel like giving in to you."

With her full strength, she pushed away from him. He couldn't resist her strength; she still had more blood in her than he did. He tumbled to the ground, and laughed as his ass hit the cement. The smile on her own lips showed she wasn't serious. She never was. This act had played itself out in many different rooms in many different cities and countries over the many years they had been together.

"You will obey me, insolent fool, or I will hang your still talking head on a pike." She walked to him, planted her foot on his chest.

Vincent grabbed her foot, and pulled her on top of him. He rolled over, to trap her between the floor and his massive body. "You made me the way I am, madam. Would you kill your own creation for acting in the way you taught it?"

He crushed her with his weight, then stopped any response with a hard kiss. She reacted immediately, and dug her nails into his chest. He grunted into her mouth as he felt the welts she gave him. He pulled away, no longer hiding his desire.

There was a smile of absolute happiness slowly taking over her face. "Let me up. We're not making love in the dungeon."

He gave her a hyena's smile. "I wasn't thinking of 'making love'."

Her eyes narrowed. "You can be rather crass sometimes, Vincent. Besides, there are things I want to do that would be rather uncomfortable on a cement floor. We're moving to my room."

Grumbling at the unadventurous woman, he pulled them both off the floor. He stood with her in his arms, and smiled as they left the dungeon. "You should learn what can be done in a room with shackles."

He carried her up the stairs to the first floor, then moved quickly to the grand staircase. Her bedroom was at the top of the stairs. He kicked the door closed behind them, took three large steps to her bed and threw her onto it. She watched as he unbuttoned and unzipped his jeans. Once undressed, he jumped onto the bed, and grabbed his sire to him. Her body fit well against his, but he realized as he bit into her neck that he wanted to feed off Natalia. As Lorraine's blood flowed into his mouth and down his gullet, he lost all thought. Desire consumed him, but thoughts of Natalia still crowded in his mind.

3

Natalia woke up feeling fitful, hot, thirsty, nauseated, and confused. Disoriented and groggy, she expected to find herself in Zechariah's cabin. Since the bed was comfortable and nothing smelled like pine, she knew that wasn't the case. Her vision swam, and it made her feel as if she were moving. Natalia turned on her side toward the edge of the bed. The small movement caused her to become woozy. She groaned and tried not to throw up. Pain entered her senses, and the groan grew louder until she nearly screamed. It ended in a squeak; she was too weak for more than the small noise. Pain radiated from too many different parts of her body.

A dark shape came into her field of vision and cautiously helped her to lay down on her back. She felt hands on her body, as if performing an examination. Cold hands touched her arm closest to the edge of the bed. She tried to look at the person, but couldn't make out their features. She tried again, but failed as dizziness took over and her breath became haggard.

Ben mopped her brow with a small towel. She was sweating buckets. Before moving her back to a better position, he checked the IV in her arm. In her frantic movements, she had not pulled the needle loose. He then removed the old bandage on her leg to check her wound. It was healing well, and there was no sign of infection. There was a knock on the door as Charlie entered. Ben began to douse her wound with peroxide and bandaged it.

Charlie held the door open for a man carrying a plate of food. The human, whose name Charlie had forgotten, placed the plate down on the folding tray next to the recliner. The human then sat in another recliner and waited for Ben to notice him. Charlie went to the edge of Natalia's bed to get an update. "How is she?"

"Feverish, disoriented, very thirsty. How about you? Did that nap do the trick?"

"Yeah." He had been sedated for the night. "Still no infection?"

"No."

Charlie considered the situation. "She had a really bad infection a long time ago. Could it be affecting her now?"

Ben gave him an annoyed look. "No."

Charlie felt rather irritated by Ben's tone of voice but slammed a mental door on the thought. It was only a few days until the full moon. He was cranky but didn't want to be sedated again. "So, what is it?"

"I'm guessing poison."

"Orlando was shot too. He's doing fine."

"Charlie, Orland and Natalia were shot by two different people at two different times." Ben realized it might be best to get Charlie out of here, but understood the man's concern. "We have the woman who shot her. We're trying to get some information from her, but I'm not sure she'll be useful. We'll figure it out."

"Should we tell Vincent?"

Ben gave the werewolf a sharp look, then took a calm breath. If he remained calm, the werewolf would as well. He answered gently. "Anything Vincent needs to know, Joseph would have already reported to him. And as he flew to New York to retrieve a healer, it seems redundant to tell him that she needs healing. At this point, it seems best to see if she gets any worse. Vincent can't get back here any quicker and she's been the same all night."

"So, we wait?"

"Yes, we wait."

Charlie had to admit the man was probably right. He was nervous about Natalia's condition and without Rebecca, there was no one to calm him. To try and relax, he sat in the recliner and placed the nearby tray of food on his lap. He started to pick at the steak, not sure he was hungry anymore.

Ben finished dressing Natalia's wound and repositioned her on the bed. She groaned a bit then lay still, sweating. Ben took a good look at the IV and realized she would need another bag soon. He wondered, at times, where all the medical equipment came from, but learned long ago, not to ask questions. More often than not, things like this were stolen. Since the bag did not need immediate replacement, Ben nodded and stood up.

As Charlie picked at his food, Ben strolled over to the human and nodded kindly to him. The man sat on the edge of the recliner and held his arm out to the vampire, who took the limb gently in his hands. Ben knelt, and removed a small dagger from his boot. He appraised the man's arm carefully and looked for an area not as riddled with cut and bite marks. Once a location was chosen, he made a small cut and took his evening meal. He had been awake all night and would need to stay awake all day, probably. He needed the blood, and the man's tasted fine. Once done, Ben stood, and the human wrapped a bandage around his arm. The vampire bowed once again, and the human left the room. Ben looked at Charlie who still hadn't eaten any food.

"Charlie, you're in no state to be in this room. You need to get some air. Or maybe some real sleep... not sedated sleep. You shouldn't stay in this room. I can tell how worried you are and it's affecting your mood, and mine. Go call your wife. That'll probably help you feel better."

Charlie nodded. "That's a really good idea. Do you need someone to take over for you?"

Ben shook his head. "Not yet. I'll get someone if I have to."

Charlie nodded again and rose from the chair.

Ben gave him a reassuring look. "From what I've heard, she's a fighter. She'll be fine."

Charlie made a noncommittal noise and left the room without his dinner. Ben took a seat in the recliner. The vampire sat in quiet contemplation, and watched the sleeping human toss and turn fitfully. She was dreaming. He wondered what flitted through her feverish mind.

CR   BD

It was close to sunrise. Ben and one of Vincent's humans had been taking care of Natalia for a full day. Ben had not been able to coax Natalia awake enough to feed her. He was attempting to give her applesauce when someone knocked on the door. Joseph came in without waiting for an answer. His shirt and pants were wrinkled, and his pant cuffs were caked in dirt and dust.

"Don't come closer." Ben pointed to his boss's dirt covered pants. "An infection could kill her."

"What's wrong with her?"

"Poison, most likely. The Slayer who shot her ended up killing herself before we could interrogate her. How's Orlando?"

"He felt well enough to patrol with Rebecca during the day. How did the Slayer kill herself? Was she not searched and tied?"

Ben pointed to his mouth. "The woman had one of those fake teeth with poison in it. That's why we think Natalia was poisoned."

"Have you tried her blood?"

Ben gave him a hard look. "I don't think Vincent would be pleased with that."

"If you took just enough to see if she's been poisoned, he wouldn't object." Joseph started toward the bed.

"Seriously, Joseph, go change. Your pants are covered in dirt."

Joseph gave Ben an irritated look but left the room. He came back minutes later in clean clothing.

"Where's Elving?" Ben asked as Joseph came closer to the bed.

"He's seeing to Orlando and the other werewolves. It's almost the full moon. They're deciding whose turn it is to go out. The rest are deciding where to spend the night. Go help them." The last was an order.

Ben put the container of applesauce and spoon on the table, got up and left.

Joseph knew that every room in the house was wired with cameras and microphones. Vincent liked to make sure guests didn't plot against him in his own home. Joseph reached into his pants pocket and took out the small remote control he always carried with him. Vincent gave him the device when the surveillance equipment had been installed, in case Joseph wanted to have some privacy with Mierka. The device also came in handy when he and Vincent needed to have private conversations. While there were common apps to control such things, phones could be hacked.

The sequence of numbers he entered into the device controlled the microphones and cameras for this room only. In the security room the only thing the guard might notice was the video screen changing to a different room. Rebecca was there now, watching the screens intently. She had convinced the on-duty guard to take a break. Joseph ordered her to the security room to distract the guard; she decided to take over the watch.

Rebecca watched as the screen flashed black then came back on and showed one of the other bedrooms. Her hands hovered over the keyboard as her curiosity tried to take control. It was unusual for Joseph to demand privacy. Now that he asked for it while in the same room as their boss's woman, Rebecca was concerned. Her hands formed fists as she stared at the delinquent screen, but she knew better than to override the code.

Most vampires who visited Vincent in his home or office knew he kept everything bugged. Some, such as Christopher and Edwin, always demanded to have the cameras and recording devices turned off when meeting with him. They didn't know that his top people had override codes for such situations.

Rebecca's hands curled again and inadvertently caressed the keyboard. Vincent always allowed Joseph his privacy and advised Rebecca never to listen in on his longtime friend unless given specific orders to. She had no such orders for this instance. Rebecca hung her head, sighed and pulled her hands away from the keyboard. Whatever Joseph was doing, it was not for her to know. She sat back in the chair, and waited for the screen to come back on. Half an hour later, the room came back into view. Joseph stood by the bed and slipped his hand into his pocket; Natalia still tossed and turned behind him.

Owen came back to the security room about fifteen minutes later. Rebecca turned the chair over to him and went to the back door, still unsure of what to do. A wolf howled off in the distance, which made her hair stand on end. A shiver ran up her spine as a gentle hand caressed her back. She turned around to greet Charlie.

"Morning."

"Missed you." His arms stole around her and pulled her close. He had a wolf's grin on his lips. She slipped her arms around his neck and pulled him down for a kiss. When it became more aggressive, Rebecca pulled away.

"We can't do this now, Charlie."

"I know." He took her hand and led her into the kitchen. "I just got up. Want some breakfast?"

"Yes, I do. How's the patient?"

"Don't know. Ben ordered me out of the room last night so I could watch over her today. But I'm going to need some help."

"What's up?"

"I'm too riled up. It might be better if I don't watch her alone."

She looked at her husband for a moment, then frowned softly and spoke in a gentle tone. "Why do you think it's somehow your fault she got hurt?"

He smiled gratefully at her as his tension momentarily melted away. His wife knew him very well. He sat at the counter as she started to gather food. "It happened after Natalia hypnotized her friend. I wasn't paying enough attention to my surroundings."

He continued the story as she made breakfast. Though she listened, part of her mind was on the fact that Natalia had a human friend. Rebecca knew it was dangerous to have human friends. She had none herself. Never had. She grew up knowing what she would become and had been warned against making any unnecessary bonds. Her only friends growing up were the adult werewolves her parents knew and Vincent's crew. Her parents worked for Vincent until Rebecca was old enough to take over. Vincent convinced her great-grandfather to work for him, and her family had been working for the vampire ever since.

Rebecca brought her mind back to the present situation as Charlie finished his story. "There was nothing you could do. Sounds like the Slayer was hidden."

"Still. I don't know." He ran his hand through his thick, shaggy hair. "What if she dies?"

Rebecca looked her husband in the eye. "If she dies and Vincent is here, she'll be turned. Pretty sure she'll be turned if he isn't here." She cocked her head. "Are you worried Vincent will blame you for her getting shot?"

He opened his mouth to speak but stopped as he thought about it. During his silence, Rebecca plated some eggs and minute steaks that she cooked while he wasn't paying attention. She grabbed some coffee and milk, then sat down and started to eat before he answered.

"I think I am."

Rebecca gestured toward his food. "I think he'll be too worried about her to think about it. I'll talk to Joseph and make sure everything will be ok."

He smiled at her. "You always take care of me."

She gave him a loving smile but said nothing. He kissed her gently on the lips then turned his attention to his breakfast. Whatever happened, she always made him feel better.

4

There was a rush of activity in the house as Vincent came in from the garage. He carried about him an aura that announced to his people that any attempt to impede him would be met with immediate retribution. His suit was wrinkled, his brow furrowed. His long legs carried him quickly along his path and his hands were clenched into fists at his side.

Behind him followed a woman in a flowing yellow dress. She had a slight smile on her face and in her eyes. Her black hair streamed out behind her and revealed various tattoos. Two younger women trailed behind her, in flowing green and blue dresses. Mierka was at the rear.

Vincent led Lilly and her apprentices upstairs to the spare bedroom, and didn't waste any time on greetings. His people stayed out of his way. Joseph stood at the top of the stairs, waiting. As Vincent's foot hit the second-floor landing, his guard started walking in silence. Joseph held the door open for Vincent and Lilly, and nodded to the ladies as they walked by. He knew who they were and respected them.

The three ladies were healers from a small but growing group known as the House of the Turning Sky. The House was well respected, though other mages found their methods archaic. Most mages relied on books and scrolls handed down through the generations. The mages in the House of the Turning Sky harnessed their own will and the raw energy in the air and earth. As Mierka led the other ladies to the bathroom down the hall, Joseph shook his head. Lilly had a strong will, but he wondered if it would be strong enough to combat Natalia's.

Joseph almost ran into Vincent, who had paused in the doorway, appalled by his woman's appearance. Natalia was pale and thinner than she had been four days ago. The bed sheets and mattress were soaked with sweat. He took a breath to calm himself but stopped when the smell of the room hit him. The acrid smell of sweat and the cloying scent of death lay thick in the room. Ben sat on the far side of the bed, and checked the bandage on her arm. The IV had been removed a few minutes prior to Vincent's arrival. Ben's skin seemed to be hanging off his bones.

"The bathroom has been prepared to specifications, sir." Joseph spoke quietly, directly to Vincent.

Vincent's jaw twitched and in one smooth move he was on the other side of the bed, kneeling besides Ben. The tired vampire prudently slid out of the way, and left the room with the help of one of the humans. He had not slept for two days; he had barely eaten. He needed looking after. Vincent didn't notice when Ben left. He slipped his arms under Natalia's knees and back, and cradled her drenched body as he picked her up. Lilly followed them out of the room, the small confident smile still highlighting her features.

Joseph stayed behind to instruct the three humans who had followed their boss upstairs. Like the humans at the cabin, they had been with the vampire for many years. Joseph's orders were not necessary, but he stayed to keep out of Vincent's way. Confident Vincent didn't need him, Joseph went down the hall to check on Dr. Elving, Ben, and Orlando. Dr. Elving sat in a chair by the door, and held a tranquilizer gun. Orlando slept fitfully, but he was still in human form. Ben was feeding. Since all was well, Joseph sauntered off to his bedroom to claim his woman. Mierka waited for him wearing nothing but a smile.

CB   BO

Vincent carried Natalia into the bathroom down the hall. The only light came from the twenty or so candles set up around the room. Most gave off the scent of flowers, a few smelled of fruit. They made the room smell like a summer garden. The round tub in the center of the room was already filled with warm water. Rose petals floated on top. Lilly's apprentices stood by two tables. One table held small bottles of various colored liquids, the other had fruit. The women were in robes; their hair tied back from their faces. Vincent barely acknowledged them as he carefully set Natalia down on the black bathmat and kissed her lips. He stood, nodded to Lilly, and left the room. He wanted to stay but had business to discuss with Anthony.

Lilly removed most of her clothing as her apprentices removed their robes. Eva walked slowly to Natalia's side, while Gail climbed into the large round tub. Eva picked Natalia up, placed her in Gail's arms then climbed into the tub herself. Both ladies gently lowered Natalia into the water. She began to struggle when the tepid water touched her feverish body. The ladies had to force her onto the tub seat and hold her down as Lilly began to chant. Natalia calmed as the words continued. A few moments later she started to thrash. The spell started to take hold and tried to pull the poison out of her blood. She started to whimper, then screamed as she tried to wrench herself free of the pain. As her actions became more violent, the two ladies let her go, but stayed close in case her head slid under the water.

Natalia's body started to tremble as the spell took hold completely. She bucked off the seat and threw herself into the water. Eva and Gail reached forward and lifted her back onto the seat. The shudders became more violent, so the ladies stepped closer to try and steady her. Lilly chanted louder and faster; Natalia's shudders became quakes. A few minutes later, the ladies let her go. Continuing to hold her could harm her.

Lilly felt the will of the human as it fought hard against her. She had an incredible will, but Lilly's was stronger, or perhaps just more determined. She added another element to her spell, picked up a small bottle of oil and rewove the spell to calm as well as heal. It would hopefully assure the human that the spell was not harmful. Lilly poured the oil into the water, focused intensely on the spell, and felt the energy around her bend to her will. Natalia's body calmed as her will subsided. Lilly's concentration switched back to the healing. Her chants became even louder, hastening with intensity.

Natalia threw her head back as the tremors increased and her body heaved one final time. Acid, blood, and other liquids came boiling up her throat and out of her mouth. The viscous glob sank to the bottom of the tub and started to mix with the water. Consciousness seeped in as she leaned back and felt cool glass touch her lips. Water trickled down the corners of her mouth until she sucked it in and started to drink. She was only given a swallow or two before the glass was pulled away.

A soft voice reached her from behind, "Help her out of the tub."

Two sets of hands pulled her up and out. They set her on the bathmat on her side. She lay shivering for a couple of minutes as she was given more water and bits of oranges. A terry cloth robe was laid on top of her to help her chills. Natalia clutched at the robe and tried to control her ragged breath. As the room grew brighter, she became more aware of her surroundings. She took a deep breath as the scented candles were extinguished. She tried to sit up and was helped by two sets of hands. Her eyes rolled back as a wave of dizziness hit. She put her head between her knees and threw up.

Lilly turned on more of the room's lights and went to see her patient. Natalia leaned against the side of the tub. Eva had a glass of water for her and Gail had a tray of sliced fruit. Someone had already cleaned up the vomit. Natalia stared at Lilly, who smiled and knelt beside her.

"How are you?"

"Not sure. Everything hurts."

"Do you know where you are?"

"Vincent's home?"

"Do you know who you are?"

A small smile came to her lips, "Vincent's woman."

Lilly gave a small laugh. "You have a very strong will. I almost couldn't heal you."

"I appreciate the help." Eva offered her the glass of water and Natalia took a small sip. "Why did you help me?"

"Because Lorraine asked me too."

"Who's Lorraine?"

"Vincent's sire. Can you stand?"

Natalia talked around the piece of fruit she placed in her mouth. "I won't know until I try."

Sucking on the fruit, Natalia turned to place her knees on the ground. The women reached out to help, but she pushed them away. She wanted to stand on her own. The tub was tall enough to require steps to get in. Natalia reached out with a shaking hand and placed it on the middle step. She moved closer, put her weight on her arms and placed one foot on the ground. She pulled herself up and placed her other foot on the ground. Taking a deep breath, she pushed all the way up to a standing position. Even using the tub as support, she shook slightly as she tried to stand erect.

"How do you feel?" Her healer looked rather worried.

"Dizzy. What's your name?"

"Liliana but call me Lilly." Gesturing to each in turn, "These are my apprentices, Eva and Gail."

Natalia gave a shaky smile. "Liliana is my middle name."

"It amused Vincent, too. If you can walk, another bath has been prepared for you so you can wash up." She held out a robe. Natalia slipped it on and did not to fall. "I pulled poison out of your body. Do you know what you were poisoned with?"

Natalia tied the robe as she carefully shook her head. "I'm not even sure what happened. I remember starting to cross the street with Charlie and then falling." She frowned and looked at Lilly. "Did someone shoot me?"

"From what I gather." She took Natalia's arm to lead her to the other bathroom.

"Does anyone know who it was?"

"All I know is that it was a woman."

Natalia thought about it as she started to walk a few steps. "Judith left before Vincent came to save me. If she shot me, there's no telling what she used. She found a way to add various poisons to her bullets. She spent years perfecting the process. I have no idea how she did it. Chemistry wasn't really my thing."

Lilly frowned as they slowly continued to walk to the other bathroom. "Was she a Slayer?"

"She was."

"Why use poison in her bullets? It wouldn't do much to a vampire."

"She did it to hurt any humans she found working with Hellspawn. She didn't care if those humans knew what their acquaintances truly were." Natalia walked slowly, with small steps. She felt dizzy and weak, and wanted nothing more than to sit on the floor. She felt less disoriented if she looked down at her feet. She ignored the woman next to her and concentrated on her next step.

Lilly sensed the human's need for silence, and simply led the way. They were halfway to Vincent's room and Natalia was noticeably improving. By the time they reached Vincent's rooms, the human walked with her head held high.

Antique furniture and the scent of old, well-cared for wood greeted them as they entered the sitting room. There were two leather couches, a large wooden desk, and several glass cases filled with artwork and artifacts from all over the world. All the furniture was stained a dark red and had clawed feet. Lilly admired everything as she led Natalia through the room. Natalia didn't seem to notice anything but the way ahead. Looking around too much made her slightly dizzy.

When they entered the master bedroom, Natalia gasped at the sight of the four-poster bed. Her dream came back to her as she looked around. Though the dream had not occurred in some time, she remembered it well. She lay on a bed similar to the one before her, surrounded by sheets and drapes in various shades of red. A man appeared, a goblet of blood in his hand, and called her child. Beyond him was a balcony. She knew now that Joseph was the man with the goblet. Natalia wondered if this room was the room she had dreamt of.

The room was similar to the one in her dream, but not exact. There was no canopy on this bed, but the sheets and bedding were the same deep, blood red. She stopped thinking about the dream for a moment as the bed seemed to call to her, inviting her to lie down. The comforter looked thick and luxurious. The sheets shimmered like silk, and probably were. To stop herself from laying down on the bed, she continued to look around to try and find other similarities with her dream. There was a nightstand on each side of the bed, with a dragon lamp accentuating the dragon legged tables. A chair of the same hue as the furniture in the sitting room leaned against one wall. There were doors along each wall of the room, broken up only by the large bay window. A partially drawn curtain half-hid the view of the surrounding land.

Lilly cleared her throat to indicate they should continue. It took a moment for Natalia to move; the view had her full attention. Before moving on, she concluded that it was not the same view as in her dream. Something was missing, but she didn't know what. Lilly finally pulled at her arm. Natalia started to walk again, while she struggled to picture the view in her dream. She let the dream go and followed Lilly through the only open door. The master bathroom was larger, as was the round tub. The tub was to the left of center. There was a large square shower stall in the right corner. Next to it was a counter with two sinks. The toilet was in the left corner, mostly hidden behind a curtain.

Lilly helped Natalia out of her robe and into the tub. There were stairs for this one, too.

"Wouldn't a shower make more sense?"

"You can shower later. I want to help you with your hair. It's more comfortable for both of us if you're seated in the tub."

Natalia gave her a look. "You're going to wash my hair? No one's washed my hair since I was nine and ill."

Lilly shrugged. "The water is warm. If I wash your hair, you can relax. Eva and Gail are fetching more food. You need to gather your strength, not use it."

Natalia shook away her slight unease. It wasn't necessary. Lilly was a healer and meant her no harm. "That sounds great."

Natalia noticed a woman's razor and shaving cream resting on the foot-wide edge of the tub. She quickly ducked her head under the water, to soak her hair, and fought dizziness as she sat upright. She had to place her hands on the seat of the tub and breathe deep until the vertigo passed. Once she felt better, she turned in the seat, and presented Lilly her back. Natalia looked at her legs and knew she wanted to shave before she relaxed. She took the razor and cream and carefully went to work on her legs as Lilly washed her hair. It took three washings to clean her hair completely. Natalia was done with shaving before Lilly finished. Eva and Gail came in as she was rinsing out her hair a third time. Natalia was starting to feel lightheaded and was grateful for the bowl of stew they gave her.

"It's lamb stew. There's also bread, cheese, fruits, and vegetables." Eva held a tray with the other items, resting it against the edge of the tub. Gail set a glass and a pitcher of water to her other side.

Natalia gave a nervous but proud laugh. "I feel like royalty."

Lilly carefully massaged conditioner into Natalia's hair. "Stay with Vincent long enough and you will be."

Natalia pulled away to look back at Lilly. She frowned at her healer, "What do you mean?"

"You're Vincent's woman. After you learn the ways of his House, you'll run it."

Natalia frowned, "Sounds archaic."

"You'll be given everything you want."

Natalia tried a spoonful of the stew. It had been cooked long enough that the meat had fallen apart, and the vegetables were soft. It was very tasty. As she ate, she thought about Lilly's statement. Now that she was with Vincent, she couldn't think of anything that she wanted, except him.

She pushed the thought from her head, and decided that Lilly was wrong. Vincent wanted her for the same reason she wanted him: for sex. There was nothing more between them. He would only give her as much as she gave him. The thought didn't bother her; it just made things simpler. She settled into the seat and continued to eat the stew.

For the next half hour, she relaxed in the tub and ate. In the end, she was wrinkled and full. She ate the soup and half of the bread, cheese, and fruit. Lilly was pleasantly surprised. The human was doing better than she thought possible. Humans usually took longer to recover, even with the help of a healer. Eventually, the three mages helped Natalia into a terry cloth robe. Natalia wanted to shower, but Lilly suggested a nap instead. They dried her hair and body first, then led her to Vincent's bed. The covers were already turned down.

Natalia laid on the bed, and felt the smoothness of the fabric on her bare skin. Lilly covered her with the silk top sheet and the comforter. Natalia sighed in contentment and was asleep within seconds. Lilly left with Eva and Gail to find their rooms and settle in.

5

Agentle hand shook her awake. Natalia looked up into Lilly's face. The woman had changed her makeup. "Wake up, Natalia. Vincent wishes to see you soon."

A smile came to Natalia's face at the mention of her lover's name. Refreshed, she sat up, turned, and swung her legs over the side. There was a tray by the bed with a glass of water and a plate of bread, cheese, and fruit.

Lilly sat on a chair in front of her, to catch her in case she fell over. "Are you hungry?"

Natalia was surprised to realize she was. She nodded and reached for the butter knife, to spread blue cheese on a slice of French bread. Chewing slowly, she closed her eyes and enjoyed the rich flavor. In between bites of food, she took sips of water, and felt once again like royalty. She reached for a slice of apple and paused. Her shoulder didn't hurt, and neither did the rest of her body. She looked at Lilly.

"I don't hurt."

Lilly smiled. "I'm a healer. I took care of your wounds."

Natalia frowned, "Where was I shot?"

"In your left thigh."

A noise came from the doorway, "Lilly? A moment?"

Both women turned to see Eva standing in the doorway. Lilly looked to Natalia. "Will you be alright by yourself?"

Natalia nodded and waited for the woman to leave. She went back to looking herself over. She examined her thigh and to her arm where the graze had been. There was no bullet hole; no evidence she had ever been shot, not even a scar. She set the glass down and brought a shaking hand to the unmarred skin. These were the first wounds that hadn't left scars. Lilly mentioned healing her of the poison; Natalia hadn't considered the full extent of the spell's effects.

Natalia moved her hand to her shoulder and felt Charlie's bite mark. Her hand covered the old scar and her eyes closed. The memory flooded her mind as a shudder claimed her body. That encounter with Charlie had left her hurt and wanting. She hated the bite, but had craved his touch. She remembered the look in his eye as he had approached her those many years ago. Another shudder wracked her body as a newer memory took over. The look in Vincent's eyes when he goaded her at the restaurant had mirrored Charlie's from the night he bit her.

Natalia felt wetness on the sheets between her legs and laughed when she realized how moist she had become. "Come claim me, Vincent."

She didn't know she had spoken aloud. She shook her head and knew it wasn't what she wanted. Natalia wanted to possess him. She stood, determination keeping her steady. She wanted a shower. Though she didn't need one, part of her felt if she could stand in the shower, she could consider herself better.

Natalia grabbed the silk robe off the end of the bed and went to the shower. She found a large towel waiting for her on the rack next to the stall. In the shower were various soaps, shampoos and conditioners. There were even some small bottles of cologne. Natalia smiled. She should have known Vincent was high maintenance with all the silk and suits he wore. She laughed and stepped into the stall. She made sure the water ran lukewarm before closing the door. She preferred hot showers but knew that it was safer to have a cool shower in case her vertigo returned. Even though she felt fine now, she knew she was still recovering. Ten minutes later, she came out of the shower.

Lilly leaned against the bathtub and scowled at her. "You should've waited for me. What if you'd fallen?"

Natalia wrapped the towel around her body and gave Lilly one of her determined looks. "The water was cold, and I wasn't in there long."

Lilly saw the look and shook her head. Having felt the human's will, she knew there was no point in arguing. "There's clothing for you in the other room."

"You're not going to argue?" Natalia's desire for Vincent grew with each passing moment. In lieu of being with him, she would take a fight.

Lilly cracked a smile as she understood the woman's expression. "You're a handful. I hope Vincent knows what he's getting into."

Natalia gave the healer a devilish smile, "Probably not." Both women snickered. "May I have some privacy? I'm not comfortable dressing while someone is watching."

"Certainly. I'll be in the sitting room. There's a dress laid out on the bed for you. Vincent chose it himself."

"Thank you. And Lilly, I'm grateful for everything you've done." She gave the woman a kind look, "There's no scars."

"You have enough scars; you didn't need another one. And you're welcome." She left Natalia alone to prepare herself.

Natalia dried off and went to the bedroom. Someone had made the bed and a dress lay on top of the comforter. There was no underwear. As a smirk graced her lips, she let her robe slide off her shoulders onto the floor. She touched the dress and caressed the soft, cool silk. She lifted the dress off the bed and unzipped the back. The dress slid over her head and down her body. The fabric felt incredible next to her skin. Like being in the bed, but better since Vincent had picked it out for her. She zipped it up as she walked over to the mirror to check herself out. The spaghetti strap midnight blue dress was a little big. Likely due to her illness, she was a little thinner than usual. She wondered how long her sickness had lasted.

A final look in the mirror made her heart flutter. Breathing deeply, she tried to calm herself, since Vincent would rile her up soon enough. Natalia turned and walked into the sitting room. To her surprise, Lilly was not alone. Ben and Lilly sat on separate couches staring each other down. There was a smile on Lilly's face, which made Natalia think it wasn't serious. Lilly saw her emerge and stood to greet her. "You look lovely. Vincent will be pleased."

Ben stood to look her way. He gave her a hungry look but said nothing.

"Thank you." She dug her toes into the carpet and looked down. "Do you have any shoes I can borrow? I didn't see any in the bedroom."

"He wanted you to wear heels. I told him that it might be a bad idea, if you still felt dizzy and that I'd take care of it. What size do you wear?"

Natalia told her.

"I'll see what I can do. Ben wanted to inform you about someone named Bethany."

The name earned him a hard look from Natalia. They stayed quiet as Lilly left the room.

Ben turned to Natalia and indicated the couch he had been sitting on. "Care to sit?"

"Thank you. What's going on with Bethany?"

"Charlie wanted to make sure you knew this, but he's otherwise engaged at the moment. We've had her under surveillance." His eyes grew kind. "What you did worked. She seems to have, at least for the moment, forgotten about you."

Natalia hung her head, "Good." She closed her eyes and took a deep breath, then looked back up to Ben. "How long will she be under surveillance?"

"The plan is to keep an eye on her for a month. After that, as long as she hasn't contacted you, we'll leave her alone. Unless, of course, you believe it should continue."

Natalia shook her head. "I don't think that's necessary. It's best to let her live her life. I'll change my phone number. After that point, she shouldn't have a way to contact me."

Ben nodded. "That's all then."

"Thank you."

He stood and smiled. "If I may ask a question?"

She watched his eyes as they changed from professional to that of a man admiring a woman. She frowned slightly and wondered at his thoughts. "All right."

He paused and looked her up and down. She sat up straight on the couch, one arm on the armrest, the other beside her. The dress clung to her shapely, crossed legs. His smile came back. "Where did Vincent find you?"

"I found him." Her voice showed her pride.

"Of course you did. When you're done with him, come see me, if you desire." He held out his hand to her. She took it and he bowed low over her hand to kiss her fingers. "For now, I must bid you good night. There are things I must attend to, and Liliana has returned with your shoes."

He straightened himself, gave her another bow and left the room. Lilly stood by the door, arms crossed. Shoes hung from the fingers of her left hand. She glared at Ben as he passed her. Lilly brought Natalia the flats, but softened her features as she approached.

"Men." She placed the shoes in front of Natalia as she sat on the couch.

"You heard?" Natalia slipped her feet into the simple black flats. They were leather with square toes. They were cute, but nothing special. She wondered what shoes Vincent wanted her to wear.

"It doesn't matter what species they are; they all want the same thing."

"So do I." Natalia stood, testing the shoes, "Don't you?"

Lilly appeared to think about it, then shrugged her shoulders. "I suppose. Men are just more obvious about it."

"Don't say that until you've seen me around Vincent. Where is he, anyway?" She walked around the couches to get comfortable with the shoes. "Downstairs in his office." Lilly stood and headed for the door. "He's almost ready to see you."

Natalia held her head high. As she didn't feel dizzy, she walked at her normal pace to the door, and reached it before Lilly. "Well, I'm ready to see him. Let's go."

Lilly shook her head. She hoped for Vincent's sake that he knew what kind of woman he was about to share his bed with. She also wondered, as she led the human downstairs, if Natalia knew the kind of creature she wanted to sleep with. Lilly came back to herself as Natalia stumbled. Lilly caught her before the woman fell too far. The healer cradled the human as all around her others rushed to her aid.

6

Vincent was displeased. Anthony sat opposite him, and looked rather unnerved. Vincent had been berating the younger vampire for over two hours. Justin died while attempting to capture Judith and no one thought to inform their leader. All the people involved were currently being run through various training exercises. When Joseph was done with them, he would take the group down to the dungeon where they would be kept for 48 hours without blood. Justin worked for Anthony, but lived with and reported directly to Vincent. He knew the human longer than Anthony had.

"I still don't understand why."

"I made a mistake sir. I accept that and await my punishment."

Vincent sensed that he was holding something back. "That didn't explain anything, Anthony."

Anthony's eyes darted away then back.

"I'm waiting."

He finally answered, "I thought you would be too involved with her to worry about it."

Anthony watched as Vincent grew far angrier. "No woman has ever taken my attention so completely that I stopped caring about the people in my house. This does not happen again." Vincent stood quickly. "I'm done with you for the moment."

"What about the other people?"

"I will release them in two days."

"They suffer for my mistake?"

"Since they didn't think for themselves, they get harsher treatment. Leave."

Anthony wanted to fight for the others, but knew he could not. His boss was right. Vincent had sent six people to watch Natalia and Charlie. Any one of the five survivors could have told Vincent of Justin's death. Anthony bowed to Vincent and took his leave.

Vincent fumed as the intercom buzzed from the security room. Mierka had gone there after greeting her man.

"Stairs. Now." Mierka's tone was not to be denied.

Vincent raced out the door Anthony held open. Anthony followed, and wondered what the problem was. When he saw Natalia cradled in Lilly's arms, he felt his skin crawl. He took a breath, and pushed aside his distrust of the woman. His service to his leader mattered more right now.

Vincent sat on the stairs and carefully took Natalia from Lilly. "What happened?"

"She fainted. It happens when you think you can do more than your body is ready for."

He placed a soft kiss on Natalia's brow. "I thought you were supposed to heal her."

"And I did. The poison has been removed and her wounds are gone. But that's all I can do for her. Anything beyond that needs to heal over time."

Vincent gave the healer a hard look. "Such as?"

"Malnourishment, blood loss, lack of sleep…such things can only heal over time. Replenishing her blood and fat stores takes far more energy than I have."

Vincent looked down at the woman asleep in his arms. A heavy sigh escaped him as he looked around for Joseph. "Take her to the master bedroom. Let her sleep."

Joseph nodded and took Natalia in his arms. Bowing slightly to the healer and his boss, he walked past the two on his way up the stairs.

Vincent came back to himself and stood. He helped Lilly to her feet then thanked her for her service. He waved her away and turned back to Anthony, who stood glowering at the bottom of the steps.

"Go home, Anthony. This doesn't concern you."

Anthony held his tongue. He bowed curtly and left as he stewed in his own thoughts.

Vincent watched him leave, and wondered if he should tell his loyal friend the truth. Vincent shook his head. He wanted to trust Natalia without thought, and therefore needed someone else to distrust her for his and his people's safety.

CS BO

Joseph placed Natalia on one of the leather couches in Vincent's sitting room then proceeded to the bedroom. He closed the curtains, pulled back the sheets, and returned to fetch Natalia. She had shifted slightly, but was still sound asleep. Joseph bent and slipped off her shoes, and left them on the floor by the couch. Picking her up carefully, he carried her into the bedroom. He sat on the bed and shifted her into a sitting position as well. Leaning her forward, he grasped the zipper, and unzipped her dress.

Joseph placed one hand on her chest, at the base of her neck. He tried to keep her somewhat upright, without allowing her head to loll forward. She was breathing regularly, which worried him. She was either faking it, or really was that deeply asleep. Considering the past few days, her exhaustion was not that surprising. When her breath caught as he slid one strap over her shoulder, he relaxed. He moved his hand slowly across her shoulder blades, feeling the warmth of her skin against his fingertips. His hand followed the other strap over her other shoulder, caressing her soft skin.

Joseph's hand returned to the middle of her back and followed the line of her spine. Her skin was riddled with scars. The newest were the whip marks that cut across her back. Interwoven with those long scars were small dimples that lined her back in a pattern. As his hand caressed the marks, he assumed correctly that those were from the cage Charlie had been kept in. His hand wandered to her right shoulder to trace the obvious bite mark Charlie left. When he saw the scar of his own bite mark on her shoulder, Joseph smiled.

He shifted slightly and leaned her against his body to remove her dress. He slid the straps off her arms, slowly; rough movements would only disturb the lady. She leaned into him and placed her head on his shoulder. Her head fell to the side and exposed her neck. Joseph turned his head, his lips centimeters from her pulsating vein. His eyes closed, enjoying her warmth. Joseph wondered what his woman thought as she watched from the security room. A leisurely smile spread across his face as he continued to undress Natalia slowly.

The dress pooled at her waist and Joseph shifted to allow her to lie down on the bed. Standing beside her, he placed one hand on each side of her and grasped the dress carefully. Slowly, he pulled the dress over her waist and off her legs, and watched her face as he removed the cool fabric. A small sigh escaped her lips as the fabric whispered off her body. Joseph paused, admired her body, and wondered if he would ever have a chance with her.

Joseph pulled the sheets over her naked body as he tried to push the thought from his head. She curled into a fetal position, and gathered the blankets around her. She sighed as the cool warmth of the silk cuddled around her body, then settled back and was once again asleep. Joseph placed the dress over the back of the chair and left the room. Tense, he went to find Mierka, who laughed when he entered the security room. After some teasing, she relented, and called another into the security room.

Once satiated, Joseph went back to the humans who waited in the training room. They had been standing at an uncomfortable attention since

Mierka called him to the stairs. Joseph spent the rest of the night making them even more uncomfortable. He rather enjoyed it. It was close to sunrise when he led them downstairs. He took three into the main dungeon and shackled them to the wall. The two others were taken to separate cells. None protested, as all understood why they were being punished. Joseph left the dungeon and went to Vincent's study. He knocked before entering but didn't wait for a response, as he knew he was expected. Vincent sat at his desk, looking through some paperwork.

Vincent looked up as Joseph entered and gave his friend a level look as the man walked to the side bar and poured himself a glass of brandy.

"What did you learn?" Vincent went back to his paperwork.

"She was mostly incoherent." He swirled the glass slowly as he tried in vain to warm the dark liquid.

Vincent looked up at Joseph, annoyed with his friend's coyness. "What did she say?"

A phantom of a smile flashed across his features. When he turned toward Vincent all that was left was a glimmer in his eye. "She doesn't want to be changed. I couldn't discern why, but I believe it has something to do with the vampire she hunts."

"This amuses you?" Vincent's hands were folded on his desk.

"Yes, it does." He took a sip of brandy as Vincent stood and pushed the chair back violently. Joseph's smile didn't waiver as he continued. "She plans on staying with you for as long as you'll have her. From what I've seen, she'll be an incredible challenge. She'll drive you crazy for as long as she's here. And all the while, she'll remain human until she decides otherwise."

"Why does this amuse you, old friend?" Vincent came around the desk, and tried to hide his emotions.

"You're used to getting things your way. You won't with her. It'll be interesting to watch." He paused to take another sip of the fine brandy. "I wonder how much she'll get away with?"

Vincent stared out the window as he considered his friend's words. He wanted to argue, but knew Joseph was right. He considered how much he had already done for the human, although he only met her four times. There was something about her, as there had been with the five other women who had come before. Something had caught his attention from the moment they met. He took it for granted that Natalia would stay with him after he freed her. Now he knew she wanted to stay, but as a human, not as a vampire. He wondered if it mattered.

The memory of last night and of what he had done to Lorraine's captive came back to him. He had allowed himself to pretend it was Natalia chained to the wall. The ferocity with which he attacked and killed her had been intensified by his frustrations of not being able to be with Natalia. He didn't believe he would rip her throat out. What of the fact that she didn't want to be changed? Did it matter? He turned back to Joseph, who now sat on the edge of the desk and swirled the last sip of brandy in his glass.

"How much have any of them gotten away with, Joseph? As long as she doesn't betray me, she'll have what she wants."

"What does she want? Do you really know?"

"No, but I'll get it out of her."

"She's in the master bedroom as you asked. Will you be using that room for a while?"

"Until I trust her, yes. Bring my clothing down from my room at the first opportunity."

Joseph drained his glass, nodded, and stood to leave. He reached the door before Vincent spoke again.

"Oh, and Joseph, if you ever touch her again without her permission, I'll hang you by your toenails over the oubliette, slash your body with shallow cuts and feed your blood to the ghul."

Joseph paused with his hand on the doorknob. "Yes, sir."

Vincent listened as the door closed and watched as the sun lightened the sky in the east. After a few moments of quiet contemplation, he turned back to the paperwork on his desk, and pushed it aside. Natalia was upstairs in his bed. He had no reason to still be in his study, pretending to look over finances. He left the room, and locked the door behind him. He had to stop himself from running up the stairs.

At the door to his sitting room, he paused to try and control his ideas and desires. She had fainted earlier this evening from a little bit of exertion. He didn't know how much he would be able to do with her. Vincent took a deep breath and stepped into his sitting room. The curtains had been drawn, but it wasn't necessary. All the windows in his home were specially tinted to completely block the sun's rays. Vincent walked to his bedroom and took slow breaths to calm his mind. He had no idea if he'd even be able to wake her. The door to the bedroom was open, and light streamed through.

Vincent stood in the doorway, and silently watched Natalia, who stood by a window. She leaned against the wall and held the curtain open with her naked body. He could see her weariness in her posture. His eyes traced the line of her back, over her ass and down her legs. He closed his eyes for a moment then walked to her, silently. Her first indication that he was in the room was when his hands slipped around her. She gave a ragged sigh, leaned into him, and enjoyed the feel of his hard body.

"Never again, Vincent." Her voice was soft, but he heard her frustrations.

"Never again, what?" As he whispered into her ear, his hands roamed her torso. Her skin was warm and soft, which was lovely to touch.

"Never again, this long without you." She turned, slipped her arms around his neck, and pressed herself against him. Her lips found his, as her eyes closed. His hands pressed into her back, pulled her as close as possible, and cursed the clothes that were in the way. He continued the kiss though and decided to move slowly. There were some things he needed to discuss with her. For the moment, he massaged her back, kissed her deeply, and let her feel his desires.

Natalia pulled away first, to catch her breath. Her face was flush. "Hello, lover."

His eyes narrowed as his hunger broke through his attempt to stay calm. He growled at her as one hand went to the nape of her neck. His fingers caught her hair and brought her head to the side. He continued the growl along her neck and traced her vein with his lips. Her breath stopped as he bit her gently with his teeth. He had not exposed his fangs.

"You owe me blood, Natalia." His voice whispered into her neck, then traveled up her jaw line. He watched her reaction as he exposed his fangs to her.

"I do," she whispered. "When will you collect your payment?"

He turned her around, so her back was to his chest. Vincent lowered his head to her neck and let her feel his fangs on her flesh. Each time he pressed the tips into her skin, her breath caught in anticipation and a touch of fear. "Tonight wouldn't be wise, as you fainted on my steps not more than six hours ago."

Natalia tried to turn around to face him again, but the large vampire wouldn't let her. She enjoyed the feel of him against her but wanted to face him. His hands ran up and down her body. She'd been standing by the window for only a few minutes before he came in. Her thoughts had been to fine him. Now, here he was, going slow and easy, and all she wanted was for him to throw her onto the bed and claim her.

"What if I want you to take my blood?"

His lips were at her ear again. The cool air tickled her ear lobe. "It's not smart to tempt me with such a dangerous pursuit, Natalia."

She leaned into him fully then arched her back and neck, to tempt him further. There was an edge to his usually controlled voice; she wanted to see how far she could push him. Her hands wove behind him, and brought his head closer to her elongated neck. His hands tightened around her waist and shoulders, in an attempt to hold her still. She moved her body back and forth slightly, to rub herself against him. His arms tightened again, and his fingers dug into her flesh.

Vincent fought for control and won when he heard her gasp. He pulled back and turned her around. He took a moment to appraise her and let his eyes roam up and down her shapely body. He reached his hand out to run his fingers down her chest, between her breasts. She tried to step into his arms, but he pushed her back gently against the wall. She gave him an annoyed look, but stayed where she was and crossed her arms.

"Is there something else you want?"

"Information." His hands and eyes still roamed over her body.

"What do you want to know?"

"What brought you to my club that night?"

She turned her head away from him. "You know why I was there, Vincent."

He stepped forward and gently lifted her chin to meet his gaze. "No, Natalia. Why me?"

"Because you're still alive." Her eyes and voice held nothing but truth.

"Explain." Vincent removed his hand, backed away, and gave her room to move if she desired.

Natalia relaxed back against the wall, and gave her lover a cold look. She had wanted to be in bed with him by now. "Zechariah's group had compiled information from other Slayers. After years of investigation, he found you. There are five journals within the sixty or so that he gathered that either have an entry about you or are all about you. You've been around a long time, Vincent; the Slayers wanted to put an end to you. They thought you were responsible for the increased killings and disappearances in the Bay Area. If not directly then indirectly by not stopping it."

Vincent started to pace. "Slayers expected me to take care of the situation?"

"Not the more traditional ones, like Zechariah. But from what they knew of you, Dean and Miguel hoped you would intervene. They knew your reputation; knew that although you aren't against killing humans, you aren't going to kill or hurt a child. The current vampire in charge seems to take pleasure in such atrocities."

Vincent smirked. He was amused. "Slayers thought well of me?"

"Most vampires kill as they need, feeding as their needs or desires arise. For the most part, you stay within the laws of the society you live in. You feed from willing humans and try to avoid unnecessary deaths. You do realize how rare that is, don't you?"

He shrugged off her question. "Is that how you knew I wouldn't kill you, or were you taking a chance?"

"I wasn't sure what you would do." She stepped to him to unbutton his shirt. Her fingers whispered against the soft fabric. "But once I saw you, I knew I had to take the chance."

His hand went to rest on her jaw line, his thumb caressed her cheek. "Why?"

"It's called lust, Vincent. I've spent a lot of years staying away from men; hungering after a creature I had no way to control." Her hands caressed his now exposed chest. He was cool to the touch, as if he had just taken a cold shower. "There was a female Slayer who found her way into your household and into your bed. She described you with such shameful words. It was obvious how much she wanted you."

"What was her name?" With no small amount of difficulty, the vampire tried to control his features. He did not want to show any emotions.

"Charlene." She stopped her seduction, curious at the turn of the conversation. "Do you remember her?"

His eyes closed as he nodded slowly. "I met her in China, over a hundred years ago. We didn't spend much time together, a month at the most. I didn't know she was a Slayer."

She gave him a slow smile, full of admiration and understanding. "You completely turned her head. Her entries fascinated me. I was all for finding out what kind of vampire you were. Then I saw you, and knew I had to have you."

She stepped forward, placed a gentle kiss on his neck then bit ever so lightly. His arms wrapped around her and pulled her forward. He closed his eyes as Natalia trailed a necklace of bites and kisses across his neck. Without Lorraine's little present, her gentle touch would have made him lose control. Vincent wanted to know more about the journals and what had fascinated her, but enough was enough. He needed her.

Vincent pulled back, picked Natalia up and carried her to the bed. He threw her onto the middle of the king-sized bed. He then kicked off his shoes, and hastily removed his shirt and pants. Natalia did her own appraising as he undressed. Her eyes wandered over his broad shoulders, down his lean stomach to his muscled thighs. This was the first time she had been able to truly look at him. She watched his muscles flex and contract as he bent to pull off his shoes, socks, and pants. She turned onto her hands and knees, and he watched as she crawled toward the edge of the bed. She caught his eye and gave him a come-hither look.

Natalia kissed and bit her way up his thigh and stomach to stop at chest level. The bed was high enough to make her taller than her standing height. She and Vincent were at eye level. Natalia ran her hands up and down the side of his body slowly, to let him feel her warmth. Her hands went to his chest and his eyes closed. She curled her fingers and raked her nails down his chest. She shuddered when he bared his teeth and fangs.

Vincent placed his hands on her shoulders and pushed her back onto the bed. Natalia laughed as he followed her; closed her eyes as the full weight of the vampire pressed her down into the soft bedding. She wrapped her legs and arms around him, and sighed when the coolness of his skin made her own feel on fire. He pulled back slightly and put his weight on his arms. Vincent peered into her eyes and watched the flames that burned there.

Still wanting to pace himself, Vincent leaned down to her neck and bit her soft skin. As his teeth closed tighter, she arched into him. He stopped before breaking her skin, then bit his way up to her earlobe.

"What did you proclaim earlier, Natalia? 'Come claim me, Vincent.' Is that what you said? Do you still want me to?" Mierka had told him her words.

Natalia gasped. She pushed him back to look in his eyes. "How did you know?"

His grin was pure evil. "I have my ways."

Natalia gasped again as he plunged deep into her. She shuddered as his icy length chilled her. Vincent growled low and long as her wet heat surrounded and encased him. His eyes closed as a wave of hunger consumed his thoughts, and his desires consumed him. The image of the human he had devoured the night before swam in his head. Then came the memories of what he and Lorraine had done to each other. He opened his eyes and stared unseeing down at the human in his arms. The image of the carnage he and Lorraine had done to each other's bodies swam before his eyes again. He and Natalia couldn't do most of what he and Lorraine had done, but they could do some.

Vincent's vision cleared of his memories, and he stared down into Natalia's eyes. A devilish grin came to his lips, as he started to move slowly inside her. He watched as Natalia closed her eyes, loving the look of ecstasy that seized her features. One thing Vincent loved about new relationships: he could teach them everything he knew. Natalia had already proven to him at the restaurant that she would be willing to learn. Vincent didn't know if he trusted the human that now shared his bed. He knew only that he was going to enjoy every single moment he had with her. All thoughts left his head as Natalia started to moan with pleasure.

7

One Year Later

In Vincent's garage, in her car, Natalia sat, and redressed the new wound on her arm. She was trying to decide whether she should get out of the car or wait until noon, when there was a better chance that he would be asleep. There would be trouble for what she'd done. Natalia's hand went to her silver beaded necklace as she stared at a thin chain that hung from the rearview mirror. A blue stone pendant with a silver infinity symbol inlay, dangled from the chain. She'd found it hanging on Theodore's trophy wall under the pictures of Tina. The wall was covered with trinkets and pictures of other young girls. Many she recognized from news stories of missing children. It disgusted Natalia, but Theodore was dust now.

Natalia was tempted to call the police so that they could return the trinkets to the girls' families, but she knew that was impossible. The evidence in the house would lead to her, not a man long thought dead. Edwin seemed to control the police. If he found out she was involved in Theodore's disappearance, it would mean trouble for Vincent. It was better to leave the house for Edwin's people to deal with.

Natalia knew she didn't have to say where she had been. She could keep the necklace, say nothing of her whereabouts and Vincent would never know. It was unacceptable to keep this quiet. If she didn't tell him, Julia would never know either. Natalia finished tying the end of the bandage, and cleaned her hands with the baby wipes she kept in her glove compartment. She took the necklace off the rearview mirror. There was no way to keep it. Julia deserved to have it back; she deserved to know Theodore no longer hoarded it. Placing the necklace carefully in her fist, Natalia opened the door to her car and went upstairs to face her judgment.

As she tried to calmly walk up the stairs, Natalia twirled her own necklace. She wished she could hypnotize Vincent into giving her what she wanted. She now used her mother's old necklace. Zechariah cast her own necklace into the forest when he captured her a year ago. After taking the necklace out of the jewelry box, Natalia cut the string and sang the words. She took extra care to weave her will into the tiny silver beads. The necklace and songs were probably a spell of sorts, but Natalia knew it was all her own will at work. Her first trial with the new necklace had been on Anthony; she found she could still control him. She tried it on a rare occasion when they were alone in a room with Vincent.

The men had been in Vincent's study. Natalia walked in on them unexpectedly, and immediately hypnotized Anthony. It had been too easy, and Vincent didn't object. With Anthony hypnotized, she asked her lover why he didn't tell his main spy about her ability. Vincent suggested it was for the fun of it, but Natalia knew better. There was something else, but he wouldn't reveal his thoughts.

In retaliation to her questions, he asked why she didn't release Anthony, and she just smiled. His laughter almost tempted her to come around the desk and straddle him. A little too shy, she let Anthony go and left the room.

Natalia leaned against the stairwell wall, and paused for a moment to consider the events of the past year. Most of Vincent's people accepted her. Due to Charlie and Rebecca, she made friends with the wolves quicker than the vampires. She spent many days catching up with Charlie and learning about his wife. Natalia liked Rebecca and was glad Charlie found her. The pair also tried to help her find Donald, her mother's killer, which proved to be extremely difficult. There were sightings of him occasionally, but they only led to dead ends. Natalia considered the fact that he might have been killed but didn't want to accept the possibility. She therefore continued to search, but without her previous zeal. The truth of the matter was that she was happy. Trying to find her mother's killer brought up too many traumatic memories she was reluctant to deal with. Natalia rolled her eyes. She would be happier if Vincent let her train with his men, but that was her only real complaint.

She had the run of the house, and could mostly do as she pleased. Two cars were at her disposal. One for going out and an older one for days like this. Vincent even gave her a business credit card with her name on it, but she didn't like to depend on him. When she needed money, she used her own. Most of it was invested, but it was there if she needed it. Natalia didn't travel as much as she used to, in any event. The people she interacted with all lived in Vincent's house, and Bethany was no longer in her life. Since hypnotizing her best friend, there had been no contact.

Natalia discreetly checked in on Bethany occasionally. Bethany never saw her, which was for the best. She deserved to continue living the lie all humans lived. Natalia knew that humans were more than willing to accept a lie when the truth would prove too alarming. She told herself it was better for her friend, and it was, but Natalia still missed her. She missed the simplicity of hanging out with her but didn't want to endanger Bethany's life anymore. It was better to let the relationship go and put Bethany out of her mind.

It had been the same with her job at The Ocean's Edge. No longer in need of her waitress job, she called Richard and let him know there was a family emergency. She apologized for not giving two weeks and he wouldn't let her, stating she could return at any time and have her job back. She thanked him but knew she wouldn't call him again.

Natalia stirred as somewhere above her a door slammed. She took a deep breath, and pushed her memories away. The necklace in her hand needed to be returned to its rightful family. Natalia took one more look at the blue stone and gathered strength from the knowledge that she had done the right thing. She took one more breath, hoped Vincent would agree and started back up the steps to her fate.

03   80

Vincent watched as Anthony squared off against Kimberly. Both held staves. It was their least favorite weapon, but every member of House LeGris was expected to be proficient with any weapon they could come across. Vincent leaned against the wall of his ballroom, which was more often used as an exercise room. Currently, all the vampires who lived in his home were in the room, dressed to train. Anthony and Julia were there as well, to brush up on their skills. Rebecca, Charlie and the rest of the werewolves smirked at the vampires as they took bets. Their training session was already over, but they decided to remain and taunt the vampires as they themselves had been taunted.

Mierka and Orlando were the only ones of his household not in the room. Orlando was on duty in the security room. Mierka awaited Natalia's return. Natalia had been gone since morning, and none of the werewolves could track her. It wasn't the first time his lady pulled a disappearing act; Vincent knew she would return at some point this evening. On previous occasions, she had gone to fight either a Slayer or a vampire. Once, she fought a demon and was nearly killed. Thankfully, Lilly was now in his permanent employment. It took her three days to recover after healing Natalia's wounds. Vincent had been displeased beyond words.

Her first month in his house, they rarely left the bedroom. One or the other would try, but would be easily seduced back into the bed, shower, or tub. When they finally ventured from his rooms, Natalia discovered that Vincent trained his vampires and werewolves in his own ballroom. She pleaded with him to allow her to join them, and told him she needed the exercise to stay fit. Vincent refused outright; he was afraid someone would kill her accidentally. He thought he had dissuaded her until she finally moved the last of her possessions to the mansion. Natalia had gotten out of hand, and blamed him for her restlessness.

For a while, she asked politely. He continued to deny her request, despite her valid arguments. She felt she needed to stay in shape and keep her fighting skills honed. She still searched for Donald and expected to locate and kill him herself. Learning how to fight vampires may have made her private time with Vincent more interesting as well. He refused to share his reasoning, and instead simply dismissed her request each time.

After a month, her patience was exhausted. She disappeared for most of the day and returned well after sunset. She was badly bruised and had lost a good portion of her blood. She nevertheless walked through the door with her head held high. Upon gentle questioning, Vincent learned that she had gone to kill a particularly nasty vampire: one of Edwin's men. Once Lilly healed her Vincent lost his temper, afraid that Edwin would demand her life. But Edwin never called, and Vincent calmed down. Natalia seemed to take his words to heart but could feel the restless anger inside herself.

Natalia went out again two months later, this time after a Slayer. She told Vincent this time, and claimed the Slayer had important information. Once more bruised and bloodied, she returned after midnight with a battered leather briefcase. She refused to tell Vincent anything, stating that it wasn't his business. Their yelling match ended in bed, and each took their frustrations out through their bodies.

Vincent let the argument drop, and assigned Charlie as her bodyguard. She still managed to slip out shortly before nightfall during the full moon – when she knew Charlie would be incapacitated. When she returned once more after midnight, Natalia sported a satisfied grin and a few bruises. Vincent rushed her into his study upon her return, and thought to lecture and yell. At the first opportunity, she knelt before him, pulled down his pants, and sucked him dry. She dominated him that night, and he relished in her abilities. He gave in to her every desire and showed her a few of his own.

The night after, she once again asked to train with his people. If she could fight in a safe environment, she would still have enough energy left to satisfy him. He nearly relented until an image of her lying dead in his ballroom slammed into his head. He calmly told her of his fear that she would not be able to keep up with his people. Their age and experience put her at a severe disadvantage. Natalia asked whether it would be preferred for her to die by another's hand out in the city. Without waiting for an answer, she left the room and would not talk to him for the rest of the night.

Other than the fights about her training and her disappearances, the past year with her had been bliss. She was everything he could want in a woman: willing, adventurous, limber and intelligent. She eagerly devoured the books in his library and only asked for help when she couldn't read the language. Many of the books were first editions of classics, which she read in her youth.

With Vincent's help, Natalia rearranged the library according to fiction and non-fiction. This made it easier to find the books she considered useful. She integrated the Slayer journals as well, and sorted them in order by year. The journals specifically written about Vincent were grouped into their own section.

As Vincent found it difficult to resist her constant presence, he decided to integrate her into his business life. First, he had to stop her from fighting. It grated on his nerves that she never apologized for her actions and her harsh words. He felt as though she were trying to aggravate him.

Vincent was brought back to the present when he heard the door to the garage open and close. His heightened senses identified Mierka's distinct gait as she approached his woman. He crossed his arms and waited. Joseph signaled to Anthony and Kimberly to stop the sparring match they barely started.

Mierka's voice came through the open ballroom doors. She spoke loudly for Vincent's benefit. "He's not happy with you."

Natalia's voice was too low to hear.

Mierka's voice grew louder. "He's in the ballroom, training, but he wants you to wait in his study." Low murmur, then, "Natalia! Stop and listen to me!"

Now Natalia started to yell as well. "I'm not going to wait in his study like the disobedient child he thinks I am! He can find me now, or I'll go to him, but I will not wait!"

Natalia marched into the ballroom, angry and determined, but her expression was not the first thing he noticed. Vincent pushed against the wall to straighten himself, his eyes wide with surprise. Natalia's lower right arm was wrapped in gauze that was slowly bleeding through. Her jeans and shirt were ripped, and blood dotted the jagged edges. It was the first time in a while she had come home this badly injured. He was used to her coming home with that satisfied grin she wore so well.

"You're hurt." He sounded rather displeased.

She held her head up high and walked right past him. He grabbed at her, his anger about to boil over. She dodged him and continued to Julia. Natalia reached out her hand and placed a glittering chain into Julia's hand. Julia looked hard at the object, started to shake, looked up at Natalia, gave a small nod and closed her fist. Anthony barged over and grabbed his woman's fist. Natalia prudently backed away as Anthony addressed Julia loudly.

"What did she give you?" His voice was not kind, despite Julia's sad smile.

"The necklace I gave Tina at her birth."

Anthony's eyes grew wide, and he turned on Natalia. He still held his staff. "What the hell did you do?"

"What you couldn't."

"Natalia!" Vincent's annoyance was apparent to everyone in the room. She turned slowly and stood tall. What she had done was against his wishes, but he hadn't ordered her not to do it. "Explain your actions. Now."

"I was in the room when Anthony told you he was going to kill Theodore for what he did to Tina. I was there, Vincent, when you told him it was out of the question because Theodore was one of Edwin's favorites. I saw the look in his eye when you explained the dangerous, delicate balance your men have to keep with Edwin's lot. You saw it too, which is why you ordered him to leave the blood-sucking pervert alone. Therefore, I went. I took care of the situation."

"Edwin will order your blood. As he is my Captain, I'll have to do as he orders." Vincent's voice was deadly cold.

Natalia laughed. "Do you think I'm stupid, Vincent? I've killed five of his men so far, or didn't you know? Have you heard word one from him? No, you haven't. And you won't. When I hunt, I hunt as a Slayer, so no one knows. Do you actually believe I would endanger you or your men?"

She had a point. He was completely unaware of whether the people she "took care of" were Slayers or vampires. However, if it were somehow traced back to her, the consequences would be dire. "By killing him, you've endangered us."

"How? He has no idea." She sounded perturbed.

Vincent strolled over and grabbed her bandaged arm. He squeezed and gave her a mean look as he did so. He was angrier than she'd ever seen him before. His mood didn't improve when she ignored her pain and gave him a dirtier look. "You left your blood. That's all he needs."

"Bullshit. You're the only vampire I've ever heard of that can tell one human's blood from another. And if for some reason Edwin can, he's never met me. All he knows is that a human killed his men, not which one."

She pulled her arm away roughly and hid the pain behind her anger. The makeshift bandage was even more crimson and there was blood on Vincent's fingers. Vincent looked at his fingers, brought them to his mouth and sucked his skin clean. The taste of her was enough to fuel his never-ending need for the human who stood defiantly in front of him.

Vincent shook his head and turned away from Natalia as he tried to dismiss her. "We'll talk about this later, Natalia. But for now, know this: you'll have a great deal to answer for if this happens again."

She grabbed his arm and he let her spin him back around. He barely felt the slap she gave him. There were several gasps and one decidedly male snort from the onlookers. "No. We're going to talk about this now. I'm tired of being dismissed, and I'm tired of only being allowed to do the things that please you."

He raised an eyebrow. "What we do doesn't please you?"

It was her turn to have a cold voice. "I'm not talking about the bedroom. I'm talking about the rest of it. I'm a warrior and I need to stay in shape. How am I supposed to stay in shape if you won't let me train here, where it's safe?"

"It's not safe here, Natalia. My people have been training for more years than you've been alive." He advanced on her to try and make her back down. She stood her ground; determination seized her face. "They would kill you."

"Could kill me, not would. Your men wouldn't kill me unless you ordered them to."

"You're a human, you can't keep up."

"How old was Theodore?"

"He was more interested in hurting young ones than in learning how to fight. He didn't have the skills to keep up with you."

"So, I'm under qualified to fight your men, but overqualified to fight Edwin's. Convenient for you, isn't it?" Despite her fervor, Vincent still tried to stare her down. She saw something in his eyes and realization gripped her hard. Her anger grew, but her voice showed a second emotion he had trouble placing. "You son of a bitch. You were doing this on purpose. You knew I wouldn't stop. You could've tried harder to convince me, or you could've relented. But you did neither. You knew what I would do. You used me to eliminate your enemies while keeping your hands clean."

Vincent continued to stare her down as murmurs erupted in the room. Most came from the werewolves. He spared them a glance and they quieted, save for Rebecca who seemed to be taking bets on how this fight would end. "I do what I have to, to keep me and mine safe."

"Does that mean I'm not one of yours?" Her anger was back, a hard knot in her stomach, but her voice didn't betray her emotions.

A muscle twitched in his jaw. He had spoken without thinking, which happened a lot when he was near her. Vincent didn't want to have this argument in front of all his people. It was none of their business. "You're my woman, Natalia, which means you are one of mine."

She stepped forward. Surprised, he stepped back. "Then why let me place myself in harm's way, Vincent? If I'm really one of yours, you would never let me hunt Edwin's men."

"I had nothing to fear. I know what you can do."

"You're using me for more than your pleasure."

He shrugged, pure triumph shining in his eyes. "You said you'd be an asset."

She shook her head. "I'm not going to let you use me anymore, lover. I'm not doing this for you, and you can't stop me. I know where to go; I have contacts you haven't found yet. I'll do what I must, to keep my skills honed."

He was starting to show his feelings. His jaw twitched and he took deep breaths. His hands formed fists behind his back. All she had said was true; he had been using her, but not quite consciously. He didn't know exactly who she hunted, but as long as it wasn't anyone under his protection, it wasn't directly against his wishes. Since Edwin didn't contact him to find out if it was one of his people, Vincent let her do as she pleased. He still feared for her life but knew she could overpower most of Edwin's men in single combat.

There was something else as well. His men talked about her. Ben and Jesse were more than a little interested in her, as was Joseph. Vincent had grown rather possessive of Natalia over the past year and didn't want any of his men gawking at her. He was never this possessive, but Natalia was unique. His women were generally smart and attractive, but none knew how to fight like her. None had been quite as determined to stand against him, either. He closed his eyes as her last words penetrated his anger.

"What are you talking about, Natalia?"

"Let me fight here or I'll disappear for longer than a day."

He looked deep into her eyes and saw the truth. His anger dissipated as he called her bluff. "You are your own woman, Natalia. You may do as you please."

Natalia's anger flourished in his apparent detachment. Rage consumed her and wrapped her in a blanket of raw heat. Logic was gone; instinct took over. She grabbed Anthony's staff and swept Vincent off his feet before anyone knew what was going on. He fell to the ground, and she pressed the end of the staff against his neck. Were he human, his air passage would be blocked. Natalia and Vincent locked eyes, but neither looked to concede.

8

"Halt!" Joseph bellowed. "Back up and leave them alone, Anthony. This does not concern you."

"She's trying to kill him!" By his voice, Natalia guessed he was right behind her.

"You know very well she can't."

Vincent moved the staff away from his throat and slowly stood, eyes still locked with Natalia's. He had never seen the look in her eye before; heat seemed to radiate from her very being. He growled low, a smile on his face. He had wanted this since he met her.

"Are you all right, sir?" The concern in Anthony's voice was palpable.

His eyes never left Natalia's. "Fine. Do you know what you've done, Natalia?"

The staff rested expertly in her hands. "Challenged you."

"Do you know what happens now?" He started to circle her.

Natalia held his gaze and turned as he did. She came across his challenge rules in one of the Slayer journals. If an argument could not be settled in a friendly way, his men could land one blow to enact the challenge. "We fight. If you win, you'll drain my blood if you so desire. If I win, half of your blood belongs to me. Since I'm not a vampire and I don't want to drink your blood, I have a proposition."

"You're in no position to propose anything, human."

"I swept you off your feet fairly easily, vampire. Do you really think I can't do that again?"

"It might be an interesting fight, but in the end, I'll win." He reviewed tactics in his mind and plotted different ways of overpowering her without causing any permanent injuries.

"If you're so sure you'll win, what's the harm in listening?" The slow twirl of her staff sped up as Vincent made his decision.

"Speak your mind."

"If I win two out of three matches, you allow me to train here."

"And if I win?"

"I'll stop hunting without your consent."

Vincent stopped circling to consider the human before him and her proposal. His usual rules wouldn't work, really. He had no desire to drain her blood and she had no reason to drink his. Though he could easily defeat her, her proposal was not unacceptable. Their eyes locked again, and he realized the look in her eye had changed just the smallest amount. It was a calculating look. The woman was plotting her own tactics. A smile came to his face as a low growl once again escaped his lips. He would win the first round easily, toy with her during the second and ultimately settle the matter once and for all.

"All right. Two out of three." He turned away.

Before she could react, Natalia found herself pressed against the wall, Vincent's teeth in her flesh. Despite her best efforts, a scream ripped through her throat. The bellow of pain brought a cold, blood-stained smile to Vincent's face as he pulled away. He looked her dead in the eye and licked his lips hungrily.

"One." He reached into his pocket, grabbed a handkerchief, and threw it to Natalia.

Natalia caught the handkerchief and quickly pressed it against the bite wound Vincent made in the left side of her chest. She ripped open her button-down shirt and tied it in a way to keep pressure on the wound to stem the bleeding. She guessed correctly that Vincent knew exactly where to bite her in order to avoid major blood vessels. The handkerchief stopped the blood quite well. Anger boiled in her as she noticed the spark of enjoyment in his eyes. Bastard.

Vincent watched her dress her wound, and savored the look on her face. At this moment, she hated him. Good. It would make the fight more interesting. He backed away and assessed the situation. As the hate faded from her eyes, the same calculating look returned as she quickly surveyed the room. He wondered what she was looking at and realized how little he cared. He wanted this farce to end. He would prove to both her and everyone present that she was not capable of training with his men. As he turned from her though, he had to wonder: were his reasons for keeping her from training good enough? As he prepared himself to fight his human, he decided. If she did well enough, he would allow her to train here – though he would never permit himself to be defeated in front of his men.

Natalia had one thought in her mind: how to win. She took in Vincent's retreating back, glanced around the room once more and found what she was looking for. She hadn't expected to win the first round; Vincent had too much pride to let that happen. To win the second and third rounds, she would need to find a more appropriate weapon. She watched as he turned around, crossed his arms, and gave her a condescending look. Natalia saw his stubbornness and knew she was only going to get one chance to do this right. Training and honing her skills meant too much to her and she refused to let her feelings for her lover stop her. Natalia stood tall, approached Vincent, and stopped about five feet away from him. To her right, Joseph tried to read her intentions.

Natalia faced Vincent, studied him, and waited for a signal. He could move faster than she could see, but there was always that twitch in his jaw. She saw it and lunged to the right for Joseph's sword. The sword was quickly drawn from the scabbard, and its blade cut a path across and to the left in a single sweeping motion. Natalia felt the resistance of the sword contact Vincent's body and dove to the ground under his reach. She rolled to a sitting position behind him and swung the sword at the back of his legs. She sliced his calf muscles and Achilles heels open, and he fell to the ground as his legs gave out. Natalia stood quickly; ready to continue as Vincent turned over to sit on the floor. The first cut had sliced his shirt and chest open in a diagonal line from the left waist to right shoulder. Blood poured from the open wound. She watched as he ripped off his shirt and closed the wound.

Joseph was by Anthony's side, and reassured the angry vampire that all would be well. Vincent had enough blood in him to heal much worse injuries than this, but Anthony tensed as if about to intervene. Afraid that the vampire would get in the way of the rather interesting fight, Joseph signaled Ben and Owen to stand beside Anthony in case he needed to be restrained. Anthony gave Joseph a foul look but stood between his comrades and held his tongue. Charlie and Rebecca moved forward as well, but Joseph knew it was only to get a better look at the fight. He went to Vincent's side to confirm that his friend would, in fact, be alright.

Vincent watched Natalia's expression as he healed his legs. He hadn't expected this. At his side, Joseph whispered in his ear. Vincent shook his head. Natalia having a weapon didn't change much; he was still confident he could win. Joseph tried to help him up, but Vincent pushed him away. He stared Natalia down. There was a muttering in the room as the two lovers gave each other nasty looks.

The large vampire knew he could win this fight if he used his full speed to knock Natalia to the ground. He would have her down and the fight done in seconds. However, he wasn't done yet – and neither was she. The fight still brewed within her, and her mind simmered in hate. Vincent considered his next move. He wanted Natalia to feel as if she had a chance and knew what he could do. His men would know he was faking, but the human would not. A steady, hard look on his face, Vincent placed his feet under him and leaned forward on his hands like a sprinter at the start of a race. Knowing he could still take many hits, he waited for the fight to continue. Natalia backed up to put some distance between them. Her inscrutable expression had not changed, and she wasn't standing the way he expected her to.

Vincent wanted her to think he was going to charge low to grab her legs and slam her to the ground. Sword or no sword, she would be helpless if pinned to the ground. He expected her to reveal which way she would lunge as he positioned himself, but she stood firmly in place, and waited. Vincent tensed and launched himself at his target. She jumped straight up. He felt the blade slice into his back as she landed on him. She sprung off him and he heard her land on the floor and roll. Someone cried out in protest as another sword rang free of its scabbard. There were gasps from the werewolves as Vincent straightened and once more faced her. Six inches of steel protruded from Vincent's stomach, coated in blood.

Natalia felt the adrenaline coursing through her body as she tried to control her breathing. Owen's rapier was in her hands and Joseph's katana stuck out of Vincent's stomach. She had never fought a vampire as old as Vincent. It was a thrill to test her skills against him. He stood seething, bleeding before her. There was anger in his eyes; perhaps he realized how much he had underestimated her. Or perhaps he was considering the quickest way to kill her. At this point, she didn't care. It was more about the skill and the thrill of the hunt now. Natalia kept her emotions hidden, and cleared her mind. As she waited for her lover's next move, she became as still as a coiled serpent ready to strike.

Vincent reached around, grasped the blade, and pulled the sword slowly out of his body. He healed himself as the sword slid out of his body and tried hard to control the amount of blood that seeped from his wound. He could still afford to lose more blood, but the more he lost, the slower he would become. It would give her more opportunity to win. Joseph stood beside him again, and whispered another warning.

"She may win, with her weapon."

"Except now, I have one too." He held the sword in his hand, and evaluated its weight and balance as he wondered whether it would help or hinder him.

"It won't help. She's watching you, waiting to see when you move. You can't show her what you'll do."

"And how exactly am I doing that?" His voice grew loud. He felt his hunger rise to the surface and flow through him, as he allowed it to meld with his anger. He was still under control, but it had taken a lot to heal the last cut. He breathed deep and closed his eyes as Joseph revealed his tell.

Natalia waited patiently for Joseph to seal her fate. He most probably knew what she did: that Vincent's jaw twitched right before he moved. It was something Natalia learned in bed. There were times he would stand motionless and watch her, as he decided how to proceed. Every time, without fail, his jaw muscle would twitch before he dove for her. It was a handy tell to know about in this situation. Natalia felt the slight weight of the rapier, glad now to have the lighter weapon. The katana would have been too slow to match Vincent's unnatural speed. She stood at the ready as Joseph stepped away.

"You can't win this Natalia."

Natalia watched his body and waited for it. His shirt was off, and his tight sweatpants were ripped at the knee. She could see every muscle flex as he walked toward her. A stray thought tried to assert itself into her mind, but she pushed it aside. Thoughts about him in bed would only distract her when she needed her focus the most. She held her ground and waited for the opportunity to strike. When he was within arm's reach, she knew she would have to make the first move. She feigned to the right then dove to the left under his arm as he lunged for her. He tried to grab her, but she swept her sword at his arm and felt it land. She rolled to a standing position, then rushed forward to continue her attack.

Vincent felt his sword arm open as the rapier split his flesh to the bone. He dropped the sword, and winced as the thin blade slashed across his back three times. He turned, and reached out to grab the thin sword. As he turned and grabbed the blade, she pulled the weapon away and sliced through the flesh of his hand. He bared his teeth, and growled as she lunged forward and thrust the sword through his chest. The blade was aimed to his right to avoid his heart. Natalia pulled back a few steps to assess the situation.

Vincent growled as he healed himself and rushed forward. She slashed as he charged, and used the light weapon as she had been trained. He pulled back when blood gushed from the wound on his neck. He fell to his knees, and grasped his neck to stop the bleeding. Anthony yelled for her blood, and demanded the fight be stopped. Vincent closed his wound, and wondered if Anthony was right. He had lost more blood than he thought he would, and the hunger threatened to take over. He had to finish this. He looked up at the beautiful woman and wondered how to do it without killing her. For a split second, he saw the look in her eyes. She hid it quickly, but not quickly enough. Vincent's eyes roamed to her right arm: the bandage was soaked with blood.

The cut from earlier bled freely and Natalia was having a difficult time holding the sword in her hand. It wasn't a deep cut, but it ran the length of her lower arm. Theodore had raked her arm with his thumbnail and dug in deep. It made her whole arm throb, and Vincent saw the pain behind her eyes. She could switch to her left hand, but her right was still stronger. Therefore, she hid the pain, channeled it, and held her ground. When

Vincent stood, she held the sword at the ready. The vampire's eyes were still on her arm. He watched as a single drop of blood fell from her arm to splatter on the hardwood floor. Natalia watched his reaction but missed the significance.

Vincent growled menacingly as he bared his fags. He needed blood and wanted hers. He pounced, and grabbed her right arm. She slashed up and tried to break free, but his vice-like grip held her in place as his fingers dug into the wound. He laughed. Not willing to lose, she channeled her anger into her left arm, formed a fist, and struck him hard in the face. He rolled his head with the punch, then turned his head back and continued to laugh. He pulled her arm up, to try and make her drop her sword. She held on, and gave him a dirty look as she tried to pry his fingers free with her left hand. His laughter grew louder as he tasted victory.

Natalia smiled inwardly at his overconfidence as Vincent laughed at her apparent ineptitude. Her right hand opened to drop the sword into her left, and the blade flashed high above his head before it descended in a violent slash. He bellowed his rage as the sword carved him from neck to right hip, and Joseph shouted a warning. Vincent dropped her hand but tried to grab her again as she whirled away. Joseph was by his side in that same instant.

"You can't keep this up, sir. She has you." He was not talking quietly.

"I will not give in to a human."

"Then take my blood." Joseph held out his arm and hoped Vincent would drink, though he knew the old vampire had too much pride to show weakness.

Vincent knocked Joseph's arm away, and concentrated on healing his newest wound. Natalia watched as his eyes and wound closed. His chest was covered in blood. He reached up to touch his neck, then stopped with his hand to his nose. A slight tremor appeared in his hand as he sucked on his right palm. Her blood was on that hand. Natalia dropped her sword arm as she realized she had him. She glanced at Joseph, who seemed to understand her look and stepped away from Vincent. The sword clattered to the floor, and Vincent opened his eyes. Natalia caught his gaze, brought her left hand to her right arm, and lifted them both in front of her. She untied the wrapping and unraveled the bandage as he watched. She dropped the bandage to the floor and caught his gaze again. Vincent watched as she held her arm out. The look in her eyes was clear. He trembled as the scent of her blood slammed into his nostrils.

Natalia advanced toward him. "On your knees, vampire, or you get nothing."

He tried to disobey but couldn't. He was so hungry he salivated at the mere thought of tasting her blood. He dropped to his knees; his lips quivered in anticipation. Natalia stepped behind him, wrapped her arm around him, and placed her open wound near his lips. Her other hand slipped unseen to her boot.

"Not yet." She teased as his hands tried to bring her closer. "Concede."

"You have not yet won, human." Vincent hissed in air when he felt the cold steel against his throat.

"I don't think you have enough blood to heal a decapitation, vampire." Her voice was laced with leftover hate.

His hands gripped her a little harder. Blood oozed out of her arm. "You wouldn't."

"Never. I wanted to show you I was worthy of training here, and I think I have. Do you agree?"

He could almost taste her blood but pushed her arm away. He slowly moved her other hand away from his neck and stood. Turning to face her, he held out his hand to help her up. "I concede. The second round goes to you, Natalia." He pulled her close and twisted the hand holding the dagger behind her. There was not enough pressure to make her drop the blade, so she held onto it. "But the third will go to me."

"If you're so sure, let me go so we can finish."

"In a moment." He bent his head, brought her wounded arm to his mouth, and wrapped his lips around part of the cut. He was in enough control of himself to only take three swallows. It fueled his desire for her, as did the hiss of pain that escaped her lips. He pulled away from her arm, grabbed her by her shirt, growled at her as he stared down into her dark eyes. Natalia gasped, not from the anger in his growl, but at the humor shining in his eyes.

"What?"

Vincent spoke loudly enough for the room to hear him. "You have proven yourself worthy of fighting with my men, Natalia, but I do not take betrayals lightly. When this is done, you will find yourself in a great deal of pain, by my hand and the hands of those who work for me."

Natalia pulled away from Vincent and gave him an angry glare. "Everything I've read about your challenges states that you don't consider the challenges as betrayals. You see them as a gentleman's right."

He gave her a smirk. "This fight is not the betrayal I'm speaking of, human. Killing Theodore was not a wise move. For killing him against my wishes, you will be punished."

She gave him a seductive look and stood taller. "I think I have proven that I can handle myself against you."

Vincent hid his emotions. Natalia seemed to think the punishment would be dealt out in bed. He spanked her sometimes, for fun. She enjoyed it greatly, even when he hit her hard enough to leave a bruise. Though she apparently thought the punishment would be enjoyable, that was not the case. She didn't realize that he was about to exact her punishment in the third round. He was low on blood, but he was still far stronger than she could imagine or manage. Vincent nodded to Natalia, and waited for the end of the fight.

Natalia stood tall, and considered his words. He gave her permission to train with his men. She won, but the win seemed bittersweet. When the fight was over, she would pay for Theodore's death. She should have known that Vincent would demand punishment for breaking the rules. She didn't care. If she could restart the day and have a chance to leave Theodore alive, she wouldn't take it. Theodore deserved to die, and Julia and Tina deserved peace. Natalia believed she had done the right thing and would take her punishment. They would end the fight, then she would take her punishment. Vincent appeared weak from blood loss, and she felt she could easily overpower him. Natalia attacked first and launched herself at him.

Vincent turned back and backhanded her. His hand slammed into her chin and Natalia staggered backward. He did not hit her with full force. To do so would have surely killed her. She slammed into the wall with enough force to make everyone in the room wince. Almost everyone. Vincent watched the consciousness fade from her eyes as she crumpled to the ground.

Charlie watched in horror as Vincent used his strength against Natalia. Fear for her life wrapped around his thoughts and he felt himself changing. A growl escaped his throat and was cut short by a hand on the back of his neck. An angry voice whispered harshly in his ear.

"You attack our boss, and he will kill you. She brought this on herself. You defend her now, and I can't stop him from punishing you."

Rebecca's words penetrated his mind and Charlie changed back. He gave her a sheepish look and muttered under his breath. His wife shook her head, grabbed his arm, and pulled him out of the room. If she locked him away in the dungeon, Vincent would not. Charlie didn't fight her, and knew full well that she was right. It wasn't his place to fight Vincent. Charlie allowed himself to be taken to the dungeon, where his Alpha wife shackled him in one of the smaller rooms.

"How long?" His voice was full of defeat.

"Until I tell him why you almost attacked him. He'll decide when to let you go."

"Great," he replied despondently. Charlie watched Rebecca leave the room and heard her lock the door. He tried to clear his mind and wondered how many times he would end up here due to his concern for Natalia's safety.

9

Vincent turned when he heard a stifled growl behind him. Rebecca had the situation under control, therefore he turned back to Natalia. He waited until the two werewolves were out of the room and dismissed the incident from his mind. Rebecca would brief him later. Vincent calmly walked over to Natalia and stood over her motionless body.

He turned to his people, all of whom stood mute. Vincent did not take betrayal lightly, even when dealing with humans. "Though I wished to fight this human, I also wanted to punish her for killing Theodore. When she recovers, she will be training with us. She will be an asset to my house and family if she knows how to engage skilled vampires. We are done for the night, you are released."

He looked to Joseph as he approached. Vincent spoke to him quietly. "Fetch Lilly. Have the healer make sure there is no permanent damage, other than the mark on her breast. Make sure she keeps that one. When she is healed, make sure she understands why we didn't heal the bite mark. I'll be in my study. Bring me blood when you're done."

Joseph nodded, then picked up Natalia as Vincent left the room. She was out cold. He took her to the library, laid her down on the couch then left to find Lilly. He told her what was going on and she wasn't pleased.

"What does he think he's doing? No human can handle a vampire's full strength!"

"She does well enough in his bed." Joseph's voice was light and held a hint of humor.

Lilly glared at him as she headed out of her room and down the stairs to the library. She didn't stop to say anything more until she was at Natalia's side. She ran her hands along Natalia's body and gently felt for bruises and wounds. The back of Natalia's head bled as did her breast and arm. Those three wounds seemed to be the only damage.

"How hard did she hit her head?" She didn't bother looking at Joseph.

"Hard enough."

The small answer made her look sharply at Joseph. "Go fetch Eva and Gail. Tell them to bring me my candles."

"Will this room be sufficient for healing?"

"It'll do."

Joseph bowed, then left the room to fetch the other women. They came quickly and bought all of Lilly's supplies. Within half an hour, Natalia had recovered enough to wake up. The only wound that wasn't healed completely was the wound on her left breast. Though it was no longer bleeding, there was a thick scab. The wound would have to finish healing on its own and would leave a scar.

Once the ladies were done, Joseph looked to the ladies. "Take care of Lilly. Come back for the components later."

Gail and Eva nodded, and helped Lilly to her feet. The healer needed time and food to replenish the energy she used to heal Natalia. Once they cleared the room, Joseph knelt in front of the human. He patiently waited until Natalia was fully awake. She finally snapped awake, and her confused eyes darted around the room.

"Joseph, what..." Her head hurt slightly, and she wasn't sure of her surroundings.

"Are you awake?" His voice was not unkind.

"Where am I?"

"Library."

She glanced around the room. There were candles and other spell components but only Joseph was present. "Where's Vincent?"

"Not here."

She glared at him. It infuriated her how little the man talked. Natalia started to get up, but Joseph's hand on her shoulder stopped her.

"We're not done."

Natalia gave him another dirty look, started to cross her arms but he stopped her from doing that as well. She batted his hand away. "What do you want?"

His smile made her blood boil. "For you to understand your place. He is allowing you to join our exercises. Vincent believes you will be an asset if you learn how to hold your own against our kind. Skilled vampires, not those whelps you've been tangling with. But understand this: if you break his rules, you will be punished. Though he did not order you to leave Theodore alone, you were in the room when he told Anthony not to kill the bastard. If Vincent orders one of us to do something, the order applies to all of us who can hear him. Would you like to tell me why?"

Natalia took a deep breath. She detested his tone of voice. He spoke to her as if she were a disobedient child. Her eyes narrowed as she realized this was the second time today someone was trying to make her feel like a child. She let go of the annoyance as he raised an eyebrow, and waited for an answer. "Order must be maintained."

"That is correct." He reached out and pinched the tender wound on her left breast. She cried out in pain. Joseph pulled his hand away and gave her a hard, mean look. "You came to us looking to be saved from Zachariah. We acknowledge that you can be an asset to our house and family. Don't make the mistake of thinking that you're not disposable. Vincent enjoys having you in his bed. Understand this: if you take too many risks that endanger this house, I will take great pleasure in torturing you in many different ways before draining all the blood from your veins. Any time you consider disobeying Vincent, remember this wound; touch the scar. Let it be your guide. Now get up. We're done here."

Natalia looked up at Joseph for a moment before she tried to stand. She pondered the fact that the normally soft-spoken vampire had taken the time to offer a full explanation. This was the most he had ever conveyed to her. There was an amused look on his face that seemed to suggest he understood what she was thinking. Natalia shook her head then stood slowly. "What happens now?"

"You will sleep in a spare bedroom. Stay away from Vincent until he comes to you or summons you. He will tell you what happens next."

Natalia was wobbly on her feet but was able to follow Joseph out of the room. He led the way to an unused room on the second floor and ushered her inside. He didn't follow, but went to Lilly's room to ensure the healer or her apprentice knew to check on Natalia. Done with this task, Joseph went downstairs to bring Vincent blood.

☙ ❧

Vincent was in his study for no more than a minute before there was a knock on the closed door. "Come."

The door opened to reveal Rebecca. She walked into the study, then closed the door behind her. "Charlie's in the dungeon, sir."

"Why?"

"He wasn't comfortable with the fight and considered helping the human that saved his life twice." Her voice was rather matter of fact.

Vincent stared at Rebecca for a moment and wondered if she understood what she had said. "Is he going to be a problem?"

She paused to carefully consider the question. "He feels very protective of her and his loyalties may be suspect."

"He never gave me his full loyalty, Rebecca. He gave it to you. Would he protect her over you?"

Rebecca blinked as a quizzical expression caught her features. "I…"

Vincent held up his hand to silence his Alpha. "Don't answer. Fetch

Charlie. Bring him here."

The woman nodded and left the room. Moments later she returned with Charlie, his head down. Rebecca closed the door behind him, then went to stand with her man as Vincent questioned him.

"You thought to attack me."

"Yes, sir."

"She asked for the fight."

Charlie nodded. "I was thinking with my emotions, not with my head."

"This makes me question your loyalties, Charlie. If the situation presented itself, would you protect Natalia or me, first?"

"Natalia." His answer was too quick, and he knew it. Charlie shook his head, spoke again, and hoped Vincent would allow an explanation. "You're far stronger than Natalia. I doubt you would ever need my protection."

Vincent said nothing for a moment and drummed his fingers on the desk. He wasn't surprised by the answer. "If the situation presented itself, who would you protect? Natalia or your Alpha?"

Charlie turned to Rebecca and held his hand out to her. She took his hand and knew what he was going to say by the look in his eyes. "I spent too many years looking for my wolf. Why would I ever risk losing her?"

Rebecca gave him a triumphant smile that quickly faded when Vincent started to clap. The werewolves turned to face their master. He had a bored look on his face and was leaning back in his chair. He clapped slowly, as if amused. He was not. He stopped clapping and continued to give the pair a hard look.

"Very nicely said. I'm sure your wife will reward you for your words at a later date. This doesn't change the fact that you are more loyal to the women in this house than you are the vampire who rules it. What are we going to do about this?"

Charlie looked down and felt Rebecca's reassuring hand in his. "Whatever you have to, Vincent."

The vampire stayed silent for a few minutes and wondered what he really wanted to do about Charlie. He could easily kill Charlie but didn't think that was a worthy punishment. Also, Vincent wasn't sure Rebecca would stay loyal if he sentenced her husband to death. Vincent had known all along that Charlie's loyalty was to Rebecca, not this house or its master. That was never a problem. If the werewolf happened to be more loyal to Natalia than himself, Vincent wondered if he could use that to his advantage.

Vincent used Anthony's distrust of Natalia as a means of allowing himself to associate with the human without worry. If there was someone in his family who was devoted to her safety, then why not allow that to happen? Vincent preferred to use his people's strengths to his advantage. This was no different.

"You almost attacked me to save her. Rebecca was wise enough to know your mind and saved you from your own death. She threw you into the dungeon and released you herself. I believe that her quick actions are enough punishment for your stupidity, and she has helped me to understand your place in this house better."

Charlie stood silently and waited for more.

"From now on, you will be Natalia's protector. Should a situation arise in which I am attacking her, you will turn to your Alpha first and ask her for the best course of action. Is that clear?"

Charlie was stunned. Not only was he being spared further punishment, he was being assigned as Natalia's guardian. The werewolf fell to his knees and bowed low in front of Vincent. Though the desk hid the man, Vincent still appreciated the gesture.

"I will protect her to the best of my ability and always ask my Alpha for guidance when I'm unsure of a situation."

"Good. Now get out, both of you. I need time alone."

Rebecca pulled Charlie to his feet and the two hurried out. Outside the office, Charlie grabbed Rebecca and gave her a strong kiss. "Thank you."

She smiled. "Thank me upstairs."

Charlie grinned, picked his wife up in his arms and practically ran up the stairs to their bedroom.

CB ED

Vincent was alone for some time before Joseph knocked on the door. He didn't wait for an answer but came into the room, with two human males. The humans sat silently in the chairs facing Vincent. No words were necessary. One, the elder, placed a small dagger and a roll of gauze on Vincent's desk.

"Would it be safer for you to take from me or them, sir?"

The men didn't appear to notice the question. They were well trained. There were many times Vincent's humans had been in a room with Vincent and Joseph. Sometimes Vincent fed from them; sometimes he fed from Joseph who then fed from the humans. It was a sign of good faith that Vincent knew when he was too hungry to feed safely from a human.

"You made a wise choice in bringing men. I'll be fine drinking from them."

Vincent rounded the desk as one of the men stood and presented his arm. Vincent took the dagger, gave the man's arm a small cut, and brought the bleeding wound to his lips. He drank five mouthfuls of blood then let the man go. The human took the gauze and moved out of the way. Joseph tied a bandage in place as Vincent drank from the second. He then similarly bandaged the second man.

Once the men were bandaged, Vincent nodded and let them go.

"Where is she?"

"In a spare bedroom."

"What did you do?"

"Made sure she understood the rules."

Vincent returned to his chair and pondered the situation.

"She won't disobey you again."

"Yes, she will. Just not in the same way."

They were both silent as Vincent's words sank in.

"Should I let her live, Joseph?"

"I follow your command, sir. I cannot tell you how to live your life."

Vincent glared at Joseph.

"You're not done with her. If you were, you would have killed her tonight."

Vincent took a long, slow breath and let it out in a deep sigh. "Leave."

Joseph bowed. "As you wish, sir."

A moment later, Vincent was alone with his thoughts. What was he going to do with Natalia? Was he done punishing her for killing Theodore? Was this really about Theodore? Or was it more about the fact that he had underestimated her. No human had ever caught him off guard enough to sweep him off his feet as she had with the staff. Very few vampires were able to do that either. She surprised him, and perhaps always would.

Still agitated about the situation, he reached for the intercom. Mierka was in the surveillance room. "Would you like to know what he did, boss?"

"Every minute."

There was a sound of fingers hitting the keyboard as Mierka brought up the camera views that would replay Joseph's interaction with Natalia. Vincent stood impatiently. "I'll be there in a minute."

"Yes, boss."

By the time he was in the surveillance room, the playbacks were ready. Vincent watched Joseph punish Natalia and nodded at the end. He felt she would think twice before disobeying his orders.

"So, what are you going to do with her now?"

Vincent gave Mierka a sideways glare. "Is that any of your business?"

She smirked, leaned back in her chair, and put her feet up on the desk. With an exaggerated sigh, she placed her hands behind her head and gave Vincent a large grin. "Anything I see on the screens is my business."

Vincent glared at Mierka one last time then left the room. He wasn't sure where his steps would take him until he stood outside of the guest room. He entered without knocking.

Natalia sat on the bed, and quickly slipped on a robe when the door opened. She stood and turned to the door, ready to yell at the person who barged into her room. When she saw Vincent, she fell silent. He shut the door and took two steps forward.

"Hello, Vincent." She tied her robe closed and wondered at the vampire's inscrutable appearance.

"Natalia." For a moment, he considered disabling the security cameras but decided against it. Mierka was watching, but she could be trusted to remain silent.

"Joseph said you would tell me what was going to happen next."

Vincent nodded. "He's right."

"Are you going to punish me now?"

The vampire started to pace slowly in the small room. "Your punishment is done, Natalia. This is your first offense, so I'll explain the rules. If you do something that I would consider a betrayal, then I or Joseph or Mierka will punish you, depending on the severity. Small betrayals deserve small punishments; large betrayals deserve more. I'm not here to punish you; I'm here to find out if I'm ready to be with you again today, or if I will have to wait until tomorrow."

Natalia nodded slowly, and allowed his voice and words to ease her troubled mind. She looked away to consider his words, then gasped softly with surprise. He was suddenly only a step away from her. She didn't hear him move. Natalia looked up at the magnificent vampire and felt her heart race. His jaw twitched and he turned away. She closed her eyes as disappointment and a tinge of fear raced through her mind. She wanted him to touch her, if only for a moment, to reassure her that everything would be fine. Today had been a horrendous day; she wanted it to end well but knew it would not. Natalia opened her eyes and faced Vincent, who now stood by the door. She would sleep in this cold room tonight; his face confirmed it.

Vincent watched as his human came to the right conclusion. They would sleep in separate rooms tonight. He wanted her blood; more than was safe to take. And after he took her blood, he wanted to make her scream in pleasure and pain. He wanted to show her who was in charge of this house, who she answered to, and whose word she would follow from this day forward. Much to his frustration, Vincent had a feeling that she would never truly follow his word: she had her own agenda, and she was going to see it through. As this thought ran through his head, Vincent opened the door and left the room.

Joseph waited for him outside. He leaned against the railing, arms crossed. After Vincent closed the bedroom door he started to walk to his own chambers. Joseph followed him to the sitting room, through his bedroom, the bathroom, into the maze and to the bedroom he had not used in over a year. Vincent stopped and gave Joseph time to enter before he closed the door and sealed them inside.

"Is it safe to keep her when she has her own agenda and will continue to defy me? This may cause too much dissension in the ranks."

"She does as she pleases to further her own cause but has only openly defied you this once. You may argue, but generally have the sense to do so in private. We all know that you allow her a certain amount of leeway, but tonight proved that you are still in control. Your lover challenged you, but you showed her and all others in your house that you will punish her if she steps out of line. You have not lost face."

Vincent nodded. "Then she stays."

Joseph bowed then left the room. Vincent stayed where he was, as he tapped his fingers on his thigh. He thought about the situation for a few more minutes before he turned his thoughts to other business.

☙ ❧

The next night, Vincent found Natalia in the library. She sat at the desk, completely absorbed in a large tome. He stood in the doorway and watched her silently for several moments. When she did not look up, he walked over to her and whispered her name.

"Natalia."

She heard her name as if the wind spoke it. When Natalia looked up, her heart and breath stopped. Vincent stood not five feet from the desk and continued to approach. Last night, when he left her, the look on his face suggested disappointment. Now, there was lust. Natalia closed her eyes and took deep breaths to calm her racing heart. She slept poorly last night and woke often to reach for a vampire that was not there. Not long after sunrise she woke for the last time, gave up trying to clear her mind, and decided to shower. As she did not want to use her bathroom, and potentially disturb Vincent, she asked one of the humans for help. They showed her the spare bathroom and lent her clothing as well.

Showered, she went to the kitchen, allowed someone else to make her food and came to the library. She had nothing better to do all day than read. Natalia knew it was past sunset the moment she saw Vincent. Before his appearance, time meant nothing. The day had been a series of written words and brief naps flavored with the concern that Vincent would not want to be with her tonight, either. And now, here was Vincent.

Natalia stood to greet him when he reached the desk. He was dressed to train in black shirt and tight workout pants. He didn't wear shoes. She shifted uneasily in her ill-fitting borrowed jeans and loose t-shirt. As he looked her up and down, a small smile threatened the corners of his mouth. Still unsure of her lover's next move, she nevertheless understood she would share his bed again.

"Hello, Vincent."

"How are you, Natalia?"

"I'm…" she was going to lie, but why bother? If she lied to him, he might think she could take him on. Natalia allowed herself to slump a little and let her unease show on her face. "Terrible. I'm terrible. I didn't sleep and I'm still not sure where I stand with you."

Vincent stepped to her and placed a hand on her cheek. He gave her a

63

pitiful look, but his voice held a tinge of humor. "Poor Natalia. Did Joseph scare you? Did it help you understand anything?"

She slapped his hand away, and glared at him in almost mock anger. "Where do I stand with you, vampire?"

"I would hope by my side. As I stated last night, your punishment is done."

"If it was done last night, why didn't I spend last night in your bed?"

The look in his eye changed, and became deadly. "There are certain things that I cannot do to you while you remain human. Were you a vampire, you would have spent last night in my bed and I would have punished you myself."

Natalia suddenly found herself face down on the desk, with her hands behind her. Vincent pressed firmly against her. He continued to speak to her and whispered into her ear.

"If you were a vampire, the punishment I would have dealt out to you would have left you quivering in fear, while you screamed in pain and begged for more. Do you think it wise that I not allow a fragile human into my bed last night with such vicious thoughts coursing through my mind?"

He moved again and Natalia found herself facing her vampire lover. One of his hands was around her back, the other wrapped lightly but firmly against her throat. "Make no mistake, human. If I don't take you to my bed, it's because I have no desire to rip you apart until you are able to recover from such massive damage. Understood?"

Natalia nodded as fear and curiosity shone in her eyes.

"Good." He released her and took a step back. "Go change. You will be watching us train tonight and for the rest of the week. At the end of the week, we will formulate rules for when you participate. After training, we will retire to our bedroom and spend some time alone. Agreed?"

She nodded; amazed he was able to change his mood so quickly. "You treat everyone the same way, don't you? It doesn't matter that I sleep with you. I disobeyed an order and you punished me. You didn't give me any chance to talk my way out of it or sleep my way out of it and you never will."

"Did you expect to be treated differently?"

Natalia paused before she answered, and pondered the question. When she decided she wanted to join Vincent's house, she knew how he operated. It would mean a swift death if she did anything to harm his people. She turned the full force of her dark eyes on the vampire. "It would be an insult if you treated me differently. I appreciate that you did not and hope this means you feel I'm worthy to be a part of your house."

Vincent smiled. "If you weren't worthy, Joseph would have killed you the night we met."

Natalia's eyes widened in surprise as Vincent left the room.

10
Two Years Later

Natalia ducked as the staff sailed toward her head. Before he could finish the strike, she used her own to sweep Ben off his feet. The vampire fell hard as his weapon clattered to the ground. Without hesitation, Natalia aimed a powerful blow at his chest. Ben grabbed the end of the staff before she connected, and tried to pull the weapon from her hands. Natalia held on, and let him pull her forward. Using the momentum, she rolled over him, let go of her staff and retrieved his weapon. He was on his feet before she was, but she expected it. The vampires would always be faster than she was; as a result, she had to be smarter.

Ben was her last conquest with the staff. He had been using the weapon since he was human over one hundred years ago. It was his favorite weapon, and his skill was widely known in Vincent's household. Most of Vincent's vampires were reluctant to fight with staves even though they were typically too well fed to be taken down by a simple wooden stake. Natalia thought the fear was psychological. Whatever kept them from using the staff gave her the advantage as her own skill improved. She had already defeated everyone else in one-on-one combat with the weapon. Ben was her final test.

Natalia knew Ben's confidence in his abilities would prove to be his downfall. She had watched him fight for over two years and each time she saw him, she felt she missed something. Most of the vampires tended to leave some part of themselves open to attack. It had taken her the better part of the past two years to learn how to win against most of them in a match, even though all she had to do was land a single blow.

When one vampire fought another, they could do as much damage to each other as they wanted. As long as no one was drained of blood and became ghul, anything was allowed. The rules didn't work when fighting a human. When Natalia first started to train with the vampires, the match was over as soon as the first blow landed. As her skills increased, it became two out of three rounds, as it had been with Vincent. She lost many matches in the first ten months of fighting. The first match she won was against Anthony, with the staff. He was able to move faster than her, but she learned to predict his movements. The blow she landed resounded with a loud crack as her staff broke in two. Anthony had been very upset; she laughed with pride. Her reaction did nothing to endear her to him, but she didn't care.

Now she faced Ben. During the short fight she focused solely on defense. She blocked every blow and watched him intently the whole time. The blow to the chest had been her first strike of the match. Now as he stood and smirked in front of her, she once more watched as the staff came her way. And…there it was. Natalia narrowly ducked under the staff and rolled backwards to get outside his reach.

Ben let her roll out of the way and watched her every move. Over the past two years, he had on numerous occasions told her how much he loved to watch her fight. Each time, he kissed her hand. In his many years of experience, he found that when fighting a woman, he could catch a glimpse of how she would perform in bed. Natalia's movements on the training floor were nimble, graceful, fluid. She was very skilled.

As she positioned herself, he wondered why she was not yet a vampire. Were she a vampire, the fight would have ended already and she would have been victorious. He was more skilled than she, but her determination was stronger. She stood before him in all her beauty, wearing far less than everyone else. The vampires were dressed in black long-sleeved tight-fitting exercise outfits; the werewolves were in sweats. She was dressed in nylon biker shorts and matching top. The top looked more like a sports bra than a shirt. The outfit exposed her flat stomach and toned limbs. It clung to the rest of her body and left little to the imagination. He imagined anyway, and considered how it would be to strip her of her skimpy clothing. He knew most of the men in the room had had similar thoughts. He gave her a sly smile as she nodded her readiness.

Natalia waited, and allowed him to attack first. He always did, to test her skill and help her improve. As he swung at her, his staff dipped down and exposed his left side. She switched her stance and gripped the staff with both hands near one end. As she forced her frustrations into the swing, she aimed high. The makeshift bat connected with his head with a solid sound that echoed briefly in the large room. Ben was knocked to the ground. The elation on her face fell with him as she noticed blood ooze onto the hardwood floor.

"Ben!" She cried out, dropped the staff, and rushed to him. Joseph was beside them in an instant and pushed her aside.

"Leave him. He's fine." Joseph's voice, as usual, held no emotion. He knelt to speak with Ben quietly.

She felt herself being pulled back by warm hands, probably one of the werewolves. She heard Charlie's voice whisper in her ear. "That was awesome!"

Natalia turned and gave him a dirty look. When she turned back to assess the situation, Ben had already started to heal his wound. He sat up, waved Joseph away, and wiped the blood off the side of his face. His head turned slowly as he tried to find Natalia. Their eyes locked when he found her, and he gave her a small nod. Joseph helped him stand, but it didn't seem necessary. He was fine. Ben held his hand out to Natalia, and took her hand gently when she reached out. He bowed to lightly kiss the back of her hand, and caressed her warm fingers with his cool ones. His eyes remained locked on hers.

"Absolutely wonderful, Natalia." He stood straight, and stared intently into her eyes. His voice teased her. "It won't happen again."

"Yes, it will." Her face showed her elation. She tucked her joy away for a moment. "But are you ok?"

"It takes more than a blow to the head to stop an old vampire like me, Natalia." He released her hand. "If you'll excuse me, I find I'm rather hungry."

Ben walked away, to be replaced by Joseph. He spoke quietly, just to her. "The next time you break a vampire's neck in this house, they'll be healing the wound with your blood."

Her eyes grew wide at the realization of what she'd done. Her voice was too low for anyone but Joseph to hear. "Yes, sir. Forgive me, sir."

Joseph accepted her apology with a discrete nod as the others started to crowd her. Charlie laughed as he collected his winnings. He always bet on her, despite her low winning average. Joseph spoke again, but louder this time for all to hear.

"Congratulations. In the past two years, you have fought against most of the vampires in Vincent's house. You will never fight Mierka or Dr. Elving, as neither fight in these battles for their own reasons. Vincent has allowed you to fight him on occasion, with varied results. At this time, there is only one other vampire you have not fought who wishes to fight you. It is now time for you to fight me."

The crowd quieted as the implication set in. Joseph never fought against anyone unless he felt it would be a challenge. All waited for his next words, but Natalia spoke first. She knelt in front of him, her face awash with respect.

"I'm not ready, sir." She felt his hand on her shoulder and she lifted her head to meet his gaze.

He spoke quietly again. "You are more ready than you realize." He raised his voice. "Rise, child and accept my challenge."

She did as she was told and tried to calm the knots out of her stomach. Natalia knew she wasn't ready. As the others moved back, she felt her confidence slip. She witnessed a fight between Joseph and Vincent once, and it proved to be a bloody and violent hand-to-hand battle. When Joseph won, Vincent turned and looked for her. Both men were very low on blood and therefore ravenous. Mierka stepped in front of her, and kept Vincent from quenching his thirst on the delicate human. Joseph, in complete control of his actions, left the room to feed, and took a disgruntled Vincent with him.

Now, the formidable vampire stood about five feet away, and held a sword out to her. Natalia felt a nudge on her shoulder as Charlie, a huge grin on his face, pushed her toward their fighting master. Natalia felt herself going pale as blood rushed away from every part of her being.

"I have a request." Her voice mirrored her shaky confidence. Joseph continued to hold the sword to her but raised an eyebrow. She was stalling and he knew it. "Can we wait until Vincent returns?"

"No. He would never allow this fight to start. Take this rapier and face me as I demand."

She wrapped her hand around the hilt, and tested the weight of the blade as Joseph released it. "Won't you get in trouble then?"

"I'm the master of the fight. I do not intend to be stopped by the master of the house." He bowed to her. "We will fight each round until there is a clear winner, not to the first hit. Best of three wins. Ready?"

Natalia stood tall, and stared down the end of the blade at her opponent. She took three deep slow breaths to steady herself, then bowed. "Ready."

The room hushed as Joseph advanced slowly. He started to circle, and she let him. He and Vincent had similar fighting styles. They liked to circle their prey while they waited for the weaker challenger to show fear. Knowing she had to take him down with smart tactics and some trickery, she dipped her sword down. Natalia let the sword shake and changed her blank expression to show her true feelings. Joseph simply laughed. He knew her ploys. As his eyes closed for a second, she lunged forward and slashed at his extended arm. It killed his laughter. He didn't know all her ploys.

Joseph held Natalia's gaze as he healed his wounded arm. There was a slight smirk in her eyes, as if she were gaining her confidence. He mirrored her smirk, amplified it, and wondered at her next move. He flinched, but she didn't buy it. She stood her ground, one hand behind her, the sword held at her side, and waited for him. He stood stock-still for several more minutes as he assessed her. He could hear the werewolves as they murmured and grew impatient behind him. His own energy was boundless;

he could wait an eternity. The other vampires in the room had all been through this before, though none recently. They all knew what to expect. He was testing the human, to see how long she could stand still.

Natalia realized he was testing her as she held the sword in her right hand, with the end pointed down to her feet. Her feet were shoulder distance apart, with the right foot in the lead. The smirk grew as time passed; Joseph's actions gave her more time to prepare. With each plan that ran through her mind, the smirk grew. By the time he came at her, she knew how to win the first round.

Joseph ran at her and watched as the sword stayed still until the last possible second. Before he reached her, she dodged out of the way and flicked the sword up. He didn't bother to block the blow; he knew how many times she could slice him. He was more concerned with testing her than winning anyway. Joseph felt the sword as it caught him in the leg. It was by no means a serious blow, but the wounds she dealt to his back were. She cut him four or five times before he turned around. He backed out of the way of the sword, and she advanced with the same smirk on her face.

Natalia had learned a lot since her first match against Vincent. For one thing, don't stop slashing when up against a vampire; it gave them time to recover. She fought a few before Vincent, but none who were the same age or had the same skill of Vincent and his lot. As Joseph retreated, she slashed him a few more times, and tore up his shirt and skin. The smirk grew and her random thoughts faded as she emptied her mind of non-essential clutter. As the warrior inside took over, the smirk faded to a coldness that made Joseph smile and Charlie shudder.

The werewolf watched as the smirk left her face and remembered a time when nothing but humanity accented her features. She had never looked this inhuman, even the two times she saved him from Zechariah. Charlie studied the woman he once loved and knew for certain she was gone for good. She belonged on this stage and others like it, fighting, plotting, winning. He felt a chill as he stared at her expression, and wondered how it had come to this. He felt a tap on his shoulder and turned. His smile returned as he beheld Rebecca.

"Hey. Thought you were watching the monitors." He kissed her cheek lightly.

"I was. Boss is home. Told him we needed to talk to him." There was a slight twinkle in her eye.

"You didn't tell him?" He walked with her around the outside of the room towards the door to give the fighters a wide breadth. He saw Natalia slash into Joseph again as she aimed for the vampire's torso.

"Not yet. Thought you might like to be there."

"Thanks." He glanced back to the fight before they left the room and laughed as Natalia slashed Joseph again. She wasn't letting up. "What's he think of this?"

"He's not happy with it but trusts Joseph not to mess her up too much."
Rebecca led the way to the security room where Vincent observed the
battle. Most of the center monitors displayed the fight, and the vampire
watched his woman intently. Joseph had removed his torn shirt, so the red
lacerations he received were easy to see even on the small screens. A young
man sat in the chair, also entranced by the fight.

"She's human?" His voice held nothing but disbelief.

Charlie recognized the voice but had trouble placing it. Rebecca spoke
first, and announced their presence. "Sir? Can we speak privately?"

Vincent turned, as did the young man. Charlie nearly choked when he
recognized the human. He didn't say anything but waited for Vincent to
speak. "Is this something that everyone will know of eventually?"

Charlie and Rebecca looked at each other. Charlie shrugged and gave
her a knowing look. Rebecca turned back to her boss. "Yes."

"Then speak freely, Markus is part of my family now."

Charlie took another look at the man and wondered if the ex-waiter
from The Red Thread was indeed still human.

Rebecca leaned back against the desk, chewed on her lip and plunged
ahead. "I'm pregnant." Vincent raised an eyebrow; Markus made a noise
and Charlie blushed. "Do you remember how my mother was when she
was pregnant with me, sir?"

Vincent slowly nodded his head in affirmation. Rebecca's mother
became dangerously unpredictable in her later months. "You're leaving
then?"

"As long as you approve." There was a hint of sarcasm in her voice.

Vincent snorted then smiled. "And Charlie?"

"I'd like to go with her, until she sends me back." Rebecca's mom
hadn't been able to stand her husband in the last two months of pregnancy.
He had been too much of a risk at that point as well. Charlie was warned it
could be the same with him.

"Will you go to Montana?" Vincent owned 60 acres of private, secure,
and secluded land in Montana. Rebecca's parents had retired there.

"With your permission."

Vincent reached his hand out to the Alpha of his werewolves. When
Rebecca took his offered hand, he stepped forward, brought her hand to
his lips and kissed her hand. "Go with speed and goodwill, werewolf. Your
family will have a home with me for as long as the line is sown."

"And my family will continue to serve you, vampire, for as long as your
blood stays true."

Vincent stepped forward again, grasped her shoulders, and kissed both
her cheeks as a Frenchman would. He let her go, turned to Charlie and gave
the werewolf a slight bow. "You may both leave when your affairs are in

order. For now, let's join the others. Natalia has won the first round."

He left the room, and expected the men to follow. Rebecca stayed behind to watch the monitors. She adjusted the screens to all have different camera views but kept the main one focused on the fight. As the three men walked down the hallway, a tiny Natalia and a tiny Joseph squared off again. Rebecca winced in empathetic pain as the blur that was Joseph slammed the human against the wall. When Vincent entered the ballroom, Joseph had her pinned to the wall. Her sword arm was trapped behind her, and his hand was wrapped around her throat. Each had now won one round. Rebecca settled back in the comfortable chair to watch the next match, which she suspected would be between Vincent and Joseph.

11

Vincent restrained himself from running to Joseph to pull him away from Natalia. His friend would not harm his woman, and in fact was letting her go now. Vincent strolled to the others with Charlie and Markus in tow. He waited for the others in the room to quiet as he faced the pair at the wall. Natalia displayed no emotion as she shook herself off, and checked for wounds. When she realized all was well, she turned the intensity of her warrior look on Vincent which made him growl. He would have an interesting night when the match was done.

Natalia watched as the vampires and werewolves behind Vincent greeted a man she didn't recognize. Someone asked him a question and he just smiled large to show off his fangs. There were several shouts of welcome, which she ignored in favor of the fight. She turned back to Joseph, who faced his master.

"Let's finish this, vampire."

Her voice was slightly hoarse from the stranglehold he had given her. He didn't choke her, but came close. She wasn't surprised by his actions. The first round had been to test her, the second to make the third more intense. Since Vincent witnessed her loss in the second round, she hungered for victory all the more. The thought of Vincent made her brain twitch, and a new strategy came to mind. A slow seductive smile took over her features and she stared at Joseph, who waited patiently once again.

Joseph saw the smile and understood that his plan worked. He prepared himself for what was to come. Vincent also saw Natalia's smile and gave a low, long growl. He wanted to be the recipient of that look.

Natalia's whole demeanor changed as she walked toward Joseph. Every part of her body screamed seduction. "You may have won the last round vampire, but I'll win the match. I have something to compensate for your loss. Would you like to know what it is?"

Joseph narrowed his eyes, and hid the smile of triumph with a look of desire. Vincent narrowed his eyes quizzically, not sure where she was headed with her soliloquy, not sure he wanted to know. That look on her face was all too familiar.

She was within arm's length of Joseph now, her hands behind her. She stopped and very carefully cut her thumb on the rapier. She gave an exaggerated look of pain to emphasize her actions. Sure of herself and of the vampire's hungry look she brought her injured hand to his face. She placed her bleeding thumb on his lips, and let the other fingers rest near his jaw line. His eyes closed as she traced his flesh and left blood on his lips. She pulled her hand away.

"Lick your lips clean, vampire. Sample the consolation prize."

He did as instructed and nearly broke. The taste of human blood left him wanting much more. He reeled in his hunger, opened his eyes, and allowed his desires to show. The first round had taken a good deal of his blood. He allowed her too many slashes to test her skills. He underestimated how much the rapier cuts would cost him. A great thirst was upon him, and she offered no more than a drop of the precious liquid.

"Is that all you offer?" There was a tinge of barely concealed aggressiveness to his desperate voice.

A look of triumph flashed across her face. She didn't think the ploy would work on Joseph, but apparently, she was wrong. She let the seduction go further than necessary, as Vincent's eyes dug into her. A jealous lover might prove to her advantage as well. Natalia returned her thumb to Joseph's lips. He caught her hand lightly, wrapped his lips around her thumb and started to suck softly. She closed her eyes with pleasure, then pulled her hand away, to take control of the situation.

"Watch yourself, vampire."

"But I want more." His tone showed the truth.

Natalia stole a glance toward Vincent, who scowled mightily. He looked both annoyed and aroused. A shudder passed through her. Being in control of a situation always turned her on. She looked back to Joseph, the seductress taking over. "How much more?"

"How much do you offer?" His voice was petulant. She knew she had him.

Her hand went to his face to trace the line of his jaw. "How much do you want?"

Joseph grabbed her wrist, spun her around, and tightened his other arm around her. His words were a triumphant shout. "All of it!"

Natalia held back a scream as his teeth plunged into her shoulder. She looked at Vincent, her eyes wide with wonder. Mierka struggled with Vincent as he tried to come forward. She heard a metallic ring as the rapier fell from her hand to the floor. Her arm, no longer encumbered and heavy, reached up to caress Joseph's neck. The bite hurt, but her head spun as he sucked slowly. She looked back to Vincent as numbers ran through her head.

As the number six flashed by her consciousness, she understood. She always counted the swallows Vincent took. Occasionally, he took eight, but in general, Vincent never took more than seven swallows of her blood. Joseph was on his eleventh, more than was safe.

Joseph felt the human stiffen as she finally understood the danger. He held her a little tighter, and wondered how she would try and escape. He would let her go before too much longer, as he did not want to irrevocably harm her. He took slow sips, to give her ample time to react. He felt her relax and was disappointed. He had hoped she would escape his trap. As her free hand slid down his body, he knew he had won. A groan sounded in the back of his throat as she caressed his erection. Lost in the act of feeding and seduction, he pulled her closer.

Joseph sighed with pleasure as her hand slid down between his legs to his inner thigh. As her hand slid back up, he knew he had to let her go. It was too late; he was too wrapped up in the taste of her to understand her true intent.

Natalia wrapped her hand around his balls and squeezed as hard as she could. Her nails dug through the thin fabric of his pants, and he shrieked in pain. He pushed away from her, and dropped to the ground. Natalia sank to her knees from the blood loss. Even through the pain Joseph understood that the fight wasn't over, and he was glad. He saw Vincent kneel beside Natalia as the new blood flowing through his veins healed his slight wound.

Vincent had to punch Mierka to get by her. She tried to explain why Joseph and Natalia sparred, but Vincent did not care to listen. He knelt beside his woman, concern evident on his face. He grabbed a handkerchief from his pocket and placed it on her wound. Though Joseph had bitten her neck, the wound was close to her shoulder. Vincent maneuvered the piece of cloth under her sports bra strap to staunch the blood flow.

"Natalia. Are you well?" His voice was low. He didn't want the others to hear.

She helped to position the handkerchief, but wondered if it was helping. "Fine. Need air."

Once the makeshift bandage was secure, Natalia pushed Vincent away. She breathed deeply to keep her vision from fading. She had judged once that Vincent's seven swallows were about a pint of blood. It was no more than what blood banks took when someone donated blood.

Joseph managed almost twenty swallows: over two pints of blood. She was lightheaded and needed to rest, but knew the fight wasn't over. She understood now what Joseph had planned when he asked her for a match.

She had to get up and finish the fight. Natalia heard a sound behind her and knew Joseph was standing. She slowly opened her eyes, and tried to get to her feet. Vincent tried to help her, but she once more pushed him away.

Vincent looked back and forth between the pair as Mierka walked to him. He assessed the situation and grew angry as he saw what was happening. "Are you both mad? This fight does not continue!"

"Of course, it does. There's no winner." Natalia's voice was strong, though her face was pale and showed weakness.

"No winner? He took more of your blood than he should have. You're weak, Natalia. Yield and go rest."

She was on one knee, to balance herself before she tried to stand. Her movements were slow, but as Joseph hadn't attacked, she could take her time. "Not going to happen, lover. Get off the training floor."

He ground his teeth and knelt in front of her. "What are you trying to prove, Natalia?"

She brought her head up and gave him a cold look: a warrior's look. She met his gaze, held it, and she stood as if unhurt. "That I am worthy of fighting for this house."

Joseph grabbed her from behind and threw her against the wall as Mierka pulled Vincent back. Natalia looked up quickly from the floor and caught Vincent's eye. There was pain in her look and voice, but there was determination as well. "I fight because I can, Vincent. Don't stop me."

As she spoke, she grabbed the staff that had fallen next to her when she hit. She used the staff and wall to pull herself up. There was a buzzing in her ear that blocked the angry exchange between master and servant. She concentrated on breathing and on tactics. There was no way to attack; she didn't have the energy. Her only course of action was defense, and she couldn't do that either. She had lost a lot of blood to Joseph, which meant he probably felt just fine. Natalia stood now, her back to the wall and the staff at her side. As she considered her options, she stared at the point of the staff.

The argument grew louder, and Natalia blinked. Most of the staves used for practice had blunt ends. It was safer that way and allowed opponents to grab the end if necessary. There was one though, that had a point. It wasn't sharpened, but it did taper and could do some serious damage if the opponent wasn't careful. It was used rarely and mostly to help the vampires learn how to defend against pointed wooden objects. The staff Natalia held on to had a tapered end. She looked up as her plan took shape. She didn't have to move to win. She stood, breathed deep, and waited for Joseph to finish his argument with Vincent.

Vincent's anger with Joseph was palpable. His friend refused to give any kind of explanation. From the look on Joseph's face, he wasn't going to explain until the fight was done. Vincent contemplated picking Natalia up and carrying her out of the room, except that she wanted to finish the fight. She demanded to be treated as an equal in the training room and worked hard to achieve it. There were different rules when she fought to keep her from dying, but none of her opponents gave her any slack. They used their skills and helped her to test her own. To stop the fight now would be an insult to Natalia.

Vincent ground his teeth, as he relented. "If in the end, you don't have a very good explanation…"

"You will take my blood in retaliation." Joseph stared at Vincent, and knew he won. He turned to Natalia, who leaned meekly against the wall. She didn't look well, but he could still see the warrior. The tension in the room thickened as Joseph ran to his prey.

Natalia waited to get the timing right. She wanted to faint, and knew it was almost over. At the last possible second, she grabbed the pointed staff, swung it up, and held it perpendicular to the wall. Too late, Joseph saw what she was doing. He slammed into the staff, unable to stop his forward motion. It sank deep into his abdomen. Natalia, too weak to hold on to the staff with Joseph's weight on it, let go. The end of the staff dropped to the floor and lodged in the crook of the wall and floor. Joseph didn't have time to react before the motion sank the staff deeper into his body to poke out his back. He grabbed the staff before it could cause any more damage. He took a tentative step back to move the staff away from the wall. Joseph fell to his knees, then fell to his side. Natalia still stood, but barely.

Vincent ran to the pair as Mierka, and Charlie ran out of the room. Vincent, torn between concern for his friend and concern for his lover, knelt between them. They were close enough he could check on both of them at the same time. Natalia sank to the floor as Vincent reached for her. He looked toward Joseph as he took Natalia's wrist in his hand, to feel for her pulse. It was weak but steady. His hand tightened around her wrist for a moment then let go. She would be fine. Joseph was still on his side, in a pool of blood.

"Don't move; Mierka brings blood." His voice was surprisingly steady, despite his anger and worry.

"Need blood now. Natalia's too close." Joseph's voice was dead calm, but there was a cavernous hunger to it. Vincent unbuttoned his shirt sleeve, pulled the fabric to his elbow and slit his wrist with his fingernail. The pain was light in comparison to the frantic turmoil of his mind.

Vincent placed his bleeding wrist to his friend's mouth. He caught Kimberly's eye and nodded her over. She came quickly. "Joseph, Kimberly is going to pull the staff out slowly. Can you heal yourself as she does so?"

Joseph nodded, as he continued to suck on his master's wrist. Kimberly stepped over him to get to the correct side of the staff. "We're going to have to move him back. I don't have enough room."

Joseph let go of Vincent's wrist and pushed himself back a little. He grasped the staff, and pulled it out enough so that the end no longer stuck out of his back. He flipped over onto his back, already partially healed.

Kimberly watched as he moved. "That'll work too." She straddled him and grasped the staff. "Fast or slow, boss?"

"Do it quickly." Joseph heard several people run into the room and felt better. Mierka was back with blood. His lover was by his side before Kimberly could pull the staff out, and indicated she should wait.

Two humans knelt by his side, the closest bearing their wrist to him. The human pulled out a dagger and slit his arm carefully. Joseph grasped the humans' wrist and sucked on the blood. Joseph took what was safe, then pulled back and looked to the other human. The second man took out his own dagger, slit his arm and presented the wound to the downed vampire. Joseph grasped his arm as the first human pulled back, gauze pressed tightly to his wound.

When he had taken enough from the second human, Joseph closed his eyes and blindly nodded to Kimberly. She grasped the end of the staff and pulled it out slowly as Joseph healed his wound. They timed it well, and he bled no more. Once healed, Joseph opened his eyes, to look for more blood. As the two donors slipped out the door, two more came forward to feed him. He smiled his thanks and took what they gave gratefully.

Charlie, not as quick as Mierka, came in as Kimberly stepped away from Joseph. She still had the staff in hand. A third of it was covered in blood. Charlie smiled in admiration as he knelt next to Natalia. Vincent had a hand on her ankle, but he seemed more interested in staying between Natalia and Joseph, probably for her protection. Charlie placed a full water bottle on the floor next to her, along with some beef jerky, but kept the orange juice in his hand. He really didn't know what to give her but figured the orange juice would be good for quick energy and the beef jerky good for iron to help her blood loss.

Charlie placed the cold glass of orange juice to her lips, and helped her hold the glass as she sipped. Her eyes fluttered as the icy liquid slipped down her chin onto her neck. Natalia pushed the glass away and sloshed the liquid. She opened her eyes fully and stared at him.

"You ok, Nat?" He spoke softly, but Vincent turned when he heard the question. Joseph was fine and wouldn't attack Natalia. Now he could concentrate on her.

"Yes, are you alright? Do you need Lilly?" He faced her, his hand still on her ankle.

Natalia was dizzy and lightheaded. Her vision kept threatening to quit and her ears were ringing. She tried to focus on Vincent and just couldn't. "She can't heal blood loss." She took a breath. "Joseph ok?"

Vincent's thoughts stopped as her words echoed in his mind. Joseph was up and herding people out of the room while she sat still on the floor. He couldn't understand how the human could be worried about the vampire. Charlie answered her question as the werewolf helped her drink some water.

"He's an old vampire, takes more than a staff in the gut to stop him." There was a mocking quality to his voice as he almost imitated the master fighter.

Natalia laughed around the water bottle straw. It made both men feel better. She took some more slow swallows of water. Her stomach rolled; she felt nauseous. She took the bottle, placed it on her leg, and held it steady with one hand. She willed her vision to clear as she looked at Vincent. There was concern on his face. Her hand shook as she touched his cheek. Vincent stopped his worry as he saw the sheer determination take over. His hand stole over hers as he turned his head to kiss the palm of her hand. Natalia, still able to focus, noticed Joseph who stood nearby. She took two quivering breaths.

"Did I win?"

Vincent's eyes grew wide. He dropped her hand as if it were a distasteful piece of carcass. He moved quickly away from her as he stood. He presented his back to her, and decided to show his anger to Joseph rather than Natalia. His friend could take the anger; she could not. Without turning, he barked orders at Charlie. "Take her out of here, wolf. Make sure Lilly sees her. Stay with Natalia and give her all she needs until I arrive."

Charlie nodded, picked Natalia up in his arms and carried her out of the room. She didn't protest once, but he thought it was a good sign she asked for water and food. He took her to Vincent's sitting room, and placed her on a couch. Once she was settled, he left to retrieve Lilly.

12

Joseph stood motionless as Vincent, still rather angry, screamed and yelled. He said not a word, to allow Vincent to satiate his frustrations as he paced violently up and down the training room. His boss was so angry, he switched back and forth between English and his native French. Joseph stood and took it. He knew Vincent would be easier to handle once the fury was deflated. It took a good long time. Joseph knew his friend was calm when he went to stand by one of the tall windows.

"Would you mind explaining now, why you tested my lover when I specifically forbade it?" He still gazed out the window, hands crossed behind his back.

"We need to speak in a secure location."

Vincent turned, a quizzical expression on his face. He regarded Joseph for a moment, then shook his head and walked out of the room. Joseph followed him to the study. Once they were both inside, Vincent locked the door and took out his remote control. He entered the code to jam the audio and video feed. Once they were both seated at the desk, Joseph pointed to an invitation that sat on Vincent's desk. Vincent picked it up and read the card.

"It arrived today."

Vincent stared at the invitation, and tried not to show any emotion. "He hasn't had a Red Tie Affair since before Christopher left. This is dangerous."

"You don't think it means Christopher is coming back?"

The agitated vampire shook his head. "No." He paused in thought. "Edwin enjoys pretending to be Captain because it means no one can touch him, but he's been Acting Captain for almost five years. I have to wonder how long a vampire like him can stand only being the Acting Captain.

There are limits to what he can do. There are still too many in the Bay Area who won't listen to him. It may be that he wants to show his power, show that he <u>has</u> power. We need to be there."

"Of course, we do." The tone in his voice made Vincent look up hard.

"What does this have to do with you testing Natalia today?" He looked as if he didn't want to know the answer.

"We'll need her."

"Out of the question."

"She'll be an asset; a great distraction."

"I won't risk her life."

"Neither will I. Now that I know she won't either, I feel we can use her, if she agrees."

"It's not your decision, nor hers. She's not coming with us."

"Why? Because you think she's not ready? Or because she's yours and you're reluctant to lose her?"

"Because if we bring her, Edwin will know her." He stood, walked around the desk and started to pace.

"He won't know she's yours, if we play our cards right." Joseph continued when Vincent stayed silent. "Remember when she first fought you; she said she presented herself as a Slayer when she fought Edwin's men. If she comes with us, we can pretend the same thing. We make sure she arrives after we do and leaves before we do. She can distract Edwin and his guards as we free the young ones. Two years ago, she was far better than most of Edwin's men. Her intelligence and skills have made her as good as our best fighters. Had she the mind to, she could kill us both." His voice grew quieter. "She would have to seduce us first, but she could kill us." His voice grew to normal volume. "She can take on his men without pause. She'll walk away the victor, and I'm willing to bet she'll walk away without a severe scratch. Let her show you what she can do."

Vincent listened as Joseph finished his speech. He paced faster, toward the end. He did not like how much thought Joseph had put into placing his woman in harm's way. He wasn't willing to risk Edwin meeting Natalia. Normally, his Acting Captain wasn't interested in women Natalia's age, but Vincent was worried Edwin would try to take her out of malice. Edwin often took his people's favorites in order to initiate them into the fold his way, which was why he sent Markus to New York. Lorraine changed him a year ago and taught him the ways of the vampire. Markus was back because this was his home and he could now defend it, but Natalia was still human.

"No."

"Why don't we ask her?"

Joseph didn't want to let this go. He knew Natalia wanted to battle unhindered by rules. He saw it in her eyes every time she fought, and tonight, he knew she was ready to be tested. She fought Vincent on several occasions, and always reverted to using her blood to throw her lover off his game. They both enjoyed it, but it was dangerous. All who watched knew that Vincent would never take her blood without her permission. Joseph knew that if she continued to consider her blood a weapon, she would be easily killed in a real fight. She learned the errors of her ways tonight, and he believed she would not consider the ploy again. She was ready for the next step.

"No." Vincent stopped pacing, a glimmer of a memory in his eye. He turned quickly to Joseph. "She isn't ready." He returned to his desk in less than a second and shook the invitation at Joseph. "She only knows how to fight in comfortable clothing. And if she arrives at Edwin's function in anything but eveningwear, she'll be turned away. She's never fought in an evening gown and heels." Vincent hit the invitation against Joseph's chest with each word as he finished his tirade. "She's." Thwack. "Not." Thwack. "Ready." Thwack.

Joseph stared at Vincent, not reacting to being hit repeatedly with card stock in the chest. "Tell her about the Red Tie affair. Ask her if she wishes to participate, then have her practice in heels and an evening gown. Let it be her decision."

Vincent turned and walked back around his desk to sit in his leather chair. "Fine. I'll ask her tomorrow when she's better. Agreed?"

Joseph kept his back to his boss to hide the victorious smile on his face. "Agreed."

Vincent watched as Joseph left the room without another word. He cursed under his breath when the door closed behind his friend. He hated being manipulated.

ભ ૪

Vincent watched with trepidation as Natalia circled Markus in her beautiful crimson silk gown and stiletto heels. It was a little over two weeks until Edwin's Red Tie Affair. She practiced in a gown for a week, and learned how to move quickly in heels for three days. Tonight, she wore both for the first time. She was able to move well enough slowly, but Joseph instructed Markus to attack as if she were trying to kill him.

Vincent pleaded with Natalia for a long time, to try and make her understand how dangerous it was to fight in heels. She ignored him and told him that with practice she would be able to use stilettos as weapons. They argued about her decision every day since he told her about the Red Tie Affair. Since her decision to fight against Edwin, she became far more aggressive in bed than he had ever seen her, which made it hard for Vincent to deny her.

Now, as she pranced clumsily around Markus, Vincent had to bite his tongue not to stop the fight. He knew there was a good possibility she would fall and twist her ankle. Part of him looked forward to her injuring herself, as it would keep her away from Edwin just a little longer. Vincent tore his eyes away from Natalia long enough to turn his attention to the youngest of his family and wondered how Markus was doing.

Markus wasn't sure of his skills yet and was slightly afraid of the human who stood before him. Dressed in formal wear while brandishing a sword she looked deadlier than usual. All the gathered vampires were dressed to impress, as they needed to practice. All would attend Edwin's function, save Markus. The young vampire stated he would be a hindrance rather than an asset. Joseph and Vincent concurred, as neither wanted to risk their youngest member. He was nevertheless dressed in a new suit for practice. He faced Vincent's woman though, and she unnerved him. Her eyes were cold and calculating, too much like Vincent's. She looked like she could rip out his heart and eat it as she laughed. Vincent often wore the same look. Markus also saw her win against Joseph, which was rumored not even Vincent could do.

Natalia felt she hid her shakiness well, but knew that as soon as Markus attacked, she would fall. When Vincent informed her of Edwin's soirée, she knew she wanted to fight. As more of the vampires told her what these parties were like, she knew she had to be there. Mierka informed her that Edwin would find and capture about ten children. They would be fed on and passed around for the pleasure of his perverted friends.

Moving quickly in a gown was hard, but she found that if she wore a dress with slits up the sides, it increased her range of motion. She hadn't figured out how to keep steady on her heels, though. Natalia liked to wear heels and did so whenever she and Vincent went out. She sometimes wore heels around the house, just to drive him crazy. Moving slowly and seductively on heels and trying to walk as a warrior in them were two entirely different creatures. She felt like a child trying out heels for the first time. The sharp thin heels would be great to use as weapons, she thought. Now, as she faced down a practice threat, she wasn't too sure. She circled slowly as she used every other part of her body to intimidate, and waited for the terrified vampire to strike.

And then he did.

Markus lunged at her to knock her to the ground. Natalia jumped up to leap over him. She thought to land on his back and drive her heels into his flesh. She forced herself down, and sunk all her weight to her feet. She misjudged his intentions and missed him as he dove to the right. Natalia landed hard on her feet, and she felt her left foot threaten to slip out from under her. She stumbled forward in an effort not to twist her ankle. It didn't work. Her right foot caught in a crack in the floor and her already unstable left finally slipped. Natalia fell hard on her rump and her eyes grew wide as she heard the snap.

Vincent and those close enough to hear the snap gasped as Natalia's face became as pale as a vampire's. Vincent watched, fascinated as she kept in the scream of pain. He was by her side as she continued to struggle with the scream. He screamed for her, forming a name.

"Liliana!" It was more of a bellow then a scream, in a voice not to be ignored. The healer was already on the way over. She had been apprised of the situation and agreed that her place was in the training room while Natalia tried her new form of fighting.

Natalia's eyes were closed, and her hands gripped Vincent's arm as she did her best to hold on to consciousness. The scream still threatened to rupture from her throat and burst through her teeth. She breathed deep and tried not to think of the pain. Her ankle was broken, no doubt about it, but Lilly would heal her quickly and she would be all right. She felt herself being picked up and someone pulled her good leg out from under her. She was told to brace herself as someone placed warm hands on her calf and slowly brought her left leg straight out in front of her. She closed her eyes to stop herself from looking at her broken ankle. The gasps from onlookers made her understand how bad it looked.

"Natalia? Can you hear me?"

Natalia nodded as she heard Lilly's voice. Her eyes were still tightly shut. The healer spoke again. "I have to set the bone. This is going to hurt."

At least the woman was honest. Natalia felt Lilly's warm fingers tenderly touch her already swollen ankle. She started to shake as pain took over her very being. Agony became her only existence when the healer grabbed her ankle and pulled. The scream barely escaped her lips as the fiery cold teeth of misery sank its fangs into her consciousness and yanked her away. She went limp in Vincent's arms as the healer began her chant. He looked angrily at Joseph who was on her other side.

"She's not ready. She does not fight." His angry words brought only a solemn nod from Joseph.

C3 &O

Natalia paced the length of the downstairs hallway. It was the night after Edwin's Red Tie Affair, and no one had returned. Sunset was hours ago. Markus was in the security room, waiting for word. It was the full moon, which meant she didn't even have the company of the wolves, who were sedated and locked in the dungeon. She yelled at one too many of Vincent's humans for no good reason, therefore they stayed out of her way. They were as worried as her but were better able to control their emotions. Consequently, she paced, and waited for something.

It was an hour later when the door of the security office banged open, and Markus yelled out the door. "They're here!"

Natalia raced from the front door to the garage door as she heard it open. Vincent was in the lead. She nearly knocked him down as she flew into his arms. His arms wrapped around her, and he sank to his knees, unable to support her weight. Anthony had been able to supply them with blood, but only a sufficient amount to be strong enough to get home. He didn't have as many humans on hand as Vincent did. They stopped at several homeless shelters and dark alleys until they had fed enough to be safe before coming home, but they all needed more. It was a credit to their self-control that no humans died in the feeding frenzy.

Vincent's hands sank into Natalia's hair, and curled into her flesh. He loved the feel and smell of her. He closed his eyes as the scent of her blood brought his body to life. He growled hungrily into her hair, and tried to control himself. He couldn't take her blood; he wouldn't be able to stop. Hands pulled her away and he didn't protest.

Mierka held Natalia back as Joseph presented a human to Vincent. The human fell to his knees, dagger in hand and offered himself over to Vincent. The vampire drank the warm blood down as Natalia watched, speechless. When he was done with the first, he stood and beckoned a second.

"What happened?" Natalia's voice shook with wonder and worry.

Mierka answered as Joseph and Vincent both drank from their blood donors. "Edwin knew we were coming and knew we would try and save some of the children. It's a game we play. He takes as many children as he can, knowing we have a chance to free most of them. This time was no different. Except that once the children were safe, we ran into some demons. They attacked us and nearly killed us, leaving us for the Morning Star to finish. Anthony was able to contact one of his men to come get us. We were badly drained."

Natalia stared at Vincent and wondered why he didn't take her in his arms. "Did Edwin send the demons?"

"It's possible. I think he's trying to take over as Captain. He knows I want him dead. He could have sent them to kill us, but I don't think he has what it takes to control demons." Vincent dropped the second arm and looked around for more. As he passed Natalia, his hand squeezed her thigh. The aphrodisiac was starting to take hold. "Now please go upstairs until we're through feeding. Your blood would taste rather lovely right now."

Natalia looked around for the first time, and saw the vampires around her. All gave her hungry looks, Mierka included, who had pulled her away from Vincent. Natalia pulled herself to full height, and tried to look imposing. She turned and walked away glad when the security office door opened, and Markus came out to walk her to the stairs. He stayed at the bottom, and kept watch until she was at the top.

Vincent drank his fill, and instructed the others to do the same. It took 24 humans to satiate their thirst. They came willingly when called as was their duty. Vincent went upstairs to be with Natalia and left Joseph to deal with the others. She waited for him on the bed, dressed only in a hungry smile. He was on the bed before he was completely undressed.

☞ ☜

Sometime before sunrise she fell asleep in his arms. Her back was to his chest, a satisfied smile on her face. He lay awake, his arms wrapped around her, and felt her breath push her chest in and out. He had learned something tonight: his life, and the lives of his people were at stake. It was time to take over, and he wanted Natalia to help him. The look in her eye when she rushed into his arms had shown him all he needed to know. She was upset at being left behind, at not being able to help, at not being there to know what had happened to him. She loved him. Or so he surmised. If it were love, it would bind her to him even more than before. If it were love, he could control her for an eternity, if he desired.

He closed his eyes, nuzzled her hair with his nose, and smelled the fruity scent of her shampoo. As her fire penetrated his chill an ugly worm of a notion crawled into his mind. It started to wriggle around his psyche, and threatened his pleasure filled thoughts. He gathered her closer to drink her heat and bring her the eternal cold of his kind. It would be sinfully easy. The sleeping human would feel nothing, probably wouldn't wake until he fed her his own blood. And then it would be too late to abort.

Vincent brought his favorite human as close as he could, and exposed his fangs as he dipped his head to her vulnerable neck. His lips parted slowly to the soft rhythmic pulsing of her vein. His teeth scraped her delicate olive skin, which made her arch her neck. She was such a willing victim. His hand traced down her elongated neck as his head pulled back. Both Natalia and Charlie told him of her reaction to the werewolf's attempt to change her against her will. She had thrown Charlie out of her life. Would she do the same in this situation?

Vincent continued to caress her neck, then allowed his hand to follow the curve of her breasts down to her stomach. He believed she would leave. Not only leave but disappear. He had a great network of spies, but even they had problems following her when she wanted to be left alone. She would disappear, perhaps never to return. He embraced her again and let her touch burn away his intentions.

He wanted her to stay. If it meant she remained human and risked her life to help him gain control, so be it. He would talk to her about changing her if she was dying during a fight, but he would never change her without her permission. Vincent wrapped his cool limbs around Natalia's warm body, and inhaled her scent as he took a deep breath.

"With your permission Natalia, and not a second before." He kissed the back of her head gently and fell asleep with his favorite human wrapped in his arms.

13

One Year Later

S o where are you going tonight?"

Natalia looked up from the library desk and glared at Charlie, who was dressed in his usual: white t-shirt, jeans and work boots. He stood nearby and looked restless and dangerous. "Out. Why are you asking?"

Charlie shrugged and Natalia groaned inwardly. She could almost read his mind. "Vincent thinks it might be better if I left the house tonight. Thought maybe I could go with you."

She gave him another glare. "Why would I want to take an agitated werewolf with me on an information gathering mission?"

He moved quickly to the desk, knelt on the other side from Natalia, and grasped his hands together as if pleading to her. "I'm bored. I'm restless. I've got nothing to do here. If I don't get out of here, I'm going to start fighting the vampires, and that's just asking for too much trouble."

Natalia gave Charlie a pitiful look. He came back from Montana about a month ago. Rebecca was still taking care of the twins on Vincent's ranch. As her husband seemed to grate on her every nerve and made it hard for her to watch the newborns, she sent Charlie back here. Without Rebecca, Charlie seemed a little harder to control. Vincent didn't seem to appreciate having the werewolf without the Alpha but understood Rebecca's need for space. Charlie's frustrations often transferred to Orlando and Doug, who were generally more controllable. If Charlie felt like he needed to get out, maybe it was best to get him out.

She sighed. "Maybe I can use you, but Charlie, you're going to have to travel in wolf form and hide in my backseat."

He brightened somewhat. "What are you looking for?"

Natalia shook her head. "That's the problem, I'm not too sure. Since

Edwin's Red Tie Affair last year, I've been finding pieces of information on a possible confrontation between the Slayers and Vincent's people, but nothing concrete. There's a Slayer in the city that may have something more, but I'm not sure. I've been tracking him for the past three months and I think I have his routine down. The past three weeks, he's been prowling Golden Gate Park for vampires. I'm going to break into his apartment while he's out and rummage around."

Charlie could only give her a wide-eyed look.

She rolled her eyes. "Don't lecture me, Charlie. I know what I'm doing."

He held his hands up in defeat. "I didn't say anything."

They stared at each other across the desk. Charlie nearly grinned and Natalia's look dared him to say something. Finally, he did.

"Look, I need some time away from here, even if all I do is sit in your car in wolf form. At least I'm out of Vincent's way, and we can pretend I'm doing my job."

Natalia rolled her eyes again and sighed as she realized she did want Charlie to come with her, but it may cause problems. "All right. Be ready in one hour."

Charlie grinned and stood up. "Great! I'll go tell Vincent."

Natalia placed her head in her hands, and wondered why she thought allowing an unpredictable werewolf to come with her on a stealth mission was necessary.

ℱ Ⅎ

The pair left Vincent's an hour after sunset. Natalia didn't have Charlie change into wolf form, but informed him that if she told him to, he wouldn't argue. From her research, Natalia knew that her target didn't generally leave for his rounds until midnight, and always turned most of his lights off before he left for the night. When they reached the Slayer's apartment, they parked in a nearby public lot and left the car. They walked close enough to the apartment building to see the Slayer's lights were still on, then went hand in hand to a nearby restaurant. Though it was late evening, the restaurant was still serving, and the pair fell into an old pattern, acting as if they were a couple.

Natalia sat facing the apartment building, and waited for the lights to go out. They paid for their dinner long before there was any change in the apartment, but stayed at the table until the apartment went black. They walked away from the restaurant and went around the back of the apartment building. In the parking lot, they watched as the Slayer, Jeffery Tathers, climbed into his car and drove away. Natalia and Charlie said their good nights at the apartment building's back door. Charlie went to Natalia's car, climbed into the front seat, made sure no one was around and changed to wolf form.

Natalia went inside the building, as if she belonged there. The back door didn't have a lock. Inside the building, Natalia went right for the stairs. She didn't want to get stuck in a conversation with an overly curious passenger in the elevator. Though this was a large apartment complex there were only four stories and only eight apartments per floor. In her other visits, it seemed as if the residents knew each other. The elevator was therefore a bad idea. Jeffery Tathers lived on the third floor; the stairs didn't prove much of a problem. On the third floor, she headed down the hall toward his apartment, and dug out keys as if she were headed to her own apartment. In front of his door, she quickly took a look around, to make sure no one was in the hall. She used her lock picking tools to unlock his door then slipped into his apartment and shut and locked the door.

There were three lamps in this room: one on the side table, on the other side of the couch from the door, and one on a desk covered in papers. Natalia shook her head as she marveled at the ease of this task. She walked to the desk and gathered the papers. She didn't know if any of this was what she needed, but she wasn't going to take a chance. Why flip through the papers here when she could just take it all and look through them at her leisure, safe at home?

While she gathered the papers, Natalia caught glances of a description and paused when she saw the same description a third time. She flipped back to the other descriptions and saw it again: short, female, Asian vampire, black hair and eyes. Hunts in new bars for single males but doesn't pick them up until the target is drunk.

Natalia's heart stopped. Jeffery was after Kimberly.

She didn't know much about Kimberly and her man Owen. They fought well and followed Vincent's rules, but seemed to need to hunt in the city far more than any of the other vampires. Vincent, Joseph, Mierka, Dr. Elving and Ben only took their blood from the humans in Vincent's house. When she had first entered Vincent's house, Natalia asked the vampires for information on their hunting techniques so she could make sure not to track Vincent's people. Owen targeted the homeless, being careful never to kill anyone; Kimberly preferred to pick up drunken single men in newly opened bars. She never killed her prey either, but it was still best not to have anyone recognize her. Going to new places lessened the chance that someone would remember her.

Natalia went back through the paperwork and saw Jeffery's notes stated there was a new bar near Golden Gate Park. No wonder he had been there more in the past few weeks. Knowing that one of Vincent's people was in danger, Natalia slammed the papers back onto the desk and ran to the door. She had the presence of mind to lock the door on the way out, then raced down the steps, out the back door and to her car. She yanked open the car door, fell into the seat, and startled Charlie. The wolf yelped as she slammed the door shut. He changed to his human form, but stayed low to ensure no one saw him.

"What the hell?"

"He's hunting Kimberly."

Charlie shifted into a sitting position, adjusted his ripped clothing, and stared up at Natalia as she started the car and headed out of the parking lot. "You can't know that."

"There was a description of a vampire he's following. Short, Asian female, hunts in new bars for drunk single men. That's her. She told me once that's what she prefers. Easy mark, bad witnesses." She was on the street now, trying not to speed. Natalia wanted to get there quickly, but had to follow the speed limit. There were too many police officers around, and traffic was thick. She did not need to get pulled over, or get into a car accident.

"Why don't you call her?"

"Can't. If I tell her what's going on, she'll kill him. We can't let her kill him on the streets or in a park."

"Why not?"

"Whenever a Slayer is found on the streets or in a park, the body disappears, and a secret organization takes over the investigation." She slammed her hand on the steering wheel. They were at a red light and Natalia felt each second that passed as a knife in her mind. How the hell had she missed this? "If we can get him away from her, bring him back to his apartment and kill him there, the Slayers will take care of their own and no one outside of the Slayers will know about it."

Charlie repositioned himself, buckled his seat belt, and tried not to look too worried. "How do you know all this?"

The light turned green, but Natalia was not the first car in line. She turned to give Charlie a frank look. "I've killed Slayers before, Charlie. When I kill a Slayer, I watch the papers to find out if anyone notices. The first time I killed a Slayer in his apartment, the story never reached the papers. The first and only time I left a Slayer dead in a park, the papers stated the investigation was being handed over to a special department."

Natalia turned her head to look out the window and carefully continued to Golden Gate Park. Charlie didn't say anything more until she parked the car a while later.

"What are you going to do?"

"Take down my prey. Stay in the car, you'll only get in the way." Natalia rummaged in her backpack, pulled out a plastic sandwich bag stuffed with a wet cloth. Charlie didn't ask about it as Natalia carefully placed it into her front pocket. She turned to Charlie once she had what she needed. "Turn wolf; hide in the back seat. I'll let you know if I need help when I get back."

"You're not telling me your plan, are you?"

She held his gaze. Her tone of voice demanded he follow her

instructions. "Change to wolf; hide in the back seat. Await further instructions."

With that, she was out of the car and headed across the street.

☙ ❧

As she walked, Natalia let her pace slow; let her expression melt from one of hurried worry to that of pleasantly calm. She let a smile shape her lips and let her steps take her two blocks to the new bar. In the dark, the neon sign on the front showed the name of Liquid Green. Natalia walked past the bar, listened to the loud sounds as they seeped out the door and continued down the street. She couldn't go in. Kim would know her immediately and wouldn't pick a victim. Natalia looked at her watch. It was too early for anyone to be drunk enough to be a target. She walked back to the park and slipped into the bushes unnoticed. She wore dark jeans and a black shirt. Her clothing would be good enough to hide her in the darkness.

Once Natalia was well enough in the bushes that no casual observer would notice her, she climbed a tree and settled into its branches to watch the bar. The bar was almost right across the street, and she could see the people coming and going. She could also look around well enough to spot any hiding spaces. There were none except for the trees and she was the only one in them. Finding a comfortable spot, Natalia took one last look at her watch. It was close to midnight. She would probably have to wait an hour before Kim made an appearance.

☙ ❧

Kim did in fact leave the bar about an hour later. She had her arm around the waist of a man who couldn't walk straight. The vampire was beautiful in her little black dress and high heels. Perhaps too nicely dressed for this area, but the man didn't notice. He was dressed more appropriately in jeans and a sweatshirt from one of the local colleges. Kim was leading him across the street, not paying attention to her surroundings. Natalia climbed down from the tree to better follow in the shadows and bushes.

After Kim and her victim entered the park, Natalia hung back, watched her surroundings, and waited for Jeffery to show himself. When he finally did, it was from the direction of the bar. He'd probably been inside the bar, waiting for Kim to leave. Natalia let him follow the couple first, and carefully pulled out the sandwich bag from her front pocket. At first opportunity, she would use the chloroform-soaked cloth to take him down. Natalia kept to the bushes on the side of the path, and followed the threesome.

It took a while, but finally Natalia saw what she needed. Up until now, only her side of the path had bushes. The other side had trees that weren't thick enough together to hide herself and her actions. Now, there were bushes on both sides. She pulled the cloth out of the bag, placed it into her right hand, left the bushes and slipped up behind Jeffery. He didn't notice her, and she was able to wrap her arm around his head, place the chloroform cloth to his mouth and nose and pull him into the bushes on the other side of the path. Jeffery wasn't a large man, about as tall as Natalia, which made it easy for her to move him around. In the bushes, she used her full weight to keep him quiet, until the chloroform made him pass out.

Knowing she didn't have too much time, Natalia stuffed the cloth back into the plastic bag, shoved the bag into her pocket and pulled Jeffery up to a standing position. She slipped his arm around her neck, and placed her arm around his waist. It made it look like she was trying to walk him back to her car. He was about her built and weight, so it wasn't that hard to pretend to walk him out of the park.

At her vehicle, she placed him against the car on the passenger side, and spoke out loud, as if she were unhappy with her passed out boyfriend. Once the car door was open, she placed him on the seat, and did the best she could to position him correctly in the seat. It was dangerous to have him in the front with her, but she didn't have any other choice. She needed to control the situation and couldn't if he were laying in the back seat. This way, she could have the chloroform at the ready.

When he was buckled in, she closed the door, went to the driver's side, climbed in, and drove away. "Charlie, if you can hear me, change."

A moment later, "Is he dead?"

"Not yet. We're taking him back to his apartment. I want to ask him a couple questions."

"About the confrontation?"

"Yeah."

"How are you going to get him into his apartment?"

"You're going to pretend to be drunk and we'll take him up there. It's not that hard to act drunk. You do have a change of clothing, right?"

"Yeah, back here."

"Change and get ready to help me."

"I don't like this."

"I can let you out here if you want. Pick you up when I'm done." She sounded serious.

"Nat, this is really creeping me out." His voice was muffled as he pulled his shirt off and pulled on the new one.

"As I said, I can let you out here."

He gave her an odd look through the rearview mirror. "Nat, I'm here to help as you need, but it's just a little weird for me. I still picture you as the girl that saved me from the gilded cage. Seeing you like this…"

Charlie shook his head and shrugged, not sure of what to say. Instead, he unbuckled and unzipped his pants, pulled off the ripped pair and started to put on the new pair. Natalia didn't comment, and decided to pay attention to the road instead. She was able to reach Jeffery's apartment quickly and without incident. Once there, she pulled out a new chloroform cloth from her backpack and placed it against his nose and mouth. She left it there for a few minutes, then put the cloth away.

"All right, get out and help me, but stumble around a bit like you've been drinking."

Charlie nodded, opened the back door, and stumbled out of the car, as he gave a fake laugh. Natalia followed, pulled her backpack out of the backseat, and climbed out of the car. She started to talk at Charlie; annoyance and fury resonated in her voice. She rounded the car and helped Charlie pull Jeffery out of the car. The pair stumbled to the building and inside. They used the elevator, as it was safer and simpler to do so. At this time of night, there was no one in the hall to stop and question them. At Jeffery's door, Natalia dug into his pockets and pulled out his keys. She still berated the men, just not that loudly. Charlie, unnerved by the whole situation, kept quiet.

Once inside the apartment, Charlie placed Jeffery on the couch and Natalia went to the desk. She gathered all the papers and stuffed them into her backpack. She turned toward the coach, narrowed her eyes in thought, then took a slow, deep breath. When she looked at Charlie, the determined look on her face made him cringe.

"Carry him into the bedroom. It's the one down the hall to the left."

"Nat. You have what you want, right?"

She indicated Jeffery with her head. "He may have more information that's not in these papers."

He gave her a terrified look. "Nat. We need to leave. It's not safe here. He's a Slayer."

Natalia shook her head. "I don't think so. I think he's a vampire hunter. If he was a Slayer, I wouldn't have been able to sneak up on him as easily."

Charlie covered his face with his hands. Part of him really wanted to stay and watch, to witness whatever it was Natalia planned on doing. The other, larger part wanted to pull her out of this apartment, get to the car and drive like the devil chased them all the way back to Vincent's. When he pulled his hands away from his face, he gasped in surprise. She stood right in front of him, and reached out to him. Her hand felt warm and soft on his cheek. He was astonished to find out he had to look up to look into her eyes. When he did, the very familiar look in her eyes made him shudder in need.

She smiled at him, whispered to him. "Trust me, Charlie."

He shook in his shoes and moved away from her to hide his discomfort. He pulled at his pants and tried to will away his erection. As it was no use, Charlie bent to the man on the couch, picked him up and carried him into the bedroom. Natalia watched him, and tried not to laugh. Perhaps it wasn't fair to control her ex-boyfriend like that, but she wanted to have her way. A smug little bounce in her step, Natalia followed Charlie into the bedroom.

Natalia pulled some rope out of her backpack as she walked into the bedroom. Charlie placed the man on the bed. She walked around the bed, and tied Jeffery's hands and feet to the bed's metal frame with sections of silk rope. Done, she sat on the bed and pulled out a small black canvas case about the size of a personal organizer. She unzipped the case, to expose various syringes and vials of different shapes.

Charlie stared at the contents, very uncertain of what she contemplated. Did he trust that she knew what she was doing? Absolutely. Did he really want to watch while she did it? The werewolf had to admit, he wasn't too sure. Charlie shook his head and waited to see if he had to intervene. He wondered what Vincent would think about all this and realized the vampire probably wouldn't care, as long as nothing could be traced back to him.

Natalia pulled out a small paper tube, gripped one of the flattened sealed ends, and ripped it open. She placed the open end under the sleeping man's nose and waved it back and forth. Even standing a few feet away, Charlie could tell it was smelling salts. He covered his nose against the sharp scent that permeated the air. It made him want to growl. Natalia didn't react in the least, just kept waving the salts in front of Jeffery's nose until the man started to react. She stopped using the salts when he coughed and jerked his head away. She cocked her head to the side and pulled her hand away from his face. She grabbed a few tissues out of the box on the nightstand, wrapped up the smelling salts and stuffed the bundle into her backpack. When he opened his eyes and stared at her, she gave him a gentle smile.

"Hello, Jeffery. Did you have a nice nap?"

He tugged at his hands and legs and twisted his head to try and decipher what was going on. "Who are you? How did you get in here?"

Natalia shook her head. "That's not how it works, Jeffery. You're the one that's tied up. I'm the one asking questions."

When the ropes didn't give, Jeffery turned his attention to the two people in the room. He barely glanced at Natalia before looking at Charlie. His eyes narrowed. "Hellspawn."

Natalia smiled when Jeffery's eyes turned back to her. He took a long, hard look at her before he glared at her. "You."

She looked surprised. "You know me?"

"You were the one we were warned about. The One Walking the Edge."

"That's the third time a Slayer has called me that, but this is different, isn't it? And you're a Slayer, aren't you?" She narrowed her eyes at him. "Why didn't you sense me coming?"

Jeffery shook his head. "I won't answer your questions."

"Change Charlie."

"What?" He didn't sound like he wanted to comply.

Natalia turned her head and he saw that same determined look he was so familiar with. This time though, it was different enough to raise the hairs on the back of his neck. There was a dangerous look that conveyed an order and a seduction that shouldn't be there. This human should not give him this type of look. It was too much a mirror of Vincent that Charlie was suddenly very afraid of Natalia. So much so that when she raised a single eyebrow, Charlie became Blitzkrieg.

Natalia turned her head back to Jeffery. "I'm going to kill you. There is no doubt about that. The manner in which I kill you is still in question. Cooperate and your death will be quick and painless." She stood, turned to Charlie, reached out, caressed his snout, then scratched behind his ear. "I think though, that he would really appreciate taking some frustrations out on you." She turned back to the bed, sat back down, and gave Jeffery a very seductive smile. She licked her lips to accentuate the anticipated bloodbath. "I would love to see what he would do to you. If I let him."

Jeffery closed his eyes and started a whispered prayer.

Natalia slapped him hard on the cheek. "That isn't what I want to hear. Tell me what you know about me."

The Slayer looked to Charlie, whose lips were drawn back in a snarl, and watched saliva drip from the creature's mouth. He knew, beyond a doubt, that he would not survive this night. He looked back to Natalia and wondered: would it really make a difference if she knew? It was his fault for using the phrase in the first place. The voices in his head were not happy with the turn of events but let him know others were alerted to the situation. Though he would lose his life tonight, perhaps one of these two would as well. Jeffery nodded and started to speak.

14

I'm a Slayer. I hear the Angels and I kill Hellspawn for God at His request. I wasn't able to hear you because we're only alerted to the comings and goings of Hellspawn. I have also sworn to protect humans from the truth in the darkness. Though not all of my brethren care for the human race, I do. I recognize that we all begin as humans and are tainted or blessed as needed. Because of my self-appointed role, I'm able to tell when a human is nearby, to ensure that I don't expose them to the truth. You, you are neither fully human nor tainted by Hellspawn. I would accuse you of being nothing, but that wouldn't be the truth. You are the One Walking the Edge, and I'm not able to predict where you will fall."

"And you're telling me this, because?"

"I have no reason to keep it from you."

"What does this all mean? Can the other Slayers sense me?"

He tried to hide the answer, but she saw it in his eyes and drew back in surprise. She whispered the answer.

"You don't know." The implication made her skin tingle. This knowledge opened up whole new avenues for her. After she joined Vincent's house, she had assumed she would be a known vampire's woman. She approached Slayers with the thought that they knew she was Hellspawn. Jeffery's story showed her that they might not know her, might not even see her. It meant she could approach Slayers for knowledge and leave them alive when she was done with them.

Natalia looked back to Jeffery, and realized she didn't like the look on his face at all. She lifted the case off her lap, peered down at it and pulled a vial and a syringe out of the case. "Charlie, love. I need you to change into your human form. Do you understand what I'm saying?"

Charlie's brain buzzed with the desire to rip into something, but he heard the order and did as told. Once human he looked over at Natalia and watched as the tip of the syringe plunged into the rubber stopper on the vial. "Nat? What are you doing?"

"That's not the question you should be asking, Charlie. The question you should be asking yourself is," she looked him dead in the eye, "do you really want to know?"

Charlie swallowed hard and kept his mouth shut. He watched as she pulled out the filled syringe and put the vial away. She then tapped the syringe, pushed the plunger a little to release the trapped air and brought the syringe to the Slayer's arm. "Any last words, Jeffery?"

"God sees everything you do, Natalia. One day, you will face your Maker. You may wish to think about what you do before you continue on this path."

"He'll have to wait a long time for me."

Natalia plunged the needle into Jeffery's arm, and pushed the plunger. Once it was empty, she pulled the syringe out and put everything away in the black case then placed the case in her backpack. She then calmly looked up at Charlie, who had an expression on his face that conveyed his discomfort. He looked almost comical with that odd expression and the ripped clothing. She almost laughed but sobered when she heard a noise from the living room.

"Charlie, did we lock the door when we came in?"

The werewolf paled. "I don't know."

Eyes still set in the direction of the living room, Natalia stood and picked up her backpack. Behind her, Jeffery started to tense as the drug took effect. She talked to Charlie without looking his way.

"There's a second bedroom, down the hall to the right. There's a balcony in that room. Go."

Charlie moved quickly but quietly. He didn't look back, just hoped that Natalia would follow. He reached the second bedroom, carefully opened the door and stepped inside. That was when he looked back. Natalia knelt at the other end of the hall to look into the living room. Charlie stopped the urge to call out to her, and did as she instructed. He went to the window, pulled open the sliding door and stepped out onto the balcony, with no idea what to do next. There were balconies lining this side of the building. It didn't face either street he and Natalia had walked on, which is why he hadn't noticed before. He stood there in the dark, and tried to see the next step. The door snicked closed behind him and he nearly jumped.

Natalia pointed to the next balcony as she whispered, "Can you jump?"

Charlie nodded, as he didn't trust his voice. He climbed the railing, jumped, stumbled, and fell onto the wooden lawn chair that took most of the balcony. Natalia landed next to the chair, and gave Charlie a triumphant smile when she saw how he landed. Both turned sharply when they heard the door on the Slayer's balcony open. Natalia dropped her backpack to the floor, quickly joined Charlie on the chair, grabbed him to her and kissed him passionately on the lips.

He tried to pull away, but felt her legs entwine in his, felt her body against his. Her hands were on his back, under his shirt, and touched the inside of his legs. He shuddered when her hand found his hard erection and old feelings he had forgotten came back to him. His arms pulled her closer, and he fell into her kisses. He briefly wondered at their actions as they were in danger. Before his caresses could get any more exploratory, Natalia pulled away and looked toward the other balcony.

"You know, a picture lasts longer." Sarcasm dripped from her voice.

Charlie looked to the balcony in time to see a young woman turn and head back into the apartment. As soon as the door slid shut, Natalia slapped his arm.

"Change and get to the car as quick as you can."

He didn't think, just let her words guide him. He was Blitzkrieg in seconds. The creature jumped over the balcony to the ground three stories below without thought. He rolled, turned wolf, and plastered himself close to the building. He headed to the back of the building and the public lot next door.

Natalia watched him go then made sure her backpack was securely on her back. She stood up and went to the edge of the balcony. She grabbed the top of the iron bar railing, lifted herself up and swung one leg, then the other over the top. Natalia turned to face the balcony, gripped the bars very carefully and allowed herself to slide/drop to the balcony beneath her. Once her feet were on the edge of the railing, she let go of the balcony above her and jumped into the empty balcony without a problem. She took a few deep breaths then repeated the steps to end up on the first-floor balcony. From there, it was an easy jump to the ground.

On the ground, she hugged the wall, but ran quickly to the back of the building. At the corner of the building, she knelt and looked around the corner. As she saw no one, she stood and walked leisurely to her car. She opened the door, nodded to Charlie in the passenger seat and dug out her keys as he stared at her. They were out of the parking lot and well on their way before Natalia realized that Charlie still stared at her in disbelief. She glanced at him out of the corner of her eye.

"What Charlie?"

He shook his head, looked out the passenger side window and shook his head again. "We have to tell Vincent everything we did tonight."

She turned to him briefly then looked back at the road. "I know that. Why would that be a problem?"

"You kissed me. You had your hands, well, in some pretty interesting places."

"Sorry, Charlie. We had to look like we had no idea what was going on with the world. Stargazing wouldn't have worked. Most times, people don't like interrupting a couple making out on their own balcony. It was the only thing we could do to get away clean."

"I don't look forward to telling the boss. He gets pretty jealous."

"Let me tell him then. Don't worry about it, Charlie. You'll be fine."

He didn't believe her, but what could he really say or do that would make her understand his trepidation? Charlie let it go and settled back into the seat for the long drive back home.

⚃ ⚂

The pair found Vincent in his small study when they reached home about two hours later. Traffic leaving the city proved thick. Everyone was on their way home from the bars. The vampire sat in his study, and looked over finances on his laptop, newspapers, and various bits of paper. The knock on the door brought him to the present. He made one or two more changes on his computer, then stated, "Come in."

He smiled when he saw Natalia, but practically ignored the werewolf.

"Hello, Vincent." She sat in one of the chairs and placed her backpack on the floor beside her. Charlie took the other chair, and nervously looked about.

"I expected Charlie to report to me. I didn't expect you, Natalia, as you never report anything to me." There was a bite to his tone of voice. It made Charlie even more nervous; it made Natalia smile seductively.

"We wanted to let you know what happened." Natalia answered innocently.

Vincent raised an eyebrow. He did not believe his human in the least. "Report, Charlie."

"No." Her voice was no longer innocent.

Vincent's eyebrow crept up again but was accompanied by a hard look.

"I'm capable of telling you what happened, Vincent."

"Without editing?"

She gave him an innocent look, and placed her hand on her chest as if shocked. Neither Vincent nor Charlie bought her act. She smiled at both men and started to talk. "You need to talk to Kim about her choices in hunting spots. The Slayer I was tracking tonight was following her. He knew where she would be because she always picks her victims at new bar openings."

Vincent sighed. "What happened?"

Natalia related the story, and included her mistake in not realizing whom the Slayer hunted until the last moment. She continued the tale without dialogue, but gave Vincent details on what she and Charlie did that night. She paused when she came to the part about jumping to the second balcony to escape the other Slayers. Natalia looked to Charlie, then to Vincent and continued the tale.

"When we were on the next balcony, we heard the door to the Slayer's apartment sliding open and I knew there was only one way to make the new arrivals not suspect us. Charlie had fallen onto a lawn chair. I fell on top of him and started to kiss him. I wanted it to look like we'd been there for a while and weren't paying attention to anything else."

Vincent stared at Charlie as Natalia spoke. The werewolf didn't look as if he wanted to be in the room at this point. He refused to look at Vincent. Instead, Charlie chose to stare intently at his legs as he picked at the fabric of his ripped jeans. Natalia looked at miserable Charlie, then at her lover. She didn't want Charlie to be punished for her actions.

"Vincent, what's done is done. You have a problem with what happened, then tell me about it. Charlie doesn't need to be here at this point. It wasn't his idea. Dismiss him."

"No." Vincent's voice was hard, not to be denied.

"It wasn't Charlie's doing."

Vincent stared at the werewolf, and dared the man to look at him. Charlie didn't comply; he looked at Natalia, a hopeful look on his face. "Perhaps I wish to hear from him as well."

Natalia stood, walked around the desk, placed her hands on Vincent's cheeks, and forced him to look at her. "He would tell you the same thing. There is no reason for you to interrogate him. This is done. I'm not about to be trapped between a volatile werewolf and a difficult vampire. Release him and talk to me about your jealousy."

Vincent stood quickly and pressed Natalia against the wall, one hand against her chest to keep her still. He leaned in closely and sniffed her. He pulled back, stepped away from her and went to the window. "You smell like the werewolf. Go shower before you dare approach me again."

She heard the bite in his voice and rolled her eyes in irritation. "If I go shower, does that mean that Charlie will be allowed to leave?"

He turned to face Natalia. "No. He and I will discuss things like men."

Charlie saw the deadly look on her face and loved her all over again. The determined look was on her face. Not the seductive one from earlier, but the ready look he knew well and respected without thought. He sat back in his chair and waited for her next words as calm descended around him.

"I'm not leaving until I have your word that you will not harm him. This wasn't his fault." She crossed her arms and stared down her lover.

Vincent stared back. His jaw twitched as he came to a decision. An evil glint came into his eyes. "On my word, I will not harm your guardian. Now go shower and wash his scent off you."

She saw the glint and did not like it. "I want your word no one else will harm him either."

The glint was still there. "Not one hair on his body will be harmed."

Natalia did not like that glint in his eye one bit. She stared him down for a moment, but the look did not leave. The vampire planned something, but Natalia couldn't tell what. She had his word, though, that Charlie would not be harmed. She sighed and looked down. His word was his word. Natalia looked at Charlie. He nodded once, and Natalia looked back to Vincent. "I'll hold you to your word, vampire. If anyone harms my guardian for doing what I ordered, I won't be pleased, and neither will you."

Natalia rounded the desk, grabbed her backpack, and left the room. She slammed the door shut behind her.

"Stand up and face me, Charlie."

Charlie complied, stood up and faced Vincent. As he knew better, he didn't leave the chair between them, but moved out of its way. No reason to make Vincent demand him to move.

"What did you do to my woman, werewolf?"

Charlie was pleasantly surprised to realize that Vincent's voice was mild. There was no hint of anger or frustration to be heard, but sometimes that was just as dangerous. "It's as she said. When I jumped to the other balcony, I landed badly and fell onto the lawn chair. Natalia jumped over. We heard the Slayer's balcony door slide open, she fell onto the chair with me and...well..." he looked away from Vincent, took a deep breath then looked back, "she started to kiss me and grope me, like we were interested in each other."

He looked away again, swallowed hard, then looked back. Charlie took two startled steps back when he realized Vincent stood directly in front of him. "It was the only thing we could do to make sure the other Slayers didn't think we had been in that apartment. When Nat pulled away, she looked at the Slayer's balcony, told the girl looking at us to take a picture and scared her away. We were able to get moving after that. We made out to save our skin!"

Vincent took a few menacing steps to Charlie, and invaded his space, which caused the werewolf to stumble back to the door. With his back pressed against the door, Charlie gave Vincent a wide-eyed crazed look. "Would you have preferred if we were caught? Or seen and chased in San Francisco? She knew what she was doing, sir. It was a smart idea!"

The vampire crossed his arms and leaned in just a touch more. "Did you enjoy making out with my woman?"

"How the hell do you expect me to answer that?!?" Charlie yelled; he couldn't help it. He was sure his voice carried outside the office.

Vincent grinned maliciously while Charlie breathed deeply to calm himself. A smile on his face, Vincent backed up to lean against the nearby chair. "I expect you to tell me the truth."

Charlie let himself slump to the ground as he continued to breathe deep to stop himself from turning Blitzkrieg. After a couple minutes, Charlie looked up at Vincent. "At first, I was worried about what Rebecca would say, then about what you would do, but in the end, she just feels too good and knows how to distract men way too well. Of course, I enjoyed her. She's a beautiful woman that I used to screw on a regular basis. How would you feel if an ex-girlfriend came up to you and started making out with you for no reason you could discern?"

"I'm not happy with you, Charlie."

Charlie stood, angry and annoyed. "You know what, Vincent? Screw you. She'll be in your bed tonight and what about me? I'm going to spend the night in my bed," he raised his right hand, "with my right-hand man. My wife, who would be more than happy to remind me that I'm hers after an incident like this, is conveniently in another part of this country. You get to leave this room, find your woman, throw her into your bed and claim her and make her scream your name. I've got I don't know how long before I see my wife again."

Vincent nodded slowly. "You may go, Charlie."

Charlie blinked, surprised by Vincent's mild tone, then bowed. "Thank you, sir."

Vincent watched the werewolf leave then followed him out the door. Charlie didn't go upstairs but went to the kitchen. Vincent went upstairs to his rooms to find Natalia. To his surprise and irritation, Natalia was in the sitting room. The papers spread out on the desk held her attention.

"Natalia? Did I not ask you to shower?"

She looked up, gave him a brief smile, then looked back at the papers on the desk. "Something has me worried. I wanted to take a closer look at these papers." She looked back up at her lover. "Did you hurt him?"

"He did not deserve punishment."

"I'm surprised you think that way. You seemed hell bent on harming him. There was that glint in your eyes."

Vincent smiled slyly. "Charlie is afraid of me. I used that."

She rolled her eyes and looked back to her newly acquired Slayer notes. "As long as you didn't harm him."

Vincent stared at Natalia for a moment, as he thought of her actions. He wasn't sure if he should allow her to study the papers or if he should pick her up and carry her to the bathroom. "What has you worried?"

"Remember I told you it seemed as if the Slayers were possibly looking for a way to confront you and your men?"

Vincent nodded.

"They were following Kim." She gave Vincent a very worried look. "What if they were following your other men? Or Anthony's men?"

Vincent's desires vanished as the implication set in. "Is there anything in the paperwork?"

"That's what I'm trying to find out. I need some more time."

The large vampire walked to his human and slipped his arms around her waist. "Does it really matter tonight, Natalia? Everyone is here. The Slayers aren't coming here. If they are, my guards will take care of them long before they reach the house."

"Is Kim back?"

"Joseph is on surveillance duty. As soon as he heard what happened, he would have called her and ordered her back here. She's on her way." His voice was soft against her ears; one hand caressed her jawline and neck.

Natalia's eyes closed at his gentle, cool touch. What would she gain by reviewing the information tonight? "Should I shower first?"

"Let me wash you."

Her gasp of anticipation was enough of a response.

ʒ ʒ

Six Months Later

"Natalia." Vincent whispered her name softly, but knew she would hear. When she did not move from the desk full of papers, he frowned and tried again.

"Natalia?" When she didn't answer that time, frustration clouded his judgment, and his voice was louder than he wanted it to be. "Natalia!"

She didn't look up from the desk, but reached out and picked up a notebook to examine it better. "What do you want, Vincent?"

"The sun has been up for nearly three hours. You stated you would join me."

She frowned at the notebook then finally looked at the vampire. He stood in the doorway to their bedroom, a dark look on his face. His arms were crossed, which caused his black silk robe to stay mostly closed. Natalia turned back to the notebook, her previous thoughts still tearing through her mind. "I'm close to this, Vincent, I know I am. I need more time to think."

The pages on the desk fluttered with the wind he caused. He reached out and tried to take the notebook. Natalia held on to it tightly, and turned from him as he tried to take it again. He glared at her again, but she didn't see: her face was buried in the notebook. When he spoke, his voice was dead calm. "Natalia. Look at me."

She did for a second, then turned back to the notebook. "What do you want, Vincent?"

"For you to look at me."

His words and tone of voice finally penetrated, and she turned and gave him her full attention. He stood very close to the desk, arms at his side, the glare still on his face. She smiled. Glare or no glare, he was very handsome. His robe had fallen open, and showed more skin than he probably realized. The open robe made him look more and less menacing at the same time.

She smiled at her lover. "You are a very handsome man."

He raised an eyebrow. "Why have you not come to bed yet?"

Natalia placed the notebook on the desk, and kept her hands on the page. "There's a lot of information here, Vincent. There's something here and I want to find it. This is important."

"What is it?"

She gave him a look to convey her own annoyance with his lack of memory. "These are the papers and notes that I have been gathering from Slayers and vampire hunters for the past nine months. Notes on who is following whom and possible attack points."

The glare fell from Vincent's face. "Go on."

She grabbed the notebook again, and held it up to Vincent's face. "This is full of notes on your people, Vincent. As I have told you before, Jesse, Ben, Dr. Elving, Kim and Owen are being followed. The only reason Joseph and Mierka aren't being followed is because they know to look for things like that. No one is following you because you don't leave the house without your bodyguards. I've also found notes on some of Anthony's people, but most of his people know what they're doing, and are able to mislead or simply lose their trackers. The Slayers are also following Edwin's lot, but I'm more worried about your men."

Vincent frowned. "I thought you killed those following my men."

"I killed the vampire hunters that were following them, then the group responsible sent Slayers to follow your men. I killed the Slayer following Dr. Elving. When a new one started to follow him, I gave up. I can't keep killing Slayers. Someone's going to notice what I'm doing and then they'll not only hunt me, they'll stop talking to me. I'm not going to risk the tenuous relationship I have with the Slayers. And this," she shook the notebook, "is not just about that. This group of Slayers is plotting something big. That's what I'm trying to find in all this paperwork. What are they plotting and when will it happen? For the past few months, that's all I've been trying to find out, and I haven't been able to figure it out and that, to me, feels dangerous."

A glint came to his eye and Natalia braced herself. "If you haven't been able to find the connection in the past few months, what makes you think you'll find it now? Come to bed Natalia. None of this matters right this moment."

Natalia threw the notebook at Vincent. He caught it deftly then placed it on the desk. "Damn it, Vincent! This could mean the lives of your men are at stake! Don't you care? Can you think of anything other than your pleasure?"

An interesting smile came to the vampire's lips. "There was a time that all you cared about was your pleasure."

It was her turn to glare. "I'm not coming to bed yet. I'm not tired and I want to try and figure this out. Kim almost died because I wasn't vigilant enough about one Slayer's activities. If I don't figure this out, how many are going to die?"

"Have you asked Anthony for help?" Anthony was his best spy and knew how to put clues together. In his human life, he had been a detective.

"I gave him a copy, but this is in notes and shorthand I'm familiar with. After I gave him a copy, he sent Julia to tell me he couldn't even read the notes. Vincent," she gave him a terrified look, "I don't want anyone under my protection to die."

Vincent's left hand went to his chin to curl in front of his mouth. He took a good look at Natalia to reassess his woman, and tried not to draw attention to her choice of words. He narrowed his eyes at her, then nodded. "All right, Natalia. Come to bed when you're done."

Natalia watched as he turned and left for the bedroom. She blinked in surprise, shook her head, picked up the notebook and started to study it once again.

15

Six Months Later

Vincent leaned against the back bar on the first floor of The Red Thread, and watched as more of Edwin's people poured into the front entrance. Edwin insisted that no guards were necessary. Only those he invited would come through the doors. Mierka watched the entrance from the security room, but as Vincent's people didn't know all of Edwin's people, it was still a security risk. All invited were dressed for a night on the town, as was he. Vincent wore a midnight black tux that had a silver-colored silk handkerchief in the pocket, a silver-colored silk shirt and black tie. He hadn't wanted to look his best but couldn't help it. It wasn't in his nature to dress badly for a gathering such as this, even if he didn't want to be involved.

Two years ago, Edwin hosted his last advertised Red Tie Affair. He held one last year, but Vincent and his lot were not invited. They learned about it the day after the party, when the bodies of twenty children were discovered in an abandoned warehouse, mutilated beyond recognition. Six months ago, Edwin gave Vincent an ultimatum: host his coronation at The Red Thread or face carnage worse than the year before. To keep more Slayers out of the area, Vincent agreed.

Edwin would be declaring Christopher officially dead. There was no proof, but the Captain had been gone for over seven years. Before his disappearance, Christopher had been a public man, and had his face in the papers to keep his businesses in the public eye. Since no one, human or vampire, had heard from him since he left on his last expedition, he had been officially declared dead by human laws. Edwin jumped on the bandwagon.

Edwin wanted Vincent to do so as well.

Vincent knew that by hosting the coronation, Edwin's men would believe Vincent accepted the young vampire as his Captain. No one knew the older vampire had been coerced into it, no one ever would. To keep his own safe, Vincent would play along. He put his plans to take over in motion after the bodies were found, but it would take far longer to actually be able to implement them. Comrades needed to tie up loose ends where they were before they could come to the area. His people, Natalia included, were slowly killing off the worst of Edwin's people. They had to be careful; all the deaths had to look like Slayers were responsible. The process was expected to take a long time. Every time they killed one, Edwin changed two more. It was a frustrating situation.

Vincent knew he had to step up the plan but was reluctant. Any overt action could start a war between the two factions. Vincent was confident he would win a war against the younger vampires but didn't know how many humans would die in the process. He loathed killing humans, as it always brought more Slayers. He had contemplated blowing up his club, or inviting Slayers, but knew the absence of his people or important non-human guests would alert Edwin to an ambush. Also, Edwin had invited the new Mayor.

Somehow or another, Edwin learned how to control humans with his blood. Vincent heard rumors of being able to do this, but never explored the possibility. He always thought it best practice to allow humans their minds. It ensured a better relationship; a more loyal relationship and was therefore far stronger. Edwin seemed to just want loyalty and didn't care how he attained it.

Vincent snarled as Edwin walked through the door and immediately came toward him. The vampire wore a neon purple shirt and black pants. He gave Vincent a large grin as he approached. Edwin slapped his shoulder in lieu of saying hello and laughed heartily. "Going to be a grand affair this evening, don't you think, Vinny?"

"As well as to be expected." Every time Edwin called him Vinny, he wanted to slice the pathetic vampire's neck open. He took a step away, as he did not appreciate the touch.

"You don't seem happy to see me, Vincent. You're going to have to change your attitude if you plan on living in my city and having businesses here."

"I'm hosting your party, what more do you want?" He looked over Edwin's shoulder, and watched as a few more guests walked through the door.

"Did you bring me a present?" His voice dripped with humor, but Vincent felt Edwin expected something from him.

"What did you have in mind?" He didn't hide his contempt. There was no one around them; he wouldn't hide his feelings.

"My other Lieutenants did. Don't worry, if you forgot, I'll just come by your home in a couple of days and pick someone out then." He laughed heartily, but falsely, which made Vincent cringe. The older vampire didn't like the tone in the younger's voice. "Oh, come on, Vincent. At least now you get to try and kill me again."

Vincent turned sharply and gave Edwin a look full of disbelief.

"Now, now, don't bother lying. I've always known where I stand with you, Vincent. Let's not change the game with lies."

The large vampire relaxed back against the bar. "Since you know I will kill you, why force me to have your coronation at my club?"

"Because you're not stupid enough to kill me here. No, you'll wait for a better opportunity."

"Then why not kill me or order me out of your city?"

Edwin gave him a conspirator's smile "I know what you and your people are doing to the ones I've changed. I know it's not Slayers. I'll scream loudly that it is, but I'm only fooling the idiots."

Vincent narrowed his eyes. "Then why change more when one dies?"

He laughed. "I can't make it <u>that</u> easy on you. And the longer you're busy with them, the more time I have." Edwin paused for a moment. "You and your lot are quite useful. There are so many that I changed, or my people changed without thought. We left them to their own devices, knowing they wouldn't last very long. And we were right."

The grin on his face showed how he felt he was using Vincent. Vincent didn't care. He let a moment of silence pass then asked the one question he wanted answered above all else.

"I don't understand something, Edwin. You enjoyed being the Acting Captain for so long, why the change?"

"The humans think Christopher is dead. We haven't heard from him in years. Why not?" Edwin looked to Vincent then rolled his eyes. "I really wish you were more like me, Vincent. We could rule the world. Haven't you ever enjoyed a young girl before?"

Vincent glared at Edwin. "When I sleep with a woman, I want her to be old enough and experienced enough to tell me yes or no. I do not enjoy children."

"What about a seventeen-year-old? Or sixteen? Fifteen's legal in some states. Hell, if you're in other countries, you can get them as young as you want."

The cold look of hate on Vincent's face stopped Edwin's grin, but only for a moment. "As I have stated on numerous occasions, I prefer women. I would not take a child to my bed or any other location."

Edwin crossed his arms. "Do you realize that you are the only vampire I know that will admit to my face what you really prefer? That's why I respect you Vincent: I know where I stand with you. You always answer truthfully." He indicated some stragglers as they entered the building. "The people that follow me say yes to whatever I suggest. At first it was great, but now, I find it tedious. They do, too. A lot of them no longer listen to me. That's why I'm doing this, Vincent. That's why I'm putting my head on your chopping block: because they don't listen to me anymore and I grow tired of it. I'm done being Acting Captain. They <u>will</u> listen to what I say."

Edwin gave Vincent a menacing smile, walked away, and loudly called out to someone who walked in with Joseph. Edwin and his friend headed upstairs; Joseph walked over to his boss. He wore a simple gray suit with a black shirt. Joseph didn't deem a tux appropriate wear for this occasion.

"What did you learn?"

Joseph walked around the end of the bar and poured them each a glass of brandy. The good brandy was upstairs, but this would do just fine. He walked back around the bar, handed Vincent a glass, and waited until Vincent took a sip to answer the question. "His Lieutenants were each instructed to bring a human as a gift for their new Captain."

"What's he expecting to do in my club?" Vincent didn't hide his anger.

"I was given an invitation by one of our spies. He's calling this a Red Tie Coronation. He expects you to roll over and play dead."

"Where are the humans?" Vincent slowly twirled his glass. The motion was smooth and controlled, as was his voice.

"The gifts are with the vampires that brought them. Most understand whom they are with and what will happen to them."

"Most?" Vincent held up the glass to one of the ceiling lights, and examined the liquid as it continued to swirl.

"There are three that are rather young and may not know what awaits them. They have collars around their necks and are chained to their captors."

"Can we get them out?" He took a sip of the brandy, but wished for Natalia's blood.

"Possibly, but we need a distraction." Joseph still swirled the glass in his hands, as he fruitlessly tried to warm the liquid.

"What do you suggest?" Vincent drained the glass. He knew what was coming.

Joseph drained his glass, set it on the bar, faced Vincent and simply raised his eyebrow, as if to suggest there was only one true distraction.

Vincent growled low in his throat. He had wanted to keep her out of this, but knew she was the only option. He gave Joseph a disgruntled look, pulled out his cell and sent Natalia a text.

16

An hour later, Vincent leaned against the wall in the private room. He stayed out of everyone's way, as he did not want to associate himself with most of those present. He spoke to the Mayor, and found the man was indeed under Edwin's spell. Vincent had dismissed Anthony so the man could investigate the circumstances.

Vincent glanced around the room, spotted his people, who tried to reassess the situation at hand. Those who saw him nodded, but tried not to convey too much. Mierka, Ben, Jesse, Owen, and Kimberly were arrayed around the room, to position themselves near the three young girls who had no idea what was going on. Markus was in the security room: Vincent wanted his youngest safe. Joseph mingled to talk to all the other 'presents', and make sure they actually knew what was going on.

As Vincent watched, Joseph wandered over to him, and joined him against the wall. "All but the three know what is expected of them. A few offered me their blood."

"How do they seem?" Vincent heard a familiar laugh from the door. He glanced in that direction, but there were too many creatures in the way, and he couldn't see who approached.

"Exuberant. They're looking forward to being sacrificed."

"Do they know they're to be sacrificed?" He turned his head to look at Joseph, as he wished for all the information.

"They know what's coming sir. I would tell you if I felt anything different. Stop taking your frustrations out on me, I tire of it." Joseph chided his master then egged him on. "When will Natalia be here?"

"Soon. She was at one of Anthony's safe houses, waiting for instructions." He heard the laughter again, and his body reacted. He craned his neck to catch a glimpse. He stood taller as the crowd parted and revealed Natalia. The night improved tenfold.

Natalia's dark hair, which was tied up in a French twist, sparkled in the light. The hairdo revealed her long neck in all its beauty. Her dress was black velvet with silver vines and flowers. The dress tied around her neck, which revealed her bite mark riddled shoulders and muscular arms. Her silver necklace was just under the string tie, almost hidden by the velvet. The dress was so short: it barely hid her ass. She held a black and silver rose made of feathers, and twirled it slightly in her hand. Her shoes, stiletto heels, matched the silver of the dress. He caught her eye and she smiled. She was almost to him. To try and stay in control, Vincent started to breathe. As his eyes raked her body his only thought was to wonder where she had gotten the dress.

Natalia stood before her lover, reached out with the rose and drew it slowly down his jaw line. He closed his eyes at the softness and let his lover draw him to her with the rose. He was rewarded with a kiss as soft as the feathers of the rose. His blood boiled as she reached out to grab his belt and pulled him closer. She pulled away from the kiss, and smiled an evil smile. She acknowledged Joseph without looking at him.

"Hello, Joseph. You summoned me, Vincent?" The defiant, warrior look was in her eye. Vincent grabbed her to him, gave her a crushing kiss. Joseph caught the rose as it fell from her hand.

They pulled away when a decidedly annoying voice spoke up. "Is this your present Vincent?"

Natalia spared a glance at the smaller vampire who stood to their left, then looked back at her lover. "Yes, I am. He'll have fun unwrapping me later. Won't you Vincent?"

Vincent growled through his grin. Edwin looked at the two, not sure what to make of the woman in Vincent's arms. She looked too old for his taste, but something about her grabbed his attention. Infuriated with being ignored, his voice was thick with loathing. "Isn't she for me?"

Natalia turned her head to the younger vampire who tried to intimidate her. Vincent informed her earlier of how old Edwin was and how much combat training he had had. A fight against him would be easily won, she surmised. She wasn't afraid of his inferior skills. "I'm here for Vincent's pleasure," she turned back to Vincent, "and for mine."

Natalia smiled again as she wrapped Vincent's black tie around her hand. She started to walk backward, and pulled him toward the private corner. Edwin protested at the insubordination. Joseph, a smile on his lips and in his voice, engaged the Captain in conversation as the lovers walked away. As Edwin wasn't certain he wanted the older woman, he allowed the distraction.

Natalia led Vincent through the crowd by his tie, as she enjoyed the look in her lover's eye. She still walked backwards; Vincent's hands were on her waist, and helped guide her to their destination. They worked out the plan weeks before the party. If she were needed, she would show up dressed to impress, and seduce Vincent. They hoped to anger Edwin, have him follow them, and yell at them. As they argued, Vincent's men would take any young humans into the empty storage room for safe keeping. The children would be taken to a hospital at first chance.

As Natalia led her lover to the private corner, Vincent realized the folly of their plan. She was too damn sexy in her black and silver dress. He didn't want the plan to work; he wanted to screw the hell out of his woman.

As they strolled into the private corner, Vincent wondered again where she had gotten the dress. He had picked one out for her; she left the house earlier this evening dressed in it. She had not carried anything with her. She must have had the dress at the safe house, or perhaps had it brought to her. He preferred this one; it revealed far more of her. And it was velvet. Vincent shook his head and took a few deep breaths. He was obsessed with her dress.

When they were in the private corner, she let his tie go. Natalia smoothed out the tie, a smile on her lips. With the tie lying flat against his chest, she pushed away from him to stand against the wall. Her hands were behind her, between the wall and her ass. The position pushed her chest out. She gave him a seductive look through half closed eyes.

"Remember the first night we met, Vincent?" Her voice was quiet and softly caressed his ears. He moved closer to hear her better, but also because he understood what she was doing.

He placed one hand around her neck, and pressed his body against hers. She pulled her hands out from behind her and wrapped her arms around his neck. He growled into her ear. "Of course, I remember. How could I forget?"

"What did you want to do to me that night, Vincent?" One hand was in his hair; the other maneuvered its way into his pants.

"Before or after you slammed your knee between my legs?"

She laughed softly. "You gave me no other choice. You had me trapped."

"I believe I was the one trapped, dear woman." Vincent gasped as her warm hand encircled his frigid erection. His eyes closed as he placed his hands flat against the wall next to her head. He whispered into her ear. "And I believe you have me trapped again, madam."

She licked her lips slowly and gave him a smoldering look.

Vincent's voice tried not to sound seductive. "The plan isn't working. Edwin didn't follow."

Natalia's hand slid out of his pants and the other came down from his hair to meet at his zipper. "We have time before the ceremony."

Vincent pulled back slightly to try and control his desires. He needed to keep an eye on the situation; needed to know the children were safe, not play with his lover. His hand went to her bare thigh, to caress her soft skin. His hand slipped under the dress, which was an intense mistake. She didn't have any underwear. His groan turned into a growl as a new plan came to mind. Edwin thought Natalia was his present. This whole evening was to show everyone who was in control. Why not let them see?

A plan formed itself in his mind. This night need not be Edwin's coronation; it could be Natalia's coming out party. No one knew what she was capable of. The past two years Natalia and Joseph spent much time convincing Vincent she could handle herself well enough to show Edwin she existed. Why not let that happen tonight? He gave her a devilish smile as he helped her unzip and unbutton his pants. She looked surprised as his right hand went around her throat and he once more pushed his body into hers.

Vincent growled low, as if angry. His left hand slipped between her legs and encouraged her to spread them. She did and her dress slid up enough to expose her. Her laughter turned to a gasp of pleasure as he slid inside her. She shuddered as he slowly pushed his way deep inside. Her arms went around his neck, to hold on tight. Vincent wrapped his arms around her, whispered into her ear.

"Let them hear you, lover. Let them hear how much you enjoy being with me. Tell them all who you belong to; that you are mine to use as I wish, when I wish. Scream my name, Natalia. Scream it loud."

Vincent slipped in and out of her as he talked, slowly at first then faster to match the cadence of his speech. He thrust deep within her with his last three words, and caused her to cry out. Those closest to the private corner heard her and stopped their conversation. Neither Natalia nor Vincent cared at that point, as they were too wrapped up in each other's bodies. Vincent continued to stroke deep into her, faster and faster until she indeed screamed his name. His name was echoed by several impressed voices which increased his climax until he bellowed her name. Natalia laughed out loud, and satisfaction rang in her tone.

Edwin's voice penetrated their thoughts. "What the hell are you doing? You don't have a present for my coronation, and you feast on this human before I have?"

Natalia laughed again as Vincent slipped out of her. Without a word he pulled his kerchief out of his pocket, cleaned himself off and zipped up. He then reached between Natalia's legs and wiped her clean. "I didn't know I had to wait for your word in my club."

Edwin's expression grew hateful as Vincent's hand stayed between the human's legs, which caused her to shudder. The still Acting Captain spoke through clenched teeth. He enunciated each word, forcefully. "I'm your Captain. You're supposed to obey me."

Vincent slipped his hand out from between Natalia's legs. The look in his eyes revealed his annoyance at the younger vampire. Vincent was not one to obey anyone. About to put Edwin in his place, he caught sight of Joseph who stood just beyond Edwin's shoulder. Vincent stopped the angry flow of words. He pulled himself together, and folded the kerchief to give himself more time to relax. He placed the kerchief in his breast pocket, readjusted Natalia's dress, stood tall and looked down at his soon to be Captain.

"I have not yet feasted on her. I have but enjoyed her body." He hated the words; made it sound like he didn't care for her in the least, but it was the safest thing to say. Natalia, aware of how things were done, watched as her lover went from leader to follower. She hated the transformation but stayed silent. Her hand went to her necklace. Out of annoyance, she started to slowly twirl it.

"So, she hasn't been fed off of today?" Edwin's words were slower, not as angry.

Natalia noticed the change immediately. She felt the change in him as well. Curious, she looked over at the distasteful bloodsucker. He was caught in the lights that bounced off her necklace. She slammed the door on her glee as her hand dropped to her side. She wanted to shriek with happiness but contained it as best she could. She looked to Vincent, but he was too busy trying to appease Edwin. She looked around for a friendly face and spied Joseph, but too many people might see if she signaled. Since quite a crowd had gathered, Natalia kept the secret.

She could control the slimy perverted vampire. Her will was stronger.

Natalia turned from the crowd, and pretended to be hurt by Vincent's words. She let a huge smile explode on her face, then took the time to control herself. Vincent would need her to react to him soon. This was the perfect distraction. They had to use it.

Vincent watched out of the corner of his eye as Natalia turned from him. He wondered at her odd behavior, then took it as her understanding he had caused the distraction. He plunged on. "I have not fed off her. As to whether another has fed off her, I don't know." A bit of a bite came through his tone as he spoke the truth. "She is troublesome and doesn't do as she is told."

Edwin watched from a cloud as the human turned around to regard him. There was an odd look on her face. He shook his head and cleared it. "Then I'll have the first taste."

Natalia snorted, walked to Vincent, pulled out his kerchief and threw it at Edwin. "This is the only fluid you'll taste from me, vampire." She leaned in close as she passed him. "Enjoy."

Natalia needed more room to move. The corner was an ideal place to talk and screw, but it was a bad place to fight. She knew that in the end, she might have to allow Edwin to taste her blood. Earlier, she told Vincent and Joseph that it would be against her will and the last possible resort. She would fight whomever she had to, to keep Edwin from drinking her blood.

Edwin stood speechless as she passed, stuffed the kerchief in his pocket, reached out to grab her, and missed. She was too fast. She was already out in the main part of the room, seemingly waiting for him. "Vinny, tell your human to obey me and give me her blood."

"I don't belong to him. If you want something from me, you'll have to actually address me."

She stood tall, and stared at him. When he turned to address Vincent, she scanned the room. She saw Mierka, Ben and Owen herd the three children out of the room. She also noticed four of Edwin's men as they tried to approach her. The other people in the room moved away from her and Edwin, and left a wide-open space between her, Edwin and the private corner. The ones trying to reach her were pushed back.

As she looked around, she saw faces she vaguely recognized, but couldn't place. As she thought she had seen them here, she let it drop, and turned her attention back to Vincent and Edwin.

"Control your human, Vincent; she's beginning to annoy me."

"I've never been able to control her, my liege. I know not how." Vincent gave his Captain a slight bow, and spoke in an apologetic voice.

"How do you feed on her?"

"When she allows."

"Why do you keep her around?" Edwin was becoming skeptical.

"Because she's great in bed." Vincent moved to the main floor, as he wanted to keep a better eye on things. He locked eyes with Natalia as he spoke, and wondered what she thought of the situation.

"So how am I supposed to sample her wares?"

"You're not." Natalia answered.

The worry stole back into her blood. She looked around again, and tried to catch glimpses of the people she had recognized. As she did so, Edwin came toward her. She let him as she lifted one foot up then the other to kick off her shoes. After her ankle healed, Vincent spent many long days yelling at her until she agreed not to try and fight with heels. Stilettos were not effective weapons. She conceded, as she knew he was right. Since then, although she practiced in evening wear, she always slipped off her shoes before a battle.

Edwin circled her but she ignored him, which aggravated him. He grabbed her arm, to force her to look at him. She pushed him away and stepped beyond his reach. He tried to grab her again, but she dodged out of the way, and stared intently into the crowd.

Natalia had seen the bald man before, but it wasn't quite right. He tried not to look at her, but his eyes wandered back over and over. She squinted at him, and tried to picture him with hair. There was something about his eyes....

Vincent and Joseph watched Natalia. Both knew something was up but were loath to say anything. The children were out of the room and safe, but they still had to appease Edwin. Natalia continued to ignore him completely as she scanned the crowd. Vincent tried to follow her gaze, but couldn't. He stood at the wrong angle. He watched her as something clicked inside her head and a look almost like fear crossed her features.

Joseph understood what Natalia was doing before Vincent did and headed for the private corner. She had recognized someone. He didn't know whom, but he needed to gather the troops. As he slipped by the crowd, he pulled out his cell and sent Mierka a text. In turn, she called the werewolves, who waited a block away with Lilly in another club. As he put his phone away, he heard Natalia yell a name he had not heard since the night they freed her.

Natalia recognized the man and hurriedly looked at the other faces. She locked eyes with the man again. "Dean? Dean! SLAYERS!"

The crowd scattered.

17

Natalia watched as Edwin's men reacted like scared children. They ran to every door they could find, not sure which direction they should go. She could see Vincent's men, who calmly stood where they were and looked around for targets. Besides Vincent's men, there were four people in the crowd who stood stock-still. Those four were her targets. She looked around a little bit more, and found Vincent, Joseph, and Edwin. All three had retreated to the private corner.

Natalia returned her gaze to the crowd, who all tried to get out the closed door at once. She heard interrupted screams and saw gray clouds around the four Slayers. Their deaths showed Natalia how young Edwin's lot was. The crowd parted around one Slayer, a young woman, and Natalia saw Mierka close in on her. The Slayer held a stake in one hand and a spray bottle in the other. Natalia guessed it was filled with either holy water or garlic oil. Natalia felt the warrior in her take over and she pounced.

The woman turned when she saw Natalia jump towards her. As she was now the only true target, the woman aimed the bottle at her. Liquid landed on Natalia's outstretched arms. She closed her eyes to slits as the smell of garlic hit her. The oil, if made right, could blind a human. Since Dean was amongst the group, Natalia knew the oil would be potent. She slammed into the Slayer, opened her eyes, drew her hand back and punched the woman in the face. The Slayer brought the water bottle up and tried to spray her in the face. Natalia slammed the woman's hand down on the floor, and used more force than necessary. She was used to fighting vampires. Out of the corner of her eye, she saw movement and remembered the wooden stake in the woman's other hand. A foot landed on that wrist before the Slayer could do anything against her.

Mierka saw Natalia launch herself at the woman, but waited until the

Slayer was down before moving forward. Once Natalia straddled the Slayer, she stepped forward. Mierka saw the woman bring the wooden stake up to stab it at Natalia, and moved. The Slayer screamed in terror as the vampire embedded the stiletto heel into the woman's wrist. Mierka smirked as flesh parted and bone crunched. The smell of blood filled Mierka's nostrils, and she sighed. She gave Natalia a satisfied smile.

"I'll take her from here."

Natalia nodded, and searched the girl before getting off her. Natalia pulled her dress down as she looked around for her next target. Most of the guests still gathered around the door. A Slayer stood in front of it, armed with a sword and a cross. The crowd was just beyond his reach. She could see Kimberly and Owen as they tried to approach the door, but the crowd wouldn't let them get close enough. Natalia looked up to judge the distance to the ceiling. She looked to Mierka who had picked the woman up to feed.

"Mierka." No response. "Mierka!" Natalia put force into her voice, and demanded attention.

Mierka pulled away from the woman's neck, and licked the blood off her lips. She gave Natalia a seductive smile but shook her head. The nearly dead Slayer dropped from her arms. "Yes?"

"The door's blocked. Can you throw me over the crowd?"

Mierka craned her neck, and assessed the layout. "Yes. It'll be a tight landing; you may be run through."

"Not if I do this correctly."

She went to Mierka, who had gotten down on one knee and created a footrest with her hands. Natalia placed a barefoot in Mierka's hands, put her hand on Mierka's shoulder and waited. In a second, she was thrown through the air towards the door. She twisted and turned until she was feet first then realized Mierka had used too much force. Natalia flew over the Slayer's head and slammed into the door, which proved to be a better idea. She hit the door and it burst open. She grabbed the door as it swung open, and caught herself before she flew over the stairs.

The crowd wasted no time and ran over the Slayer, despite his sword and cross. Natalia clung to the door, placed her feet on the railing, and waited for the crowd to thin. She looked down on them from her shaky perch, and cursed their cowardly bearing. When she was able, she pushed the door away from the railing and jumped down. She was pissed off now. She had no pity for Edwin's vampires. They were ill trained and ill bred. None had stayed behind to help in the fight.

Natalia considered the people in the room. The wolves had arrived and stood by the back hallway. They were still in human form, and awaited instructions. Mierka and Ben had one Slayer held against the wall, as did Owen and Kimberly. Jesse was facing off with Dean, who held a sword. Vincent stood with Joseph and Edwin, who did not look happy.

The Captain shook his head. "I knew you were out to get me Vincent, but this is low, even for you. Inviting Slayers to my Coronation? It was bad enough to have your tryst with your whore in front of my people, but Slayers? I'm leaving. Take care of this. You will hear from me again. I blame you for this ambush!"

Still growling words, Edwin left the corner, and made sure to avoid everyone else as he stormed out of the room and down the stairs.

The word 'ambush' flooded Natalia's mind and she allowed herself a moment of guilt for not realizing what the Slayers planned. With no time to think, she pushed her thoughts aside. There were still enemies in the room. Though all the Slayers were captured, she was only interested in one of them. Natalia headed for Jesse, to talk to Dean. She had almost forgotten about him in the past few years. She wished she hadn't. He was a good man, despite his Slayer tendencies. She knew what Vincent did to Slayers; Natalia wanted to save him from that fate.

"Leave him to me, Jesse." She glanced at Vincent. "Keep the men back, lover."

It was an order. Some time ago, Mierka informed her that as Vincent's woman, she could give his men orders. Vincent confirmed it. She never tried to give any of them orders, except for Charlie, but that was different. The wolf always listened to her. Jesse looked over at her, glanced quickly at Vincent, then backed away from the fight when Vincent nodded.

"Hello, Dean."

"So, this is what happened to you. I wondered."

"I wondered, for a while, what happened to you." She continued to him and noticed the wolves fan out behind her. They were still in human form. Charlie was in the lead, feeling ornery, she knew. Rebecca had remained in Montana to take care of her twins. Charlie went back and forth between California and Montana, but it was never often enough. Husband and wife hated the situation; Charlie wanted a fight to release his aggressions.

"I took over for Zechariah." He cocked his head. "What did you do to him?"

Natalia faced Dean now, and looked him over. He had grown older, lost weight, and his skin had cleared. "Killed him, I think. I was otherwise engaged when he was taken care of."

"He tried to save you; you callous bitch." He gripped the sword badly; she could take it from him easily.

"He kidnapped me and told me he kidnapped my friend to keep me docile. He nearly starved me and tried to beat me into submission." Her anger grew.

"He was trying to save you!"

"By harming me and lying to me?"

"Your friend was poisoning your mind! It looks like she succeeded." He looked indignant.

She gave him a baffled look. "What are you talking about?"

"He was trying to keep you away from your demon friend, to stop her influence on you." He stood taller as he spoke in Zechariah's tone.

Natalia stood, her mouth agape. "He told you she was a demon? She's human. Didn't your voices ever tell you that? Oh, wait. You never heard the voices, did you?"

"I do now!" But he didn't catch her gaze. He was lying. She wondered why, but he continued, and she let the lie go. "Sometimes the voices lie, as they're doing now."

He turned the sword and pointed it at her. She wanted to question him further, delve into his lie, but her words were ripped from her lips. From her right, Jesse appeared in her field of vision, and rushed Dean. The sword caught her eye as Jesse continued forward and Natalia finally thought she understood what it was.

"Jesse, NO!" She reached out to him, saw the blur, and knew it was too late.

Vincent watched as Jesse did as he ordered. The vampire thought that while Natalia distracted the Slayer, Jesse could tackle Dean. He watched as Jesse ran, heard Natalia's warning, and watched as the Slayer turned slowly. Dean lifted his sword as if it were weightless and beheaded Jesse easily. It was a large sword, but the way the Slayer held it, it was obviously very light. Too late he noticed these things as Jesse turned to dust. His eyes grew wide. Jesse had fed; they had all fed before coming here tonight. He didn't know how old Jesse was, but had known the shy vampire for over one hundred years. A beheading would not kill him.

Natalia's blood grew cold as she read the symbols on the blade. She hadn't thought the sword was real. But here it was; it threatened the life she led. The warrior took over, calculating and cold. She understood his last statement: he probably believed her a vampire. It was to her advantage. As long as he didn't run the blade through her neck or heart, she would be fine. She heard Charlie behind her growl. Other growls joined his. She could let the wolves take him, but she wanted to do this herself: for Vincent and their men. And she didn't know if the sword would kill the wolves, too. She glanced back at the wolves, silenced them with a look, and repeated her order.

"Keep our men back, lover. Let me take care of things." There was no emotion in her voice.

Vincent wasn't keen on the idea, as he didn't want to lose any more of his people. The woman had made up her mind, though. As she was still human, any weapon could kill her. If this were a magical sword, it might not be as deadly to a human. Why a Slayer would be using magic, he didn't know. He looked around the room, caught everyone's eye, and confirmed her order. His gaze returned to the fight as her words came back. Why had she called them 'our men'?

Natalia formulated a plan as she paced in front of the Slayer. She needed to keep him talking; he beat her to it.

"Why did you turn yourself over to the vampires, Natalia? You could have tried to find me, or others like me. We could have made a grand team."

"I'm not a Slayer. Never was."

"You hunt vampires."

"Just one." She let just a little bit of emotion through as she watched his movements.

"Why are you with them?" He sounded curious. She went with it.

"Because they're the only ones who ever showed me anything other than pain." More emotion than she wanted broke through. She lost control of her emotions and felt her anger rise.

"And now that's all you bring to others."

He said it with conviction. He was certain of what she was. Natalia regained control as his attitude smoothed out her anger. This allowed her to see his weakness. He swung back with the sword as he spoke. She stood still, drew herself to full height, and brought a seductive smile to her face. "They seem to enjoy it."

"You blood sucking bitch."

She ran at him, and aimed at his sword arm to try and disarm him. He was quicker than she expected and was able to swing the sword before her. She used her arm to knock it out of the way and gained a large cut on her arm. It stung, but it was just a sword to her. The look on Dean's face confirmed what she had deduced from the runes. Any cut on a vampire's body by this sword would kill it.

"You're still human!" He was shocked.

She punched him in the face and knocked him back a step. "Surprised?"

He stepped back from her. "Why do you protect them?"

"I protect me and mine from those who wish to harm us."

Those around her who knew where the words were mirrored from looked to its originator for some response. There was no emotion on Vincent's face.

"Doesn't matter if you haven't been changed, you stand with them." He stepped back yet another step, and readied his weapon. "Zechariah couldn't convince you of heaven, but at least I'll save you from hell."

"Hell will be a sweet reward."

Dean gave her a confused and scared look as Natalia smiled a wicked smile, and readied herself for battle. He lunged at her. There was an obvious clumsiness to his movements that betrayed his unpracticed battle skills. He aimed for her head. Natalia was able to knock the sword out of the way. With an unexpected speed, Dean brought the sword back in time to stab her in the stomach as she rushed towards him. Her face contorted in pain as she stepped forward, and drove the sword deeper into her body. She had to get it away from him, at all costs. If he were able to use it on Vincent, the people of San Francisco would continue to wallow in the misery they had experienced for the past twenty years.

With no desire to contemplate the possibility of things getting worse, she grasped for the hilt of the sword. She was still too far away and pulled herself further along the blade. Her consciousness threatened to leave her; she blocked the pain, and stared Dean in the face. There was a look of pure wonder on his face as she pulled away from him, and took the sword with her. She vaguely heard Vincent give an order as she fell to the ground. She sat and watched as a flurry of furry critters ran by her and covered the Slayer. As she held hard to consciousness and the sword, Natalia yelled for her wolf.

"Charlie!" Her voice came out red as blood bubbled up her throat. A lone wolf extracted itself reluctantly from the melee. It padded over, snout, forepaws and chest spotted crimson with blood. She saw Vincent approach as well, but carefully waved him away. The movement caused the sword to shift and cut into her a little more. She felt a warm hand on her outstretched arm. Lilly, who had been standing by in the security room, told her she would be all right. As the pain took hold of her, she questioned her healer's words. Her breathing was labored, and she felt faint. She wondered briefly what hell would be like, and knew she did have a way out.

Charlie, now human and naked, but still spotted with blood, knelt beside her. Vincent had a moment of jealousy when the wolf took her hand. "Nat?"

She squeezed his hand weakly, took a shallow breath, and tried to stay conscious. "Take the sword." Her words were red. "Guard it with your life." She breathed out more blood. "No vampire touches it."

Her hand slipped from Charlie's, her head rolled back, as her body threatened to do the same. Lilly sat behind her to hold her up, and prevent more damage. After Natalia's words, she stared at Charlie and waited for him to comply. Charlie looked at Vincent first, doubt on his face. Vincent closed his eyes and nodded once. He wished the wolf would hurry in order to allow Lilly to save his woman's life.

Charlie, not really sure of Natalia's wishes, carefully grasped the hilt, and hoped the enchanted sword wouldn't hurt him. When his hand felt normal, he tightened his grasp, nodded to Lilly and pulled the sword out. He and Lilly were sprayed with her blood. Charlie called his pack to him as Vincent eyed the sword. The wolves surrounded him and as a unit, the pack left the room.

Lilly concentrated on the energies around her, and tried to gather them.

She was worried, as she couldn't feel anything. She shook her head as she tried once more. It was no good. There were too many dark and empty spots for her to gather energy.

"I need to move her."

Vincent moved forward and knelt beside his woman. "Where?"

Lilly looked around, eyes closed, and tried to find the right spot. "Your office."

The healer lowered Natalia to the floor then stood and ran to the office to prepare it. Vincent slipped off his jacket, bundled it up and pressed it to the hole in Natalia's stomach. He snapped his fingers and held out his hand to Joseph. It took a second for Joseph to understand, but then he slipped off his own jacket and handed it over. Vincent slid the folded jacket under Natalia and rose with his lover in his arms. He carried her silently, swiftly to his office, as her words echoed in his mind.

The wolves were gathered in his office. Charlie, once more in jeans and t-shirt, leaned against the far wall, the sword by his side, hilt in hand, tip pointed down. The others were in wolf form: Orlando, and Doug to his right and left. They sat and waited for someone to make a false move. It was to Natalia's credit that Charlie and the others followed her orders. In Rebecca's absence, she became their surrogate alpha female.

The healer sat in the center of the room, naked. Small cuts ran across her chest and down her arms. Lilly had drawn some recognizable runes on the carpet in blood. He could smell it and wondered how the wolves stayed calm. He couldn't remember the last time Lilly used blood to heal Natalia. Vincent glanced sharply at the healer then at Natalia. Were he human, his face would have gone pale. As it was, his eyes grew wide as he placed Natalia on the floor next to Lilly.

Lilly opened her eyes, nodded, and raised the ritual dagger she held. She drew the sharp blade across her chest again, then dipped the bloody dagger into Natalia's blood. She used their combined blood to make a final mark on the floor and started to chant. Vincent, feeling useless, left the room to pace the long hallway and private room.

As he paced his thoughts turned back to the events of the evening. His main concern was that Edwin had not been crowned. This worried him as the man would expect another coronation party and would possibly expect Vincent to host it. And now the twit knew Natalia. He would probably demand her blood, if not all of her. Vincent would never relinquish his lover to such an atrocious creature. He wasn't sure how he would handle it, but he would not turn her over.

"Sir?" Joseph came down the hall toward him.

"Yes?"

"We have an interesting situation."

"Another one?" He sounded bored.

"Yes. You'll want to handle this one yourself." He sounded sure of himself. This indicated to Vincent that the situation did require his immediate attention. On his way down the hall, he glanced in his office. Lilly still chanted, but it ran together so fast, he couldn't decipher the words. Natalia wasn't healed, but she seemed to have stopped bleeding. He pushed aside thoughts of her and went to the next problem, which was apparently downstairs.

Vincent paused halfway down the steps. Kari, Morgan, and Janice stood by the bar. Owen sat nearby and watched them.

"What is this?" He didn't particularly like that three of Edwin's people were still in his club.

Joseph indicated the three vampires. "They said they wanted a word with you."

One by one Vincent looked all three in the eye. "All right. Start talking."

Morgan stepped forward. "We want your protection."

"Oh? From what I've seen, you can do fine on your own."

Morgan flustered and Kari stepped forward. She placed a calm hand on Morgan's shoulder. "You don't understand how it is, Vincent." She looked down, composed her thoughts, and looked Vincent in the eye again. "Though Edwin will say different, neither he nor Christopher changed me. I came to this area right around the time Christopher started changing things. I tried to leave, but his people found me and took me in. He told me if I stayed, I would have to work for him and do as he said. If I wanted to leave, I would leave in a dustpan."

Janice stepped forward. "I was told the same thing. I've been in San Francisco for a long, long time. I didn't want to leave. And I don't want to be with them. He's forced our hand."

"What stops you from leaving?" It all sounded like a ploy to Vincent.

"Those Edwin doesn't trust are ordered to sleep at his house. If we don't show up before sunrise, he sends people after us. They're thugs he's hired to keep us in line." Janice looked distraught. "I was late once, traffic was bad. As I drove up, six people were getting onto motorcycles. When I got out of my car and went inside, they followed me until they saw I was going to Edwin."

"I tried to get out once." Kari waited until Vincent looked her way. "I told Edwin I wanted to go find some new challenges. I told him I would be back in a week. He said I could go, as long as I took an escort. To hide what I was doing, I went to Los Angeles. He had me take two of his thugs. They were with me everywhere I went. Edwin may not appear to be that bad, but he's worse than you know."

Vincent stared Kari down. "Edwin is a monster. Nothing about him surprises me."

Kari looked away from the imposing man. Janice stepped forward and continued. "Vincent, please. I've lived a long time. All I want is to leave the area. I don't want to be under anyone's rule anymore. I don't know what these two want, but I want my freedom."

He crossed his arms, looked at Janice, and addressed only her. "And if I help you?"

She gave a sideway glance to Morgan and Kari. "Perhaps we can discuss that privately?"

Vincent stared her down or tried to. She held his gaze and did not waver under his hard scrutiny. Finally, he nodded. "That won't be necessary." He turned to Joseph, and whispered to his bodyguard. After a moment, Vincent turned back to Janice. "You will speak to Joseph of your desires. You can speak to him as freely as you would to me."

She frowned softly, but nodded. He had his reasons to not talk with her privately. Joseph appeared next to Janice, gave her his arm, and led the lady away.

Vincent turned to Kari and Morgan. "Well? What is it you want?"

"Not to die." Morgan answered in a flat tone of voice. He shrugged when Vincent looked his way. "I like being a vampire. I would rather not do as Edwin asks, but neither will I help you destroy him. I want to live in this city, and I don't want to be killed by your people or his."

Vincent looked at Morgan and felt the man told the truth. He then looked at Kari. She looked away before too long. "And you?"

"Same. I don't want to die, but I won't help you either. It's too risky."

"Why should I help either of you if you aren't willing to help me?"

Morgan and Kari looked at each other. Morgan nodded and Kari spoke. "We won't get in your way. If ordered to do something against you or your people, we'll let you know. We won't do anything overt though. We won't report his movements to you, but we won't report your movements to him either. We want to have our lives and we won't trouble you."

Vincent understood the answer but didn't like it. "Fine. Stay out of my way and you'll have your lives. If I find you're spying on me for him, your end will not be swift. Now get out."

Kari and Morgan both nodded and left the club quickly. Owen came to his side.

"I don't trust them."

"Neither do I, but we might be able to use them. All of my house will know of the conversation that took place here."

Owen nodded. "What about Janice?"

"I ran into her a few times in the past, long before Christopher and Edwin took over. I don't think she realizes we've met before. Or perhaps she wanted to keep that a secret from the other two. At any rate, she is what she says she is. We'll help her leave the city."

Owen nodded as they headed up the stairs. At the top, Owen left to take care of other things. Vincent looked up to see Marcus in the main room. He looked expectantly at his boss.

"Sir, I hate to add to your worries."

Vincent gently guided his newest family member to the private corner. "You don't add to my worries Markus, unless you don't speak your mind."

"I don't think I can do this, sir." His words came out in a rush.

"Do what Markus?" Vincent sounded worried.

"Fight. It's never been in my nature to jump into a fight. The first night you saw me fight here, I was trying to impress you. I knew I wanted to be a part of your house long before you knew about me. Tonight, I was thrilled that you ordered me to stay out of the way. And it's not that I can't yet, it's that I don't want to. I've been talking to Anthony about what he and his group does, and it seems more like what I should be doing." He sounded sheepish.

"You wish to gather information and be a spy?" There was no emotion in his voice.

"With your permission, sir."

"I have never stopped my people from using their strongest skills, I won't start now. I'll speak with Anthony tomorrow night on your behalf." He walked away as Markus said a simple thank you.

Vincent hurried to his office to check on Natalia as he ground his teeth and hoped not to have any more interruptions. She sat on the floor, and leaned against the couch. Lilly sat beside her, and looked just as haggard. The wolves were in the same spot. Vincent went to Natalia and knelt in front of her. He placed one hand on her knee. The other went to her cheek.

"Natalia?" He tried to hide his emotions but failed. There was worry there. She rubbed her cheek against his hand and sighed as his touch woke her up a bit.

"Vincent." It was more sigh than speech. She looked very tired, but also relieved.

Vincent looked back at Charlie, who still protected the sword. He wanted to know more about it, needed to know how a metal sword could kill a vampire and do nothing to a werewolf. When she closed her eyes and leaned into his hand, he decided. He picked her up in her arms and turned to the wolves.

"Charlie, take the sword and Lilly. We're going home. Doug, Orlando, you're on clean up." He walked out, and did not bother to wait for a response. There was no need for one.

18

The ride back to the house was awkward. Natalia came more fully awake as they left San Francisco. Charlie, after he placed the sword in the truck, ran back into the club to get the ladies some bottled orange juice and snacks from the kitchen. Lilly slept on the seat against the divider; Charlie drove, and Orlando sat in the passenger seat. Natalia leaned against Vincent, and ate a sandwich. Her lover had his hand on her far knee, as if to protect her. Natalia had spoken a few words, but Vincent's monosyllabic responses finally quieted her.

Vincent was lost in his thoughts. He wanted to question her about the sword, but her words of earlier kept coming back to him. She had called them 'our men' and repeated the words he spoke at the start of every training session. The words rattled around in his brain, and threatened to start a maelstrom. He kept silent, as he wanted to wait until they reached the house to say anything. There were some things he liked to keep private.

Once back at the house, Vincent woke Lilly, and helped her and Natalia out of the car. Charlie hurried to the trunk before anyone could take the sword. He placed it on the hood of the trunk, not sure of what to do with it. Natalia came over and started to look at it. Joseph came down to the garage to update Vincent on certain matters. They spoke quietly as Natalia examined the sword.

The sword was about three and a half feet in length, looked like a two-handed sword but was lighter than a rapier. It was well balanced, a quality piece of work. The blade had the look of a Damascus sword, but the folds of metal were red, orange and yellow. The runes on it were almost invisible unless hit by direct light. She traced the symbols, and wondered what they would do in direct sunlight. It was one o'clock in the morning. She would have to wait a few hours to find out. Natalia backed away from the car, swung the sword, and tested the weight and balance. It really was a fine sword.

The reality of the sword slowly seeped into her being as she looked around. With the sword, she could kill all the vampires in the house, in the city, and probably in the world. She was pretty sure the sword had been made by the Order of Light in the 16th century. The Order of Light had been a group of priests, monks and mages who decided they needed a little bit more help against vampires. The Order of Light was based in Siberia. They created swords and trinkets to help in the fight against Hellspawn. This sword was magic and seemed to have the same effect as sunlight on vampires. The blade simply had to cut the vampire in order to kill the creature. As far as Natalia knew, this relic was the only one left from the Order of Light's magical arsenal. It was an extremely dangerous weapon and had to be hidden from Vincent's enemies.

She looked around when she realized those gathered had grown silent. "What?"

Vincent gave her a peculiar look. She was generally deadly beautiful, but with the sword in hand, she looked even deadlier. The sword gave her a nasty look, especially with the rip in her dress. "Put the sword down, Natalia."

"Sure." She handed it to Charlie. "It needs to be put in a safe locked place. Don't let anyone know you have it. It's a dangerous weapon, especially to your kind."

"What is it?"

"A sword forged by a Siberian priest to kill vampires. The magic in it acts like sunlight against vampires. Even a tiny scratch will kill an old vampire like yourself."

Charlie and Orlando gave her looks that made her feel as if she were a Slayer. Vincent and Lilly, who leaned against the car, seemed skeptical, but believed her. Joseph was the only one who didn't seem surprised. She wondered how old the vampire really was.

"What does this mean for us?" Vincent was always a practical thinker.

"If you hide it and tell no one where it is, nothing. If word gets out that we have it…" She shrugged her shoulders and gave him a helpless look. She didn't want to contemplate the possibilities.

"We have a place to hide it. No one will know. It's a blessing Edwin's people didn't stay for the fight." Vincent looked at Charlie, who held the sword nonchalantly. He caught the werewolf's eye. "Follow Joseph. The rest of you are relieved for the night."

Charlie followed Joseph up the stairs. The rest waited to hear the upstairs door open before they followed. Orlando helped Lilly up the garage stairs and to the kitchen. She needed more sustenance, and would need many days of rest from healing Natalia's near mortal wound.

Natalia and Vincent went up the steps last, silently, each lost in their own thoughts. When they reached the first floor, Natalia pushed her thoughts aside, and breathed deep. Her hand on the grand staircase railing, she turned her thoughts to the bed upstairs. She placed one foot on the staircase, and thought to head up, until Vincent's voice stopped her.

"Come with me, Natalia." His emotions were hidden again. He noticed her body sag just a touch.

"It's been a long night, Vincent. I want to go to bed."

"Come with me, Natalia. Please."

There was a slight emphasis on the last word. Natalia turned to face him, a slight crease on her brow. She had never heard this tone before. "All right."

He held out his hand to her. When she took it, he led her to his study. Once inside he leaned against the desk, and brought her close. Vincent enfolded her in his arms and kissed her ever so lightly on the lips. His soft touch surprised her, and she pulled her head away. The look on his face bothered her and she pulled completely away. He allowed it but caught her hand and held it.

She gave him a pleading look. "Vincent, I don't feel like doing this tonight."

"And why not?"

She gave him a heartbroken look. "I failed you."

He gave her a confused look. "You nearly sacrificed yourself to the Slayer to make sure he didn't use a deadly sword on our men and you think you failed?"

Natalia missed the significance of his words and shook her head. "The notes I studied pointed to this ambush and I missed it. Had I figured out the Slayer's plans earlier, we could have stopped this before it started."

"To what end?"

"Jesse's dead."

Vincent nodded once, slowly. "And that is my cross to bear. I don't blame you for his death. You asked me to keep everyone away; I didn't listen. Despite his death, I wouldn't change this night. We showed Edwin and his men what you are capable of and Edwin did not have a chance to declare himself Captain. We were also able to capture some Slayers and take a powerful weapon away from our enemies. This night was not a failure, Natalia. It was a win. Enjoy it."

The look on her face showed she didn't want to declare this night a victory. Vincent took her into his arms again, and gently caressed her cheek and jaw line. He gave her a soft kiss on the lips but pulled back before too long.

"There is something else that I wish to talk to you about. Something you said earlier."

"What is it, Vincent?" She was tense and hid it with a slight anger. His voice was rather odd. She felt something important was coming. Natalia wasn't sure she wanted to delve into another serious conversation tonight.

The smile that came to his face was seductive, but mocked her slightly. "You were impressive tonight, lover." He pulled her to him again, trapped her as he slipped his hand down her dress. Even with the sword cut in it, it was impressive. He squeezed her cheek; he loved the feel of her hard ass. "Where did you get this dress? Much more interesting than the one I picked out."

She gasped as his cool hand brushed the top of her thigh. "We could be doing this upstairs."

He slipped arms around her to hold her closer. "There is something I wish to discuss with you, Natalia."

"Anything. Just make it fast." She gave him a seductive look. "There are other, more pleasant things I want to do."

His hand traveled up to her head to tangle in her soft, luxurious hair. "When did they become our men, Natalia?"

His words caught her by surprise. She thought back to the night's event, and remembered what she said and why. The look of surprise vanished, as she raised her head high, and gave him a proud look. "I've spent the past five years fighting with these people, learning from them, talking to them, and living with them. The creatures I see the most are the ones that live in your household."

She stopped her tirade when she realized he still smiled that sardonic smile. She suddenly wished she could take back her words and lie about why she had said what she said.

"What was the other thing you said? About protecting you and yours? You know why I say that each night before we train, Natalia. It means that in the end, I would lay my life down for the people who fight for me and give me protection. Did you say it lightly, thinking to confuse the Slayer? Or do you believe in what you said?"

Natalia closed her eyes, and tried to keep her wits about her. She wasn't sure why he asked all this but knew she should give him an honest answer. Natalia searched her mind and emotions. Once she found the answer, she opened her eyes. She turned her full dark gaze upon Vincent. Her eyes were clear and mirrored the words she spoke.

"As I said, I've spent a lot of time getting to know the men and women that live under your roof. I believe I'm meant to protect them, and I would lay my life down for the people who help to protect me."

One hand tightened in her hair; the other tightened around her and brought her as close as he could get her. He whispered his question into her ear and inhaled the fragrance of her as he did. "And me, Natalia? Would you lay down your life for me?"

She tried to back away to look at his face, but he wouldn't allow it. He nibbled her neck, and sent waves of anticipated pleasure through her body. She shook as his question dipped deep inside her mind. Would she? Would she lay down her life for Vincent? It didn't take long for her to answer his question.

"Yes."

He nibbled his way up her soft neck, his fangs still unexposed. He bit her earlobe, felt her shudder, then let her go to look in her eyes. "Why Natalia? Why would you risk your life for me, when your life is so much more fragile?"

She gave him a quizzical 'why not' look, her head cocked to one side. She blinked a couple of times, then looked down as if to look inside herself. She shook her head to clear it. He watched as she looked inward again, then shook her head again, a look of denial on her features. She backed away from him, and did not let him hold her anymore. He tried to catch her hand, but she pulled away, a look of pure sorrow on her face. She looked up at him, near tears. Her breath came fast, and her heart beat so hard he could hear it. She started to shake her head slowly as she continued to back away.

He could tell she didn't want to face the truth. His features softened as he saw her persist in lying to herself. In one movement he had her in his arms again, and held her as she sobbed. "What do you feel for me, Natalia? Let me know how you feel."

His whispered words revealed nothing but concern. She broke further and her sobs grew harder. "No."

"Why not?" He brushed away her tears and smeared the black mascara across her cheeks.

"Because if I feel that way maybe she did too." Her words were hidden in her sobs.

"Who, Natalia?" He understood what she spoke about but wanted her to say it.

Natalia shut her eyes tight, balled her hands into fists, pressed the palms into her eyes, and tried to block out the knowledge. Vincent gently pulled her hands away and held them to her sides.

"Tell me, Natalia. Tell me what you're thinking." His voice was soft, low, and soothed her nerves. She leaned into him, and let the all too familiar feel of him comfort her. She sagged into him, felt his coolness, and desired more. A sob escaped her as she allowed herself to speak the truth.

"If I love you, then maybe my mother loved Donald, and maybe she allowed him to feed off her. And maybe she liked it and wanted him to." Her voice became hushed. "Like I want you to, every time you touch me."

Vincent gently pushed her back to look into her eyes. "Do you know anything about Donald? About the man he was before he was turned?"

Natalia dried her tears, quieted her sobs, and thought hard on his words. She wasn't sure where he was going with his question. She latched onto his words, which promised an escape from her raw emotions.

"I don't know anything about him. The police never wanted to tell me anything, and I never thought to investigate. I was never interested in his past."

"Revenge is better dealt out when you know your target, Natalia." He moved her carefully away and walked around to the front of the desk. He took his key ring out of his pocket, selected a small brass one and unlocked one of the drawers. He reached inside, searched for a moment and pulled out a manila folder about an inch thick. "Donald Jenkins liked to use women. He finds a woman on his route and uses her for his pleasure, making her suffer every moment she is with him. There's more, but perhaps you would like to read it yourself?"

Natalia stared at the manila folder he held out to her, and walked to the edge of the desk. "When did you find this out?"

"Anthony's men have been compiling the information for over a year. They're still finding police reports under different names, but with the same M.O. as the police would say."

She reached a shaky hand out to it, and caressed the slightly rough surface. "Why didn't you tell me?"

He placed the folder on the desk, walked back around the desk and stood in front of her. "I was afraid the knowledge would drive you to find him." He lifted her head, and made her look in his eyes. "All I have ever done is try and keep you by my side, Natalia."

His lips were so close; all she wanted to do was touch hers to his. "So why tell me now?"

"What do you feel for me Natalia? Why would you lay down your life for me? What stops you from seeking revenge?"

She started to shake minutely. She squeezed her eyes shut again, as she did not want him to see the truth until she spoke. She took a deep haggard breath; let it out in a shaky sigh. "I love you. I stay, I fight, and I would risk my life because I love you. And loving a vampire will prove my death."

19

The words resonated in his ears and made him tense with pleasure. He crushed her to him, and gave her a hard kiss. There was no room for breath as his tongue plunged into her mouth to caress her tongue. She dug her nails into his back as if she wanted to claw his back through his clothing. He pulled away to look in her eyes.

"Would endless death be such a terrible thing?" His hand caressed her jaw line, then traveled down to her neck.

She looked into his frank blue eyes; her thoughts from earlier at the club came back to her. "What happens wh… if you change me?"

Vincent tensed. She had almost uttered the right word. He leaned in to breathe on her neck and caress her soft skin with his lips. He wanted to feel her vein pulsing with life. "Say it correctly, Natalia. Say what you really mean. I won't change you until you ask me, so use the words you wish to use."

Her voice became seductive, as it often did when he chilled her jugular with his breath. She became wet in anticipation of his touch. With such a short dress, it would be easy for her lover to plunge into her. She wished he would. Her head swimming in sexual thoughts, she dug her nails further into his back. "What happens to me when you change me? What will I be like?"

He growled deep into her neck, opened his mouth wide and wrapped his teeth almost completely around the side of her neck. He kept his fangs in; he couldn't bite her yet. He pulled away when she shuddered and gave a small cry.

"What are you expecting to happen, Natalia? What are you worried about?"

Her emotions encased her, flung her away, and made her feel out of

132

control. His questions reverberated in her mind. Her answer came in waves as she calmed herself and answered truthfully. "I have seen countless monsters in my time. Many of them were vampires."

"Do you think me and mine are monsters?" Her answer didn't bother him; most humans answered in this fashion.

"No…" But there was some doubt on her face. It made Vincent smile.

"Why the hesitation?"

"What decides the attitude of a person when they are turned?" Her words sounded serious. This was apparently something she thought of often.

Vincent looked down into her eyes, and finally understood part of the hesitation he had always sensed in her. His hand went to her hair and tenderly caressed the nape of her neck. "A human's darkest desires determine how devilish she is when she is turned. Her strong humanity acts as a counterbalance to even it out." He paused as the words sank in. "In other words, nothing changes unless the human wants it to change."

"That means men like Edwin and Theodore and Donald-"

"They acted the same way before they were changed." He paused, closed his eyes, and pulled away from her slightly. "Make no mistake, at some point you will give in to urges you didn't realize were there, Natalia. Because at some point those darkest desires will consume you." He gave her a wickedly seductive smile. "You will enjoy every moment of it. I hope to enjoy those moments with you as well."

Natalia gave him a look mixed with terror and wonder. "What kind of things have you done?"

He gave her a satisfied yet hungry look. "Would you like to touch on those desires with me?" Her look turned to anticipated terror. He shook his head as he trapped her in his arms. "I would never harm you irreparably and I will not change you until you tell me to. There are many things we've already done that you've enjoyed, that most humans would not allow. Do you feel adventurous tonight, Natalia?"

Her breath was hard and heavy. Her thoughts spun in a circle. She had declared her love for him, had declared her desire to be changed by him. Now, he offered new desires. She was intrigued by his proposition. She always enjoyed pushing him to his limits and being pushed beyond hers. "What…what do you suggest?"

"How much energy do you have?" He grabbed her by her hair, pulled her head back, and growled into her flesh.

"I'm weak, but willing." It would have been foolish to lie.

He growled again, bared his fangs, and scraped them along her elongated neck. She arched into him. "Are you willing to venture into the dungeon?" She made an affirmative noise in her throat. "Are you willing to have sex in front of the Slayers? Let them hear your pleasure? Make them jealous of you and hate you all at once?"

Her hands dug into his arms. She knew of the video and audio surveillance but wasn't sure about having actual people present while she screwed him. It excited her a little though. "If I say yes now, but want to stop?"

"I'll always stop when you ask."

That was true. She occasionally told him no, and he always stopped. Natalia nodded her head vigorously, and let her desires flood her completely. "Do as you wish, vampire. Show them I belong to you."

He growled his pleasure, and gave her a hyena smile. It chilled her to the bone as his touch never seemed to do. Vincent grabbed her around the waist and slung her over his shoulder. She protested, but Vincent simply laughed.

"This is nothing in comparison to what I'm about to do to you."

He slapped her ass hard, which made her squeak as he walked out the door and headed for the dungeon. At the door to the dungeon, he let her down, as he knew he couldn't walk down the narrow stairs with her. She laughed as he entered the code and opened the door. They walked down the steps but stopped when they reached the air vac doors. Vincent pointed out the keypad silently, and entered his code as she watched. It was the first time he had brought her down here and wanted to make sure she could get out if necessary.

When they stepped through the second door, Mierka confronted them. She stood halfway down the hall, a crossbow at the ready. Natalia laughed until the stench hit her nose. She nearly gagged but was able to stop herself. It reeked of dead, decayed flesh. Vincent reached for the handkerchief that wasn't there, and cursed himself for not thinking of the smell. He never thought of it; it didn't bother him much. He took off his necktie and handed that to Natalia. She grabbed it and used the silk to guard her nose.

"I apologize. We can leave if you wish."

"Sir, we weren't expecting you." Mierka's voice had its usual light quality to it.

Vincent raised an eyebrow and gave her a secret smile. "Who's down here?"

"Joseph and I were about to interrogate the Slayers." Her smile grew as she walked closer to the pair. "Would you like to watch?"

Vincent turned to Natalia, who seemed to be under control of her senses. "What do you wish to do?"

The smell was still too new, too strong for her to consider sex. Dean's fate suddenly lay heavy on her conscience. She turned to Mierka. "Who will you interrogate first?"

Mierka cocked her head in surprise. She didn't think the human had it in her to watch a torture. "The men will break faster if we question the woman first."

Natalia lowered the tie from her nose in surprise. "Why?"

"A grand show of chivalry, usually. Think women can't take it." She gave Natalia a sisterly smile. "Which we know to be incorrect, don't we?"

Natalia locked eyes with Mierka and returned the smile. She nodded in agreement but let her features still. "Is Dean down here?"

"The one with the sword? Barely."

"I was wondering if I could try something?"

Vincent and Mierka both gave her quizzical looks.

"What do you have in mind?" His voice was soft, inquisitive.

Natalia knew Vincent thought of the conversation they just finished of the dark desires that dwell in a human's soul. She had no wish to harm Dean, or watch him be harmed, but she could possibly learn some things. "Call Joseph out here and stay by the door or go watch from the security office. Let me do things my way."

Mierka left to go get Joseph and Natalia stepped forward to kiss her lover softly. "Please don't take offense to anything I do."

His hands went around her back and into her hair, to pull her closer for a stronger kiss. When he heard Joseph and Mierka approach, he let her go. "There are many forms of interrogation, Natalia. I know what can be done." He traced her jaw line with his thumb. "Perhaps one day I will teach you my techniques."

Natalia nodded, pulled away, handed back the tie and took a second to center and prepare herself. She wasn't sure she could do this but knew that Dean deserved better than pain. She took a deep breath through her mouth, and walked down the hall to the open door. The vampires stood sentry at the door.

There were three people shackled to the wall. Their mouths were gagged. There was a chair on the wall opposite the Slayers and several empty shackles. Dean was a mess. His clothes were torn and bloody. She could see the ripped flesh through his tattered pants. His upper half seemed unscathed, but she was amazed he was still alive. Apparently, the werewolves knew how to attack without killing. She shook her head in sympathy, went to him, and untied his gag. Natalia then walked to the chair, picked it up, set it closer to Dean and sat down. She crossed her legs and arms, and watched him with close scrutiny.

"What do you want?" His hard voice came across as defeated.

Natalia heard the pain in his voice but heard curiosity as well. It meant she could break him. She didn't use seduction during combat; she learned that lesson well. But seduction could be used to break someone. She looked at him for several minutes, and let his anger grow. The two other Slayers gave her nasty looks, but she ignored them easily.

The memory of the first time Vincent seduced her flooded Natalia's mind. She wondered if she could turn Dean in the same manner. She finally uncrossed her limbs, slowly stood, and walked to him with deliberate slowness. Dean shook which made the chains rattle. Natalia raised her hand to his cheek and caressed it slowly with the back of her hand. She stepped even closer, pressed herself against him and whispered into his ear. As she was taller, she had to tip her head forward to do so.

"Hello, Dean. Did you miss me?"

"If I were free, I'd kill you." His words were icier than Vincent's touch.

"Kill me?" She kissed his neck, nibbled his ear lobe. "Or kiss me? I remember how much trouble you had looking at me when we first met. That look in your eye told me so much."

He shuddered as her hand snaked down to the front of his pants. He could mask the emotions in his words, but not his body. Despite his pain, he had an incredible erection. She smiled and used Vincent's strategy.

"How long has it been since you felt a woman's touch? Have you ever? Zechariah was celibate, but you needn't be. Pleasure is not the devil's creation."

"It is." He spoke through clenched teeth, as sweat formed on his brow.

"Who created the devil?" She placed her hand on his thigh. Dean pulled against the chains, and tried to get free. It was no use. The shackles were meant for creatures far stronger than he. She squeezed his leg carefully. He grunted, and tried to keep some degree of composure as she continued to entice him. "Dean? Who created the devil?"

"God!" He drew the word out, a sigh of pleasure more than the name of his deity.

Natalia smiled. She understood the implication. He was almost hers. "If God created the devil and the devil created pleasure, then couldn't you say that God created the devil in order to create pleasure?"

He whimpered as she massaged his thigh.

"Do you really believe that a deity as powerful and loving as God wouldn't want us to feel pleasure? His first home for us was paradise. He created us to fit within one another. He created us to feel. Don't you want to feel good? Don't you want to know how it feels to lay naked next to a beautiful woman after making mad love to her? Don't you want to know what I feel like?"

She stepped more fully in front of him. She placed her feet to either side of his, as if to straddle him. Her dress was short enough that it wouldn't take much to slip him inside her. That wasn't her goal, but she wanted him to think the possibility existed. Natalia wondered what Vincent thought of all this. "Can you feel me? Can you feel my heat radiating, threatening to consume you? Wouldn't you like to be consumed?"

Vincent stood outside the room, and listened to it all. He balled his hands into fists, and growled as her voice became far more seductive than he wished to hear. He understood what she was doing, but he didn't like it. He ground his teeth as he heard her last words, heard her lean in and kiss the Slayer. With a bellow of frustrated rage, he tore into the room, grabbed his woman and nearly slammed her into the wall. His hand was around her neck; his face centimeters from hers. The growl that emanated from his gullet ran up and down her body. She turned the full intensity of her gaze upon him.

"Never. Do that. Again." As he spoke his angry, jealous words, he exposed his teeth, and showed her his fangs.

She narrowed her eyes, and gave him a seductive look. There was no fear in her eyes. She grabbed his waistband and pulled him closer. Her words were a husky whisper. "Why not? I had fun."

Vincent pulled her away from the wall, grabbed her wrists and trapped her hands. He pulled her arms over her head, and lifted her slightly off the ground to bring her face level with his. "I came down here to chain you to a wall. I think I'll follow through with that threat."

She laughed as he dropped her back to the ground, spun her around and pinned her arms behind her. He herded her to the far wall, as he wanted the Slayers to witness what he did to her. At the wall, he spun her around, and lifted her hands to the shackles. He left her feet free, as he always enjoyed the feel of her legs wrapped around his waist. Once ensnared in the chains, he pressed her into the wall with his body, and gave her a hard kiss.

"Does this excite you, Natalia?" Her thudding heart gave away her answer, but he enjoyed hearing it.

"Very much." Her eyes were closed; her breath came in short gasps. She strained against the chains to touch him. She tried to bring him closer by hooking his leg with hers. But he wasn't moving toward her. In fact, she found he was backing away. Natalia growled in dissatisfaction. She opened her eyes to glare at him. He backed up to the door, and gave her his hyena smile. Her face fell as she contemplated her situation.

"Where are you going?" She sounded more annoyed than angry or afraid.

"Don't fret Natalia. I wouldn't leave you chained in my dungeon unless you were the only one in it. But there's something I must retrieve."

He turned and left the room quickly. In his absence, she realized that Dean repeated lines from the bible in a low voice. It was something about the devil, she couldn't make it out. The other two stared at her with pure hate. She stared back, not the least bit worried. Vincent waltzed back in, the grin still on his face. He held a flail in his right hand, and slapped the thin leather strips in his left. Her heart and breath stopped for a nanosecond then started again, faster than before.

Vincent caught her eye as behind him, Mierka came into the room and took Dean down from the wall. Soon, the basement echoed with screams.

In the main room Natalia's pleasured screams angered the Slayers. In one of the smaller rooms, Dean screamed in damnation as Mierka used different tactics to try and extract information. His voice resonated with pain but he did not break. The third sounds came from the oubliette, where the lamentations of one long forgotten echoed, and tried to be noticed.

20

Hours later, Vincent unchained his love from the wall, as he tried not to bite her. He was hungry and she smelled so good. He could tell that her heartbeat was weak, and she was exhausted. Ever the stubborn warrior, once unchained from the wall, she insisted on standing on her own. He placed her on her feet, tied the top of her dress back around her neck, pulled the bottom down and took a step away. When she stood tall, he nodded, took her arm, and led her out the door. Joseph was nowhere to be seen, but Mierka waited in the hallway. She leaned against the opposite wall, her eternal smirk on her lips.

"Done?" Her voice was light and teased.

"Was there something you wanted?" Vincent didn't sound amused.

"The Slayer wants to see you, Natalia."

"Why?" Natalia wanted to go to bed, not talk with Dean. Every part of her body ached. She wanted to lay in bed next to Vincent and enjoy the memories.

"He says he has some information he won't share with anyone but you." She shrugged to indicate she didn't know what it was.

"Leave it Natalia. He's probably lying." Vincent needed to get some blood. It was well past sunrise.

"He's not lying. He's thoroughly broken."

Vincent shot Mierka a dirty look.

Natalia turned to the large vampire, touched his cheek to gain his attention. "I'm going to talk to him. Get what you need. I'll be up shortly."

"Natalia. I don't trust him." Vincent caressed her cheek. He wanted to pick her up and carry her to their bed. He still had some energy.

"That makes two of us. I can take care of myself, Vincent." She stepped even closer and leaned in for a kiss. Vincent obliged, and released her when she pulled away.

"I'll wait here for you. Call if you need me."

"Us." Mierka leaned even further into the wall. "He's in the next room. The door's open."

Natalia nodded, left the pair, and wondered what Dean wanted to tell her. Behind her Mierka told Vincent to drink from one of the other Slayers, since he was thirsty. Natalia paused at the door to Dean's cell, and quietly watched the praying Slayer. Dean was on his knees, his hands tight around his rosary. He rocked back and forth as tears streamed down his face. His side was to the door. His exposed leg bled.

"Dean."

His head shot up at the sound of her voice, but he stayed on his knees. When he spoke, he sounded like a scared little boy. It brought her no joy. "You've ruined me."

She opened her mouth to respond but had no words. There was no use lying to herself, or to him. She shook her head. "You asked to see me."

"I lied earlier. I never heard the voices. I didn't want the others to know I'm not a Slayer."

"Why are you telling me?" Her confusion was evident in her voice, but she still spoke kindly.

He gave her a sad look and she saw how much he wanted her to understand. Natalia frowned but let down her guard and listened. "When Judith and I found out you were with the Hellspawn, she wanted to kill you. I stopped her from killing you, but she still shot you. I hated her for that. I ran away for a while, thinking I needed to be a warrior for the Slayers." His look grew even more depressed. "I was really mad at you for allowing the others to die, but then after a while realized I was madder because you had escaped, and I didn't."

Her thoughts stilled. "What are you saying, Dean?"

"I'm not a Slayer, never was. I was a vampire hunter for a while, but then I grew up and my anger and grief faded. My kid brother was so young when he was changed, and it made me so fucking angry. But as I met more and more people like Zechariah, I knew I had to get out. Then I heard something that made me want to stay with the Slayers. I was planning on finding as much information as I could and then telling you." He gave her a shy look. "I thought we could join forces." He looked back down at his rosary. "I know that's not going to happen now. I don't want to help vampires. But I still want to tell you what I learned, as long as you make me a promise."

She waited for more, but when he stayed silent, she ground her teeth and prodded him. "I'm listening."

"Come closer. I don't want anyone else to hear me." His voice was almost too low to hear.

Natalia weighed her chances and finally gave in. She was on her guard and knew she could probably knock him out if this were all a ploy, which she didn't feel it was. Also, she knew how to make him scream if he tried to stop her voice. She knelt next to him, but stayed in a tense position, ready to move.

"Kill me."

She pulled away, surprised, but kept her own voice quiet. "What?"

"Let me die a man. It's what I am. Don't let them change me. I don't want that. My kid brother was changed into a vampire. I saw it happen. I don't think I could stand it if I was changed." He hung his head. "It's probably why the angels never chose me. I don't have the strength to be anything but me."

She had no idea what he was talking about and needed to make sure she understood the agreement. "You'll tell me whatever it is you know and then you expect me to kill you?" She shook her head. "I don't understand why you're even trying to tell me anything."

"Because maybe you can stop him. He's a pretender and needs to die. None of us have been able to stop him." He looked into her eyes and gave her a haunted look. "And soon, no one will know he's not what he says."

"Who are you talking about? Vincent?" She sat on the floor now, intrigued, and did not think about her short dress. She accidentally exposed herself, but Dean's eyes never strayed from hers.

Dean shook his head, and untangled the rosary from his fingers. "No. Vincent is what he says he is." He held the rosary out to her. "Promise."

She stared at Dean, to try and see the truth. "You want me to promise I'll kill you on a rosary?"

"Yes. It'll make you keep your promise." He sighed. "Do you still think all creatures are vile Natalia?"

"As a whole, yes. On an individual basis, it depends."

"Take the rosary. Promise me you'll end my misery."

"I don't have any weapons on me."

Dean reached back slowly and scratched his boot. She saw the glint of metal as something slipped into his hand. She tensed, but he simply held the rosary and blade out to her. His hand was palm down, which hid the blade. She could easily lie to him, take the knife and rosary, and leave the room when he was done telling her his secret, but she didn't want to lie. She didn't want Vincent and his lot to use him as they had Zechariah. They had kept him alive for nearly three months. They fed off him and tortured him. She caught Dean's gaze, sighed, and held out her hand. He had helped her on more than one occasion. She would do this to repay his kindness.

The knife and rosary dropped into her hand, and she quickly flipped her hand over to hide the blade. It was as small as the length of her hand but would do the trick. She took a few deep breaths as she rose to her knees.

Natalia had to be careful. There were cameras in here and Mierka would be alerted as soon as she got into position. She would have to answer to Vincent for this but knew she could take whatever he dealt out. A sigh escaped her lips as she knelt beside the Slayer.

"I promise. Who and what is the pretender?"

"The vampire you've been looking for is pretending to be a Slayer."

She reeled back as shock took over. She went pale, as her free hand covered her mouth. Her eyes wide, she finally understood why she hadn't been able to find him. "How?"

"Natalia?" Vincent's concerned voice boomed down the hall.

Natalia knew she didn't have time to ask more questions, but she had so many. She could hear Vincent as he walked down the hall. If she didn't kill Dean now, she would never be able to. Torn between keeping her promise and finding out more, she shut her eyes, and tried to think straight. Her hand strayed to her left breast, and rubbed the scar Vincent created some years ago. If she killed Dean, she would have to answer to Vincent. Also, she could find Donald with Dean's help, but Vincent would treat him as badly or worse than Zechariah had treated her. She looked into Dean's eyes as Vincent called out to her again. Her face a mask of pain and torture she bellowed, threw herself forward and plunged the blade into Dean's heart.

He gasped for air as she twisted the blade and made the wound larger. She had to be sure to kill him. Vincent was in the doorway, asking what had happened, but all she could hear was Dean's dying voice. "Thank you." He breathed a few short times. "Rosary, magic. Liars die."

Dean's eyes rolled into the back of his head, he took one more breath and passed on. Natalia hung her head and pulled the blade out of his body. Vincent pulled her away as he yelled at her. She didn't know what he was saying, and didn't care. Her only source to Donald was dead.

Vincent pulled Natalia out into the hall, and yelled his frustrations. He had no idea why she killed the Slayer and had no idea why that disturbed look was on her face. It was as if her one and only hope had been torn from her very soul. Mierka sat in the cell and felt for the Slayer's pulse. If there was any indication of life, she could turn him, and they could continue to question him. When Mierka shook her head and looked over, Vincent bared his teeth and snarled.

"Natalia. Natalia! Snap out of it. What did he do?" His voice was a cacophony of annoyance, frustration, and concern. He tried to be gentle, but the main Slayer was dead and Mierka had informed him that the other two could not talk. He needed to know what happened in the cell. The microphones hadn't picked anything up; they had spoken too quietly.

Natalia heard her lover, her love, asking her what happened, but she couldn't form the words. He asked her again and his frustration came through far more clearly. Mierka came out of the cell and waved Vincent away as she spoke to him. Natalia still had trouble listening and couldn't make out the exchange between the two vampires. After a few moments, Vincent let Natalia go and Mierka knelt beside her.

Mierka took the human's face in her hands and tried to get her to look into her eyes. When Natalia finally complied, Mierka spoke softly. "What happened, Natalia? What did he do to you?"

Natalia still didn't want to answer, despite the lady's kindness. She knew she had to tell them what happened, they had to know. She was too wrapped up in her own misery to care. Natalia shook her head, and tried to clear it. Self-pity and loathing never helped her do anything. She couldn't even remember the last time she felt this low. She closed her eyes as her jaw tightened. She took a deep breath, then another and another, until she pushed away all dire thoughts. She stood, held her head high and turned to face both Mierka and Vincent.

"He had information for me. Told me that if I killed him to spare him from Zechariah's fate, he'd tell me. He made me promise on his rosary." She handed the rosary out to Mierka. "He said it was magic and that liars die. I'm not sure how it works, so don't make any promises around it."

Mierka gave the rosary a wary look, then held up one finger. She turned, went into the supply room and was back a moment later with a small rectangular metal box. She opened it then held out the box to Natalia. The human gave the scalpels in the box an odd look, then laid the rosary down on top of the knives. Mierka closed the lid and slipped the case into her back pocket.

"No reason to touch it and tempt fate."

Natalia nodded then took a breath as she looked at Vincent. "Dean was a far better man than Zechariah. He helped me survive. I didn't want him to suffer the same fate as Marshal and Zechariah. I accepted the bargain and listened as he told me what happened to Donald."

Mierka made a noise in the back of her throat, but Vincent didn't show any reaction.

"I heard you coming down the hall after he told me Vincent, and I knew I didn't have any time left. Had you come into the room with him still alive, I would've lost my chance. And I was losing my nerve. If I hadn't killed him then, I would never have done it. I wanted more information than he gave me. I took his life to spare him the worse fate."

"Where did you get the weapon?" Mierka questioned her; Vincent was dead silent and presented her with his back to look inside the cell.

"He had it on him, in his boot."

"We weren't done with him." Mierka, oddly enough, still spoke kindly.

"Neither was I." There were tears in Natalia's eyes, anger in her voice. "But there are two other Slayers you can interrogate. You can get the information you need from them."

"No, we can't." Mierka sounded annoyed.

Natalia looked confused. "What?"

"The other Slayers had their tongues cut out. By the scars, it looks like they did it a long time ago. They can't tell us anything. And our interrogation practice doesn't lend itself to people writing out their answers to our questions."

Natalia was taken aback. She read of the ritual tongue removal but thought it had faded with time. It was popular with a group of Slayers during colonial times; used to ensure no one could tell their secrets when accused of being witches. Stunned, Natalia opened her mouth to speak, but Vincent beat her to it.

"Enough. Go upstairs Natalia. I'll join you shortly." There was no emotion in his voice.

Natalia looked at Vincent's inscrutable back, but could read nothing from his posture. She nodded once to Mierka, left the dungeon, and used Vincent's pass code to exit. She walked proudly upstairs, and wondered at her punishment.

C3  €O

When Vincent finally came upstairs an hour later, he found Natalia leaning against the bedroom window. She had showered and changed. She was in her off white silk robe, and her hair was loose upon her shoulders. She looked as if she waited to be reprimanded. She looked beautiful. It had been a long night and had continued as a long day. It was almost noon. He and Natalia spent more time in the dungeon than he anticipated. He and Mierka drank enough blood from the Slayers to be able to stay awake and take care of Dean. They threw his lifeless body into the oubliette. The ghul would take care of the remains.

Vincent stood by the door, and watched Natalia as she stared out the window. He came upstairs thinking of what to do next; how much punishment he had to dole out. Now, as his eyes roamed her tense form, he knew he had no desire to do so. Too many things had happened today. He undressed silently, and wondered if she heard him enter the room as she still had not turned around. Naked, he moved toward her, and called softly to her.

Natalia let the curtain drop to hide the sun, and turned from the window. She readied herself for a lecture, as she knew she had stepped out of line for killing Dean. She knew Vincent's rules, knew she had no right to kill the Slayer, knew he would punish her. When she locked eyes with her lover, she frowned, not sure what was going on. He was nude, and the look in his eyes was far from what she expected.

He was in front of her now, and enfolded her in his arms. He leaned into her and nuzzled her neck softly. He felt her tense as he nibbled her neck, but relaxed a bit as she realized he wasn't using his fangs. She pulled away just the same and tried to look in his eyes.

"Vincent. I-"

He pressed his lips to hers, to silence her. He pulled away, caressed her cheek, and peered deep into her eyes. "Hush, Natalia. No more words. It's been a long night and day. I want to be in our bed, sleeping, not arguing."

"I did something that deserves punishment, Vincent. I know what you-"

He silenced her again, and spoke softly. "No more Natalia. No more words." His hand went into her hair, to feel the velvetiness of her dark tresses. "Too much has happened today, and I want it done with. There is no need to finish this because it is done."

Natalia gave him a look as if to argue, and he silenced her by pressing two fingers to her open lips.

"If we must, we'll speak tonight. No more now, Natalia, I beseech you."

Natalia looked deep into her lover's eyes, and searched for clues to his mood. All she saw was a deep exhaustion and knew there was no deception. It had been a long day: Edwin knew of her, she had confessed her feelings to Vincent and herself, had been confronted by a ghost, then incapacitated him to save her people. Not to mention the loss of Jesse, finding out about Donald, and killing her only link to the information. She leaned into Vincent, and allowed all her tension to melt away. His arms wrapped around her tighter for a moment, then he let her go to pick her up. He kissed her all the way to the bed, but pulled away only to lay her down. He was beside her quickly, untied her robe, and pulled the silk from her willing body.

"I thought you wanted to sleep." There was humor in her voice.

"I changed my mind. Do you object?" His hand moved slowly down her torso, and caressed her soft skin.

"Not in the least."

She pulled his head down for another kiss and lost herself in the slowness of his movements. It was rare when they took things slow, but they did that day. They touched and caressed each other gently until they climaxed. When they were done, they lay in each other's arms, and satisfaction lulled them to sleep.

Natalia lay in the circle of his cooling arms, and felt as his body stole her heat. She wondered what he would do to her when he decided she needed to be punished for her arguable betrayal. He moved slightly in his sleep, and trapped her further as his arms tightened around her. She leaned into the frigidness of him, closed her eyes and let it all go. He would do as he saw fit and she would accept it. She killed Dean to keep him from suffering at the hands of the vampires in the house. She would take her punishment with her head held high. She would do it all over again if she had the chance. Her mind at ease, Natalia fell asleep.

21

The evening came with less confidence as Natalia woke to an empty bed. It was sometime after sunset. The curtains were drawn, but no light came through the windows. There was a knock at the door, and she realized that was what woke her in the first place.

"Come in." Her voice was groggy and hoarse, but the door opened just the same. Mierka came in, a tray of food in her hands. Natalia sat up in bed and pulled the sheet with her to cover her body. "What's going on?"

"You've been summoned."

Natalia frowned. Vincent rarely summoned her. If he needed her, he usually came to her, especially when she was in bed. "By whom?"

"Edwin."

"That was quick." Her face fell and she seemed bored. "So why the food?"

"You're not hungry?"

"I would think Edwin would demand I get down to see him as soon as he asked."

Mierka set the tray on the end of the bed, fetched the chair from the wall and set it with the tray to Natalia's left. She went to the window and leaned against it with her arms crossed and studied Natalia. "Do you want to do as he asks?"

"I would rather not get Vincent in trouble."

Mierka shrugged. "Vincent asked me to bring you food."

Natalia turned and sat up on the edge of the bed to check out the plate of food. There was a large sandwich and a glass of orange juice. She opened up the sandwich; saw lettuce, tomatoes and a thick cut of cooked meat, probably mutton. Since Vincent owned sheep farms, it was usually the main meat in the house. She picked up the sandwich, took a bite and enjoyed the flavor. Bite done, she turned to Mierka, who studied her with that slight smile.

"What?"

"Do you wish to be changed, Natalia?"

"Eventually." She took another bite of sandwich, not sure where Mierka was headed.

"Have you ever thought about what you would do if something were to happen to Vincent before he changed you?"

Natalia swallowed her bite of sandwich. It went down hard, as it was only half chewed. She put the sandwich down, took a swallow of orange juice and placed the glass down on the tray. She stared at Mierka. "No, I haven't."

Mierka unfolded her arms and languidly walked toward Natalia. She stood in front of her and leaned toward the human's right ear. She placed her hands on Natalia's shoulders to steady herself. She felt Natalia tense as she touched her.

"Remember this name: Jacqueline de la Fontaine. It was my first name." She pulled back slightly, kissed both of Natalia's cheeks, then pulled back to stand in front of her. "If anything happens to Vincent while you're human, come to me and ask for my protection using that name. You will always have a place with me, Natalia."

She left and did not let Natalia say a word. It took a moment for Natalia to comprehend what just happened. Thrown off by the declaration, she ate the rest of the sandwich and drank the orange juice without tasting either. It felt strange to hear the declaration now, after the events of last night. She took a deep breath, stood with pride, and held her head high. She then readied herself for her conversation with Edwin.

As she stood to flex and stretch, she thought about what to wear and wondered what would be appropriate. Vincent's words about her to Edwin last night came back to her and she smirked. She knew exactly what to wear. Natalia grabbed the silk robe off the bed, swung it on and walked out of the bedroom while tying the robe. At the door, she turned back and went to her nightstand. Natalia grabbed her cell. If she were about to confront Edwin, she wanted to know who would be in the security room. She dialed the number for the room and Joseph picked up.

"Odd time for a call."

"Not really. Who else is in the room with you?"

"Orlando. Should there be someone else?"

"If he's available, have Charlie watch with you. Give Orlando a break."

"I can do that. One moment."

She heard Joseph ask for Charlie's whereabouts to Orlando but didn't hear the response. A moment later, Joseph came back on the line.

"He's being fetched. Is there a reason this needs to happen?"

Natalia liked that he asked this after he followed her order. She didn't have to give Joseph a reason, and only gave him a partial one. "I need people watching who know me and won't reveal what happens."

"Charlie's not known for secrecy."

"He holds many of my secrets." She said with confidence.

"He's in the room. Proceed when ready."

"Thank you. Goodbye." She hung up before he could say any more. Natalia took a deep breath, put her phone on the nightstand and left the room.

From the top of the stairs, she saw three vampires standing by the door to the small meeting room. She went down the steps slowly, and assessed the three. Anthony, Morgan, and another man were arrayed in front of the door to the meeting room. Morgan sat in a huff on the stone bench outside the room. Anthony stood at the bottom of the steps, and spoke with the other man. She didn't recognize the third one but was slightly unnerved by him. He was dressed in biker leather and tried to appear intimidating. He eyed her as if she were a piece of meat. She narrowed her eyes as she approached, and gave him a defiant look. It just made him grin. She flounced by him and ignored him. Anthony grabbed her arm as she passed.

"That's not appropriate attire."

"You have no say in what I wear, vampire."

She pulled away from Anthony, and continued into the room, where Vincent and Edwin sat at a long conference table. Vincent sat at the head, and Edwin was to his right, his back to the door. She slammed the door behind her, to block the others out. Vincent hid his smile behind his hand as she came toward them. Edwin turned and assessed her. He liked the way she looked. She was a gorgeous creature.

With a leer on his lips and a twinkle in his eye, Edwin leaned back in his chair and addressed the older vampire. He watched Vincent very carefully to catch his reaction: to try and find out what Vincent really thought of this human. Was she just a good lay, or did he feel something for her?

"It is unbelievable how you always end up with the choice meat. How do you get so lucky?"

Vincent tried hard to hide his reaction. The hand at his mouth hid the twitch in his jaw, but he was unable to hide the slight narrowing of his eyes. Natalia answered for him though, and Vincent let her. It would be interesting to see these two argue.

"The women in this house are not only beautiful, we're smart as well. It's how we know Vincent is a better choice than you could ever hope to be."

Edwin turned his head to look Natalia up and down again. She had paused when he spoke to Vincent, but now she started to walk again, and moved to Vincent's right. Edwin continued to watch her every move as she carefully sat in the chair. He raised his eyebrows as she placed her legs on the table but made sure her robe stayed on her legs.

"You sure have a mouth on you. Is there anything else you would like to do with that mouth?"

"Not to you." She spoke with a polite tone of voice.

He looked her up and down again, and traced her body with his eyes. "You're a beautiful woman. It would be such a pleasure to let one of my humans impregnate you. It would be such a joy to touch your children and make you watch."

She didn't even blink. "You have humans?"

He knocked his knuckles on the table, as he tried to rattle her. There had to be something that would get that smug look off her face. "That's what I'm going to do. I'm going to take you home and use you for children. I'll keep the girls and use any boys you give me for blood."

Natalia threw her head back and laughed. She didn't feel it necessary to tell Edwin she couldn't have children. "Did you jerk off this evening with that handkerchief I threw at you yesterday, Edwin? Understand this: that handkerchief is the only thing I will ever give you."

Darkness crossed his features, but only for a moment. He turned to a still silent Vincent and wondered when he would intervene. Vincent sat in his chair, and smiled as smugly as Natalia. He needed to take both of them down a notch; maybe more.

Edwin turned back to Natalia. "Don't think for a moment that I can't take you."

"You can try, but you won't succeed. I would escape before you realized."

Edwin turned to her and gave her a malicious grin. "You will come with me willingly, if I order Vincent to give you to me."

She shook her head. "Edwin, I'm my own person. If you order Vincent to give me to you, I'll leave him." Her eyes and voice grew hard. "Then, I'll be my own person, free to kill you when and how I want, unrestrained by the rules of the two vampire societies that reside in the Bay Area. Then, once you're dead, I'll return to Vincent."

He glared at her for a moment. "You both think you're better than me. You aren't. Despite what you may think, I'm still in charge of this area. I will have you." A thought exploded in his head and his eyes brightened. "I'll have you now. I'm going to bend you over this table and take you now," he gestured toward Vincent with his head, "in front of him."

Natalia smiled a slow sure smile. It grew very seductive as she placed her hand on her chest and drew her hand slowly to her neck. Edwin licked his lips involuntarily. Her neck and shoulders were scarred. He wanted to add to those scars. His eyes followed her hand as it traveled further up her neck to stop at her necklace. A small smile came to his lips as he understood that he was going to have this woman, no matter what she and Vincent thought.

CR BO

Anthony didn't like Morgan. He liked the vampire Dex even less, but knew he had to keep them entertained. Vincent wanted time alone with Edwin, but now that Natalia was in the room as well, he felt someone should be watching. Joseph was in the security room, but Anthony preferred when there were two watching. One to watch and one to sound the alarm when necessary.

As it was, Joseph was alone in the security room but was more than able to sound the alarm. Anthony didn't trust Natalia and felt he, or one of his men, should watch her actions. Vincent didn't feel this was required; therefore, Anthony was stuck in the foyer, with vampires that weren't worth his time. He tried to start a conversation with Dex, but it was impossible. The man had no intelligence.

"We just need to change all humans so that we have true control of the city."

"And who would we drink from?" Morgan sounded as if he had discussed this with the biker before.

"Each other."

Anthony and Morgan exchanged glances. The elder vampire answered as Morgan didn't look like he wanted to say anything more. "We gain better sustenance from humans. If we change them all, then we have less food. And it would bring far more Slayers into the area."

The biker shrugged. "Slayers are easy to kill."

"Not if they're in large groups."

"My group can take any Slayer down."

Before Anthony could say anything more, all turned to look toward the meeting room door. The sounds from the meeting room concerned him. Anthony frowned and took a step closer to the door. He wasn't going to enter the room, but he didn't want anyone else going in either.

All three in the foyer raised their eyebrows when Natalia let out a loud, "No!"

Anthony rushed to the door, stood in front of it, and faced the other two men. "Whatever happens, it's not our business."

Though he staunchly faced down the other men, he wanted to go into the room. He didn't like Natalia, but that word didn't sound right. They heard her again and Anthony stood his ground. The only thing that stopped him from going through the door was that Joseph hadn't told him to do so.

"Vincent! No! Please don't let him do this to me!"

Natalia's usually pleasant if not smug voice was, well, terrified. It shook Anthony to the bone. He didn't like the sound, but he understood what it meant. Edwin was taking something from Natalia that she didn't want to give, and she wasn't fighting back. Vincent was allowing Edwin what he wanted. Her voice came through the door again and Dex grinned as if he enjoyed the sound of Natalia's voice. Anthony's hands formed into fists, but his training kept him from punching the younger vampire with all his might. His loathing for the man increased tenfold. Natalia's voice came again.

"NO! Please! Vincent! Stop!"

The biker moved forward, and Anthony put his hands on the man's chest to stop him.

"Just let me see what he's doing to her." He looked Anthony in the eye. "I like to watch."

A new voice came from the hallway near the security room. "No one's going in there."

Anthony and Dex turned to the new voice. Charlie stood in the hallway, a mad gleam in his eye.

Dex took a step toward Charlie and tried to intimidate him. "I do what I want."

Charlie grinned and started to change to Blitzkrieg form. Anthony answered for the werewolf.

"In this house, you listen to our rules." Anthony, glad for Charlie's presence, mostly hid a smile as he continued to talk to Dex. "If they wanted us in the room, we would have been invited." He indicated the fully changed Blitzkrieg with his head. "If you're not happy with the situation, he would be more than happy to remind you that you are a guest in this house and not in charge."

Behind them, Natalia cried out again. There was a decidedly male grunt followed by a harsh laugh. The men in the foyer seemed to relax. The Blitzkrieg stayed nearby, to make sure everyone understood no one had access to the room.

After a few more moments, the Blitzkrieg turned back to Charlie. He smiled pleasantly at those gathered and trotted down the hallway toward the security room. A moment later, the door to the meeting room opened. Edwin came out first, adjusted his belt and grinned from ear to ear. Dex gave Edwin a huge grin, clapped him on the back and whispered to him as they walked to the front door. Morgan shook his head and left with the other two. Anthony looked back to the meeting room door as Natalia and Vincent appeared. He nodded to Vincent, looked away then looked back.

Anthony expected Vincent to act oddly as Edwin just used his woman for his pleasure. The look on Vincent's face though, did not match what Anthony expected. The front door closed fully, and a smug, triumphant look exploded on Vincent's face. He took Natalia in his arms and gave her a kiss Anthony didn't want to witness. He looked away and waited to be noticed.

Vincent broke from the kiss before he was ready and turned to

Anthony. "Thank you for keeping his men entertained. If you have nothing else for me this evening, you may leave."

"Sir. What happened?" Anthony looked to Natalia to see if her expression would reveal anything. It did not. The human wore the same smug, triumphant look on her face as Vincent. Something had happened to their favor and Anthony had no idea what.

Vincent still had his arms around Natalia. The look on her face was priceless. He loved to see that look on her face: as if every secret in the world were hers. Vincent's smile grew a little. She held at least one of the world's greatest secrets. He turned to Anthony briefly, but turned back to Natalia to answer. "What happened isn't your concern, Anthony. Don't fret. All will be revealed in time." He leaned in and kissed Natalia. "Are you ready to venture back upstairs?"

"Will you be making up for what happened in there? That was fun but not as good as it could have been." Her voice was sly and held nothing but secrets.

"I aim to please you, as always."

"Join me quickly." Natalia broke away from him, walked slowly to the stairs and then up them.

Vincent turned one more time to Anthony. "As I stated, Anthony. Don't fret. All will be revealed in time."

Anthony shook his head as Vincent left his side to follow the human up the stairs and into their bedroom. As he snarled frustration, Anthony stormed down to the security room. Joseph was the only one in the room.

"Report."

Joseph looked up from the desk chair and raised one eyebrow. "No."

"What?" His anger threatened to overwhelm him.

"There is nothing to report, therefore, I will not report."

"What happened in that room, Joseph?"

"As you stated to the others earlier, if you were meant to know, you would have been allowed in the room."

"As his Information Gatherer, I have a right to know what happened."

Joseph stood and bowed. "If the Master of this House wishes you to know what happened, you will know what happened. As of this moment, my orders were to allow no one to see this recording. And no one will until my Master tells me differently. If you do not like his orders, I suggest you take that up with him."

"Natalia didn't act as if Edwin forced himself on her. She did something, didn't she?"

"And now the truth comes out. You're more worried about what she may have done than about what Edwin may have done."

"I don't trust her."

Joseph raised an eyebrow. "That doesn't change Vincent's orders."

Anthony glared at Vincent's bodyguard, but could do nothing. Joseph would never allow him to look at the recording or give him any information that Vincent did not want him to have. Until this moment, it had never been an issue. The two vampires stared each other down to the inevitable conclusion. Joseph smirked to himself when Anthony left.

Outside the security room, Anthony stood and thought about chasing down the werewolf. He shook his head and started toward the front door. Charlie would laugh in his face if ordered to report to him. Defeated for the moment, Anthony left Vincent's house and climbed into his limo. He instructed the driver and settled in for the ride home.

22

On the ride home, Anthony kept replaying the scene in his mind. In the room, Natalia sounded as if she were hurt. The smug look on Vincent's face and on her face once Edwin left suggested otherwise. He didn't know how that was possible, though. They could have tricked Edwin, but he wasn't sure how. The drive wasn't overly long, as traffic was light, but Anthony thought about it the entire time. He also thought about Charlie and Joseph's reactions. Though Joseph followed Vincent almost without thought, Anthony doubted the bodyguard would allow anyone to rape Natalia.

And the werewolf... Charlie protected Natalia better than he protected Vincent. If she had been hurt, Charlie would not have allowed it. Anthony thought back to Charlie's attitude before he turned Blitzkrieg. Charlie looked to be enjoying the situation, as if he were laughing. Anthony hit his hand against his thigh. The entire incident frustrated him. Despite his own thoughts about Natalia, he knew those in Vincent's household held her in high regard. They wouldn't allow any harm to come to her. He also knew that Vincent would never allow another man, especially a man like Edwin, to touch her. There had to be something.

Anthony shook his head. Every time he tried to puzzle her out, it was as if a wall came up in his mind. As if there was a block. He wasn't too worried about it but knew that if he could think around the block, he would have his answer. The car slowed and stopped. When the engine died, Anthony looked out the window. He was home. As he didn't want to wait for the driver, Anthony opened the door and disembarked. Julia waited for him on the front steps. There was enough streetlight to see by, but not much else.

"I didn't know when you'd be home. I just got back."

"I wasn't sure when I would be home either."

"You look troubled."

He walked up the steps and kissed her lightly. "Perhaps. Come inside. I don't want to talk out here."

Julia nodded and opened the door for him. The house was in Noe Valley. As with most of San Francisco, the houses were right next to each other. Most homes looked like they shared walls. Long before prices grew out of hand in the area, Anthony purchased three houses right next to each other. He lived in the middle house, and his humans lived in the ones to each side. They built connecting doorways and short tunnels to allow humans to visit without being seen by nosy neighbors.

"You're deep in thought, aren't you?"

Anthony drew himself out of his thoughts and saw they were in his study. "I suppose. Were you talking to me?"

"I asked if you needed to feed."

He shook his head as he sat down. "Not just yet."

She pulled out her cell. "I'll text and let them know."

He grunted but said nothing. There was no need. Once she was done, she sat at one of the chairs at the desk.

"What's going on? You have a strange look on your face."

He took a deep breath. "From what you've seen, would you say that Vincent would ever allow Edwin to touch Natalia?"

She smirked. "Doesn't matter what Vincent wants, Natalia would never allow it. She doesn't seem like the kind of woman that would put up with that, no matter what."

"I saw something tonight that perplexes me. Or rather, I heard Natalia screaming for help in the meeting room. Vincent and Edwin were with her. Joseph and Charlie were in the security room. They saw what happened, I'm sure of it, but they didn't try to stop it."

An odd look came to Julia's face as she shook her head. "I don't…"

He looked into her eyes as she trailed off. "Finish your thought."

"That doesn't seem possible."

He shook his head. "It doesn't, does it?"

"No one will tell you what happened?"

"No. At the end of it, Vincent and Natalia had smug looks on their faces. Vincent told me all would be revealed in time. Natalia sounded fine, not like a person violated. She asked Vincent to join her in bed. Joseph told me to mind my own business."

"What about Charlie? How did he act?"

"He looked like he was enjoying a good joke. And I will not ask him what happened as he would laugh at me if I asked him anything." He leaned back in his chair. "What do you think?"

"Something happened, but I don't know what."

They were silent for long enough that a thought popped into his mind. "You were finding out about Morgan and Kari. Tell me what you found."

"You don't sound like you're done thinking about Natalia."

"I'm not, but I have to report to Vincent about those two."

"I found Morgan easily enough. He was born in San Jose. I found an article on him around the time he was changed, probably. His family reported him missing, and then there was an article saying he was found. He hasn't been a vampire for long. I have everything I could find on him in a file, paper and computer."

"Good."

"Kari is a different matter altogether."

He frowned. "Oh?"

"I can't find anything on her, but then, I don't know what her original name is. If she was changed before she came to this area, we may not be able to find much on her. Maybe if we got her fingerprints?"

He held up his hand to negate her last thought. "Keep looking. You might find something."

"It's harder to find people when they live off the grid as most vampires do."

He made a noncommittal noise in the back of his throat.

"What are you going to tell Vincent?"

"I'll tell him what you found. And I'll look for information on her as well."

She paused for a moment, then prodded. "And Natalia?"

Anthony shifted in his chair until he was comfortable. He leaned back and stared off into the distance. "I don't trust her."

"Have you ever found anything on her?"

"When Vincent first expressed an interest in her, I found all I could. She had many aliases, but the name she gave Vincent was the real one. I have uncovered many of her secrets, but I feel there is something I'm missing. Something obvious. I don't know if Vincent knows all her secrets, either."

Julia sighed heavily and shook her head.

He turned his head sharply to look at Julia when she sighed. "You think I'm wrong, don't you?"

She looked at Anthony with love in her eyes. "Does it matter? I'll do as you want on this, Anthony."

He turned his chair and faced her; his hands folded in front of him on the desk. "Do you trust her?"

She reached up to Tina's necklace. She had worn it since the day Natalia brought it back to her. "It's hard for me not to."

"Did you ever consider that she took the necklace and killed Theodore in order to gain your trust and nothing more?"

"To what end? We barely see each other, and I love you. I'll do as you ask, and I'll follow you. Not her."

He gazed into her eyes, as a smile tried to form on his lips. There was too much to think of though. Anthony turned away from Julia to look out the window.

Julia looked down at her hands for a few minutes and finally gave him advice. Her voice was soft as if she didn't want to make the suggestion. "Why don't you have her followed?"

"That could be disastrous. If Vincent found out…"

"Anthony, your job is to protect Vincent. If he's being duped, you need to find out."

"Do you really think I should have her followed?"

"No, but someone needed to say it."

He turned back to her and sighed. "She looks for that. In the past, when someone tried to follow her, she was able to throw the person off her scent."

"What about Wayne?"

Anthony opened his mouth to refute the idea and paused. Wayne was changed two years ago. Before that, he had been in the Air Force, Special Ops. A friend of Anthony's found him about a year after he was changed. At the time, Wayne didn't fully understand what had been done to him. Despite his desire for solitude, Wayne nevertheless allowed Anthony to help him get back on his feet. For the moment, he was a spy in Anthony's network. Wayne had been a Navy SEAL. Natalia trained for seven years with ex-military people.

Anthony thought about it for a good long time, then slowly nodded. "That might work."

"I know I suggested it, but I don't think it's a good idea. He's good, but if she's shaken people off her tail in the past, she might know he's there, too."

"I know, but he's read her file. If anyone can follow her, I'm sure he can."

She shook her head, then looked at him and nodded once. "All right. Do you want to give him instructions or shall I?"

"I'll take care of it. I want to make sure he understands what's at stake."

She nodded and stood. "Do you need anything else?"

He reached for his cell in his inner pocket. "When he gets here, let him in. I'll be working on other things, but I want to talk to him as soon as possible."

"Yes, sir."

He looked up at the sound of her voice. It was more pleasant than it had been before. She smiled at him, and he smiled back. For a moment they looked at each other, and simply enjoyed being near each other. Julia blushed before too long and left the room. Anthony dialed Wayne's number and felt as if victory were in his hands. Perhaps soon, he would have the information he needed to prove Natalia was a danger to Vincent and his people.

Chapter One from Protector of the Grey House follows…

1

Vincent stared out the window of his study, and tried to peer into the darkness beyond the limits of his sight. Natalia was gone. She had been missing for three days now, and he was worried. His men had started to notice, as he yelled more and was short even with the delicate humans who ran his house.

Two years ago, after she killed Dean, she started hunting for confirmation of the information he gave her. In order to find any information, she came into contact with more and more Slayers. Consequently, she fought them and came home with bruises. She also came home with names, locations and sometimes, items that would otherwise be used against him and his people. He didn't want to tell her to stop. Her actions protected his house, but she found herself in more and more dangerous situations.

Natalia told him that she often had to infiltrate groups of Slayers. Before, it was one at a time. Now she often spoke with three or four at a time. She told Vincent she took care of the Slayers cautiously and avoided going against Slayers in groups all at once. Still, she started training for the inevitable. She fought his vampires two or three at a time. Vincent didn't care for these sessions but allowed it, as she needed the practice. It didn't help that Joseph and Mierka both thought she was doing a worthy job and helped to push the human to her limit and beyond. Joseph fought her often and Mierka gave her pointers on stealth tactics.

Joseph and Mierka believed she had a right to fight and train as if she were her own army. She fought Slayers and had to watch her back for Edwin's men, too. Edwin finally had his coronation, without the presence of Vincent and his men. He ignored them for the better part of a year, then had taken an interest in Vincent's businesses again. It was all part of the plan. If Edwin was interested in the human aspect of Vincent's world, he would not be interested in what Vincent's vampires were doing.

"No word from your spies?" He aimed the question at Anthony's reflection.

"No sir." Anthony told him about having her followed when she did not return after the second day. Vincent was angry, but not surprised. He took the information in stride and asked for any information. Unfortunately, Wayne had not reported for four days.

"Still don't understand why you had her followed." Mierka was aggravated, which was rare for her. It showed the men in the room how angry and worried she really was about the situation.

"Calm yourself Mierka, he was only doing his job." Vincent turned from the window, and regarded the only silent one in the room. As always, Joseph kept his opinions to himself, until he had Vincent's ear only. Since he wondered at his loyal friend's thoughts, he caught Mierka and Anthony's gazes. "Leave us. Go and train. We'll join you shortly."

The two left without a word; this was not a new situation. Joseph stepped out of the corner he almost hid in and poured himself a glass of brandy from the mini bar.

"You never ask my permission." Vincent accepted the glass Joseph handed him.

"I gave you a case of this." His voice grew soft. "Though only you know where it is."

Vincent was silent for a moment, still annoyed. "What do you think of Anthony's actions?"

"I think it's time you told him the truth of his first meeting with Natalia. It might be better if he knew why he didn't trust her."

"Do you think he would trust her if he knew?" Vincent set the untouched glass on the windowsill next to him.

"Possibly." Joseph slowly spun his glass, to allow the brandy to breathe.

"Then I will keep my secret."

"Why? After seven years with her, why have one of your top men be suspicious of her?"

"Keeps me from having to." Vincent strolled to his desk, but left his glass on the windowsill.

"Emily was human for far less time than that, and you had more reason to distrust her, yet no one followed her."

Vincent smiled at the name, and pulled his key ring out of his pocket as a vision of the lovely lady came to him. She was blond with green eyes, of average height and very shapely. Emily was as beautiful as Natalia, almost as smart, but had no desire to fight. "None of the women I've loved have been like Natalia. Natalia is smart, beautiful, and dangerous. Perhaps I want to make sure I know what I'm getting myself into."

"Even after seven years?"

"She's hunting a vampire and is still human. She will one day catch the vampire, but what happens when she does? Will she stay with us, ask to be turned, or will she leave and turn Slayer? None of us know and we won't know until her quest is finished."

"Is that why you haven't shown her your actual bedroom?"

"Among other reasons, as you know." He gave Joseph a pointed look.

Joseph raised his eyebrows. "You could remove those items."

"They would cause more trouble elsewhere."

Joseph said nothing as Vincent turned his attention back to the desk. He pulled open the drawer he had unlocked and pulled out a flat red velvet box. He looked down at the box, then presented it to Joseph.

"I suppose this won't make any sense to you or Mierka." His stoic expression was broken by a glint of trepidation in his eyes.

Joseph saw the odd look and wondered about it and the statement. Though the head vampire asked for Joseph's opinion on a regular basis, he never acted as if it mattered. Curiosity filled him as he placed his glass on the desk, took the jewelry case, and opened it slowly. Inside lay a silver necklace with a crimson stone pendant. There was a delicate silver inlay of a sword pointed down. The hilt was a fleur-de-lis and two lilies wound their way up the sword. "You mean to give her rank."

"She deserves it. She's been protecting us all for a lot of years and has given us more Slayer weapons than I thought existed. She may be doing all this to find the one she wants to kill, but it has been to our benefit."

A smile came to Joseph's face as he understood Vincent's nervousness. "And you're happy to have her in your life."

Vincent gave him a sardonic look as Joseph closed the box and handed it back. "That was not a factor in my decision, and you know it."

A twitch of a smile came to his lips. "Of course not. But if she has rank and knows how important she is to you, perhaps she'll stay after she kills Donald."

Vincent was silent as he locked the box back in his drawer. He looked to Joseph. "One can hope."

Joseph nodded. "When do you plan on presenting this to her?"

"Next time I see her."

Joseph nodded, picked up his glass, fetched Vincent's off the windowsill and presented the untouched liquor to his master. The two toasted to Natalia, and hoped for her quick return. They finished off the liquid, exited the study, and joined the others in the training room.

C<3 &O

It was three hours later, and the training session was at an end. Joseph and Mierka spent the better part of that time battling Vincent to help him work out his frustrations. He fought Mierka last, which proved to be a mistake. She had riled him up plenty. With Natalia still missing, he considered taking the lady to his bed. He had approached Mierka to ask her when the double doors of the front entrance slammed open.

Angry steps announced her approach. Vincent waited in anticipation for Natalia to walk through the doors and into his arms. She stepped through the door, gave everyone a dirty look, then stood still, as vehemence rolled off her in waves. She was dressed in hospital scrubs and wore men's shoes on her feet. She locked eyes with someone, Vincent couldn't tell who, and snarled. With a bellow of rage, she ran at Anthony with all her speed.

Anthony was too stunned to move and simply let her hit him. He allowed her to knock him to the ground. She straddled him, balled her hands into fists and hit him, over and over. Mierka pulled her off and held her back as Vincent pulled Anthony to his feet, none the worse for wear. Natalia tried hard to pull away from Mierka, despite the vampire's strength.

Vincent turned to her after he dusted Anthony off. "Mind explaining what that was about?"

"Did you know?" Her voice shook with unbridled wrath. "DID YOU KNOW?"

Upon seeing her, Vincent had wanted nothing more than to take her in his arms. Now he understood that would have to wait. "Know what Natalia?"

"That he sent a spy after me?" She managed to calm her voice, but only a little.

"I was informed two days ago, when it became apparent you and Wayne were missing." He stood in front of her and Mierka, and indicated Mierka should let Natalia go. He reached out and held on to Natalia's arms, to restrain some of her agitation. She calmed noticeably after he spoke. "What happened to you?"

Natalia sagged against him; she believed his words. He was known to lie to his people, but she didn't see any indication of that in his eyes. She pulled away, still upset with the events of the past three days. She looked Vincent in the eye and started her tale. "I found a group of Slayers four months ago who seemed to know a great deal about the other Slayers in the Bay Area. They'd been around and for some reason or another decided to catalogue their brethren. It helped them to decide who was best for what job or some nonsense. There was a core group of four Slayers, all of whom lived in the city and shared an apartment. It took me three months of meetings for them to trust me."

Natalia pushed away from Vincent and started to pace back and forth. She stared at Anthony with loathing the whole time. "The Slayers knew who I was, or rather, what I was. They had heard of the dark-haired human who slept with the powerful vampire. Some even knew me as Jeffery

Tathers' did: The One Walking the Edge. Lucky for me, these Slayers wanted to know why I was with you and why some of their own couldn't see me as Hellspawn. What kind of twisted human would sleep with a vampire who allowed his followers to torture and kill innocent children? I told them the truth.

"I told them about Edwin, and all his friends. They didn't believe me, so I went back to Theodore's on a hunch. His house hadn't been touched in years, but his trophies were still there. I took the Slayers there and showed them the wall and the pictures. In some of those pictures stood Edwin, performing atrocities on the young humans."

She paused as the words sunk in. Anthony was glad that Julia, for a change, was not present. She didn't need to be reminded of what Theodore, and possibly Edwin, had done to her young niece. His thoughts were brought back to the present as Natalia started to talk again.

"They believed me. They still didn't understand why a human hunting a vampire would sleep with a vampire. I told them I was lying to you and biding my time until Edwin could be killed. My plan was to wait until the worst of your kind was dead then kill you and yours when it was safe to. They loved the plan; wanted to help eliminate Edwin's group. I pointed them toward his lot, telling them where to find his people and their holdings.

"They passed along the information to those willing to do the dirty work and continued to talk to me. They finally allowed me to look at their information. I didn't tell them what I was really looking for. I told them one of their Slayers had information I needed to find Donald, but that I only had a description. Three days ago, I was supposed to meet with them to read the names of those they cataloged."

She paused again. Vincent went to stand behind her and placed a restraining hand on her shoulder. She looked as if she wanted to pounce on Anthony. "I went. I had no desire to hurt the Slayers; they gathered knowledge, not bodies. I arrived at their apartment and Wayne was there, tied to the wall. There were six Slayers there I had never met, along with the four that I had been talking to. The six new ones were dressed in tight comfortable clothing, like we do when we spar here. I figured them for warriors, rather than information gatherers. Apparently, Wayne didn't know not to look through Slayer's windows. The four I knew had seen him and called reinforcements. When I arrived, two of the warriors grabbed my arms. I let them, as I wanted to understand what was going on. I recognized Wayne but wasn't sure why he was there."

She ground her teeth and her hands formed into fists. "They spent the next few hours cutting his skin off in thin strips. When he wouldn't talk, they fed him my blood." Vincent's hand tightened on her shoulder. Anthony glanced away from her to watch Vincent's reaction. The lead vampire revealed no emotions, therefore Anthony once again captured Natalia's gaze. He listened to her story, to try and find any lies.

"He healed himself and they pulled his skin off again. Halfway through, he broke. Told them I was sleeping with Vincent but that his own boss didn't trust me. He had been sent to spy on me to reveal my betrayal so that I could be exposed. At this point, they stopped interrogating him. His words helped my story, and I felt we would both be able to escape with our lives."

Natalia closed her eyes and shook her head. "I hoped we would both escape with our lives." She took another breath and glared at Anthony. "After a few minutes of silence, Wayne started to speak again. They weren't doing anything to him. They hadn't fed him again, but they were leaving him alone. He told them what I had done to try and convince Vincent of my loyalty. The Slayers weren't pleased to learn that I killed their kind. They had stopped interrogating him at that point. There was no reason for Wayne to keep talking. So why did he? Did you tell him to sell me out? Do you want to get rid of me that badly? Or is it just that your man was poorly trained?"

She moved away from Vincent to pace again. When she looked his way, he saw the pure hate in her eyes. He saw also that she told the truth. Wayne continued to speak when there was no need. He looked to Joseph for confirmation, and saw his expression mirrored on his friend's face. Vincent's hands formed into fists as Natalia continued to speak.

"When he finished talking, they opened the black curtain blocking out the sun. They let him fry in the horrid beauty that is the Morning Star. One of them threw some ash in my face and it took four Slayers to throw me in a closet. They had to knock me unconscious to do so." She stopped to calm herself down. She wanted badly to take out her frustrations, but knew she could not. She needed to finish the story so that Vincent knew everything and could judge whether or not she could beat the shit out of his trusted vampire.

"Sometime later, one of the Slayers I had been communicating with threw some water on me to wake me. She led me into the basement at gunpoint. The original four were there to question me. They wanted to know where the vampire's truth started and where my truth ended. Instead, I asked them if it mattered. I told them they could believe what they wanted to about me, as long as they took care of Edwin and his clan. One understood and sided with me, one said I wasn't to be trusted no matter what and the other two wanted to gather more information. I asked what they planned on doing with me. They told me I would be kept in the basement until they had come to an agreement. They brought me water and chained me to the wall with a manacle around my neck."

Her hand went to her neck, where the marks were still evident. Her silver necklace had been pressed into her skin hard enough to pierce the flesh in a few areas. She was grateful her necklace had not broken.

"How did you escape?" Mierka's voice was almost too quiet to hear.

Natalia turned her head to look at the lady. She sighed heavily and continued. "The one who believed me gave me back my cell phone in secret. When I was sure they had all left the house, I used my cell phone to call the police." She paused, an odd look in her eye. The youngest Slayer, Ashley, gave her back her cell and confirmed she believed Natalia. She shook her head and continued her story.

"I reset my phone to clear all the information off it. When the police showed up, there was no one in the house. I pleaded amnesia and the police took me to the hospital, where I found out I had been missing for less than two days. I was weak and needed nourishment. The police questioned me, but I told them I didn't know how I had gotten there. They asked if my cell phone had any information about me. I told them it didn't. One officer took it, looked quickly at the empty contact list, and gave it back. They left, telling me to contact them if I should remember anything."

She took a breath to calm herself. "The thing that bothers me is that after the police left, two men dressed in black suits claiming to be with the police asked to see me. I was in a private room and a nurse told me they wanted to talk to me. I saw them through the open door. They worried me, so I told the nurse that I was tired and didn't want any more visitors. After she left, I was hit with paranoia and destroyed my phone. I flushed the pieces down the toilet, then laid down for a nap.

"I woke at sunset this evening. I slept for more than 24 hours. Someone took my clothing. All I had was the gown the hospital gave me. I called the nurse, but she had no idea what happened to my stuff. She left, and said she would try and find out. As I didn't want to stick around, I left the room. I stole my clothing from a doctor I met on the stairs. My luck his clothing fit."

"Why didn't you call? We could have sent the werewolves if it was dangerous for us." Vincent's voice was tight with palpable emotion.

Natalia turned to him, gave him a look of defiance. "I didn't know if I could still trust you."

"But you came back here." He moved closer.

"I had to know the truth. I found out that he," she nodded toward Anthony, "was here and figured I could confront you both."

Vincent stood before her, and looked down into her eyes. "And what do you plan on doing now?"

"With your permission, I would like to take my frustrations out on Anthony. The Slayers trusted me and were about to let me find the information I needed. Now, all that's gone. I don't even know if I'll be able to approach a Slayer after this. He destroyed all that I've built for the past two years. I want his blood."

Vincent took her face in his hands, stepped close to her, and leaned in. He whispered into her ear to make sure that only she heard. "You would destroy a man for doing what we created him to do?"

Natalia's eyes grew wide. She pulled back from her lover, balled her hands into fists and pounded him on the chest. "NO!"

The word reverberated in the high ceiling room. Several of Vincent's men stepped away from the pair. Vincent grabbed her to him, and let her bellow into his shoulder and neck. She calmed, but only because she had no other choice. He was right. Had either of them decided to tell Anthony the truth about their first meeting, he might not mistrust her so completely. It was their fault he sent someone after her. She sagged into her lover, and felt the solid weight of him. To contain her anger at herself, she bit down on his neck, not aware she did it.

Vincent felt the bite and his body reacted. He crushed her to him, and curled his fingers into her back. His eyes closed, and hid the passion that swan there. To control himself, Vincent pulled away from her gently. The situation with Anthony had not reached its conclusion. He spoke softly to Natalia. "Go upstairs, shower, change, relax and forget the past three days."

"I'm angry and riled up. I want release." The fires of her furious passion burned beneath the surface of her calm exterior. Heat radiated from her skin and the scent of her blood invaded Vincent's nostrils. He ground his teeth, closed his eyes, and dipped his head down to her neck. He growled softly near her jugular. His hunger grew as she whimpered and dug her fingernails into his arms.

"Go upstairs. I'll be up shortly, and you can release your anger on me." He still spoke quietly, and tried to control his own cravings.

She backed away from him. She wanted the seduction to continue, but knew it could not. She wanted Vincent to follow her upstairs, but there was unfinished business. If it were anyone other than Anthony, she would demand Vincent follow her. She stood still for a moment and gave him a look that swam with passion, anger, frustration, and determination. His jaw twitched, but he turned away from her. She turned as well, her head high as she walked out the door.

The head vampire turned to the room at large, and breathed slowly to stop himself from running after his lover. He had wanted to give Natalia her rank as soon as he saw her again, but knew the ceremony had to be postponed. He sighed heavily and decided. "You are dismissed. You have duties to attend to. Go to it."

Vincent turned to Anthony, who stood and waited for a closure to the Natalia situation.

ABOUT THE AUTHOR

Cat Stark was raised in California and now lives in Illinois with her fiancé.
She hopes to continue writing and publishing for years to come.
Find her here:
Website: catstark.com
Twitter: @catstarkwriter
Facebook: facebook.com/catstarkwriter/